STONE

THE METCALFES || BOOK 1

RONIE KENDIG

PRAISE FOR RONIE KENDIG

STONE

Quite simply, I'm in love with Stone. Another fantastic, swoon-worthy hero, powerful story, and addictive series by Ronie Kendig!

~SUSAN MAY WARREN, USA TODAY
BEST-SELLING AUTHOR

Ronie Kendig is at it again with a story that is rich, full, poignant, and fast-paced, topped with her trademark masterful character development. Readers will see a different type of villain and be shaken to their core by the way Kendig is able to give us the full story of the main character, honoring her strength and courage in a heart-wrenching way. Ronie's psych degree combined with her research and passion for human trafficking all mix together to make for one unforgettable story that will burn in your heart for a very long time to come.

~MIKAL DAWN, AUTHOR

Ronie Kendig wrests control of my emotions once again as she plunges a man of honour and integrity back into the world he fled. No one writes romantic thrillers with the relentless pace, soul-deep emotion, and dynamic dialogue like Kendig.

~REL MOLLET, RELZREVIEWZ.COM

Midas, who made this story possible. ;-)

Dedicated to the Survivors
*You are the real heroes.
May your story, resilience, and strength
inspire us to do more.*

*Defend the cause of the weak and fatherless;
maintain the rights of the poor and oppressed.*
Psalm 82:3

A NOTE FROM RONIE

Writing about such a sensitive topic, one that affects millions of lives around our globe, is complicated and tricky. Ultimately, this book is a work of fiction. However, much of the data is accurate and easily found online or through any one of the incredible organizations that fight to combat human trafficking.

Reading this book, and the ones that follow, may not be easy. In some places, it might be downright brutal. In all honesty, I avoided writing a series about human trafficking because it seems so trendy right now, and I did not want to throw my hat in the mix just because it was "the thing" to do. However, the fight against trafficking would not leave me alone. It's a fight I, as a survivor of child sexual abuse, strongly believe in. It's one I can relate to as a mother, as a survivor, and now as a writer trained to portray the human existence. My hope is that the story I've crafted can help shed light on the brutality and heartbreaking existence in which so many children, women, and even men find themselves trapped. Within these novels is also a good dose of romance and strong threads of humor designed to offset the darkness, provide a reprieve within your reading experience. They are never intended to make light of a terrible and disgusting crime. Those who are trafficked do not get a reprieve. They're fighting for their lives. And I would implore you to join that fight: volunteer with or donate to (or both) organizations engaged in this vicious, soul-eating war.

I'm very grateful to Jessica Mass, Director of Aftercare with Operation Underground Railroad (O.U.R.), and Tyler Schwab, Sr., Aftercare Specialist with O.U.R., for taking the time to talk with me and answer questions, all in the hope that I could accurately portray some truth about human trafficking and honor the organization that has inspired me to write these stories. At the end of this book, there's more information about O.U.R. and how you can join the fight. Please—be a voice!!

CHAPTER
ONE

BEXAR-WOLFE LODGE, *Northern Virginia*

Some days were meant to test a man; others meant to undo him.

Electric shears in hand, Stone Metcalfe palmed the bathroom counter and stared at the haggard face in the fogged mirror. The only familiar features were the Metcalfe blues as they'd been dubbed. But they were tired. Dog tired. The beard betrayed both his heritage and age with patches of rust and silver against dark blonde.

Lot of gray there.

Must be the lights.

He sniffed. *Keep telling yourself that, Old Man.* And he would. He'd crested the forty hill three years ago and was now sliding off the cliff toward fifty. And all he had to show for it were gray hairs as numerous as his failures.

Mom won't like the beard.

He lined up the shave gear on the counter: shears to shed the fur, foam and razor for a clean shave. Again, he eyed the man in the mirror. The beard.

Curse it all. He wouldn't even consider shaving it off if his sister hadn't stepped in to rearrange Mom's life, thereby his.

Had to admit—he resented Brooke. Again. She'd convinced him and their four siblings that the Bexar-Wolfe Lodge—now his under a private entity not easily traced to him—was the perfect way for Mom not to feel alone or useless. He couldn't argue it, though. Since her car accident eight years ago that required back surgery, Mom wasn't getting around easily these days. Still, he knew his sister's intentions weren't altruistic. Like usual, she wanted to free herself and her conscience.

But Mom … He had to face her today, and the cards were already stacked against him with the screwup that wrecked his life and career. Did he really want the beard as another strike? She'd always hated "scruffies." But the beard went a long way in hiding the man many knew as Governor Metcalfe. Reduced Stone to Jackson Mulroney, a pseudonym he'd adopted to survive here after the scandal. Crazy the way a beard changed a face …

Stone tightened his grip on the shears, noting the scent of coffee permeating the cabin.

A snout traced the length of his pants.

He side-eyed his black Belgian Malinois. "What do you think? Shave it?"

Grief gave a growl-huff and trotted out of the bathroom.

"Me, too, buddy." Stone tossed the shears back in the drawer, got dressed, and made his way to the kitchen. He fed Grief and then moved to the window to relish a cup of brew and the view of the rugged terrain spanning the distance. He had no regrets buying the lodge a year ago.

Man. Only a year? A lifetime had been shorn off his heart since. When he'd made the purchase, he had no idea the nightmare waiting around the corner.

Not going down into that dark pit today.

He'd paid the price and moved on. More like hid, but it all came out the other end the same, didn't it? He gave himself another fifteen minutes for a second mug, forcing himself to push her out of his mind. Forget her laughter. Her—

Yeah. No.

Get moving, Metcalfe. His days of running from Mom's disapproving glower ended in a few hours, so he filled a stainless steel tumbler with backup and eyed his dog. "Ready, boy?"

Barking, Grief spun a circle. Nails scritching on the wood floor, he scrambled across the living room and planted his backside at the front door with an excited whine.

Stone retrieved his Cattle Baron from the rack, set it on his head, appreciating the comfortable fit. He opened the front door, feeling more than a little proud that Grief waited for the command. A click of Stone's tongue sent the beast bolting into the cool morning to track down critters.

As his four-legged buddy jaunted off to take care of business, Stone started for the lodge, appreciating the progress they'd made over the last year in renovating the fifty-room lodge: new pool, fresh paint, spruced-up courtyard, and hiking trail. Rowe was likely up there clearing out brush so they could open the trail to guests. They'd been working on permits for a riding trail, but that was slow-coming these days. Thanks to a certain city inspector who had it in for him.

Accessing his office through the private rear door, Stone clicked his tongue again, summoning furry partner. Inside, he secured the door and watched Grief hauling in the scents sliding under the door. The assault of grease and sugar challenged his training.

"On your bed." Stone doffed his hat before powering up his computer.

Grief slunk over to his bed, and with a deflated huff, stretched across the foam. He skillfully hung his snout off the side so he could sniff the crack.

"Don't break your neck." Stone smirked and noted Rowe's

office light wasn't on yet. He'd hired the guy to be the front-man for the office so Stone could run beneath the radar and not blow his cover as Jackson Mulroney. Probably a little too close to his real name, but he'd learned long ago lies were best based in truth. And this lie was really a protective measure. Last thing he needed or wanted was someone connecting him to the scandal and bringing bad press to the lodge.

Over the course of the first hour he answered emails, returned calls to contractors, checked this week's reservations—*looking a little thin*—and studied his agenda for the day. Then, he spent time reviewing his six-month plan for the lodge and renovations as he did every morning, eyeballing the budget and praying for some lightbulb to go on, telling him how to make things happen better and faster. He itched to mark the coffee bar as "Complete," but he should delay that pleasure until he paid the contractor tomorrow. Next, he studied his one- and five-year plans. Gave a nod. Not sure his bank account could fund those plans without solid growth trajectory, but he was a year in and making progress. Still …

He swiped a hand over his beard. The lodge was all he had now. Had to make this work.

When Grief lazily—deliberately—dragged his nails over the door, as if to say "you're killing me here," Stone breathed a laugh. Glanced at his watch. Almost lunch. Mom would be here soon—and he still hadn't checked the condo after the cleaning crew hit it last night.

"Okay, boy." Stone stood and grabbed his hat. "Let's go."

They headed down the hall to the main lounge area with its open-beam ceilings and a floor-to-ceiling fireplace. He banked right, toward the front desk. Grief trotted ahead, paused at the corner leading to the kitchen, and glanced up over his shoulder at Stone.

"Get it."

Grief bolted for the kitchen door, where he skidded into a

sit at the threshold, knowing he wasn't allowed inside. A strip of bacon sailed into the air, and Grief snagged it, then sat again.

Dog had everyone trained. With a grunt, Stone turned down the private hall to the condo he'd called home the first six months after taking possession of the lodge. Though he'd renovated it then, he went ahead and updated the décor for his mom's tastes—a little more Traditional, less man-cave/Rustic. He entered the access code and opened the door. The scent of cleaning products hit him as he double-checked the bathroom, bedroom, and kitchen. All good. He scanned the stock in the fridge and pantry, supplied until Mom could make her own trip to the store.

His phone buzzed and he glanced at the screen.

A text from Rowe read, *BMW SUV entered the property.*

That was probably his sister. He texted his thanks and headed to the front desk.

Oscar looked up from his monitor. "Morning."

Stone nodded. "How're things?"

"Quiet. Had a few inquiries about trail rides, including a corporate event for thirty next week that got shut out of another hotel."

"Good, we need the business." Man. If that booked, a guy could breathe easier. He'd spent enough on the stables and horses.

Licking his chops as he rounded the corner trotting happily, Grief was quite pleased with the snack he'd conned from Alvaro. Grief nosed Oscar for some attention.

"Good morning to you, too." The day manager laughed and reached for a small jar he kept behind the counter.

"No treats," Stone warned with a laugh. "He just got fed—twice."

"Make me the villain and he'll take it out of my rear-end."

"Excuse me," a scratchy voice intruded from behind.

Stone swung aside to deliberately leave the customer to Oscar.

Instead, the wizened eyes of a gentleman in his seventies narrowed beneath a Vietnam Veteran hat. "It is you! I thought so."

The accusation in his tone was too familiar.

"How can I help you, Mr. Blanton?" Oscar intervened.

"I don't want nothing from you." Jutting his jaw, Blanton harrumphed. "But this one"—he thumbed to Stone—"needs to go back to Maryland and take that office I voted him into!"

Molten dread poured through Stone, lowering his head.

"I'm afraid you must have him mistaken with someone," Oscar said shakily, that nervous smile dancing on his bronzed skin.

"I ain't got nothing wrong. He's Sto—"

"I appreciate that you care so much," Stone said, cutting off the use of his legal name. He heard Grief round the corner and signaled him to heel, knowing he might react to the man's confrontational body language.

"Appreciate nothing! You walked out and left your constituents high and dry."

Oscar huffed from behind the counter. "Mr. Blan—"

"Easy." Quieting his employee with a hand, Stone kept his focus on the veteran. "A lot of people say I look like the governor, and I'm sure his leaving office was a difficult choice." No, not really. Though it'd gutted Stone to resign, there hadn't been any choice.

For the first time, the older gentleman seemed not quite so sure about his presumption regarding Stone's identity. "I know they hammered him—you." He wasn't one to give up easily apparently. "But you walked away from a gift!"

More like a nightmare.

"The world needs good, honest leaders," the man growled,

"and yeah, they tried to make you out to be a scoundrel and craven, but I know you're a good man."

Think again.

Gray eyes squinted at him. "You seen who's in office now?" Blanton screwed up his face. "Might as well be Hitler!"

"Allen Kovacs is a good man." Stone had uttered that line at least a thousand times since leaving Baltimore. His running mate held to similar values but had been ruthless.

A woman with dyed-red hair and a patriotic blouse came toward them, shaking her head. "Ed Blanton, *why* are you badgering these men?"

"It's him—Metcalfe."

Stone extended a hand to the wife. "Jackson Mulroney."

The woman faltered, smile wavering just as Oscar's had. "See?" she said with a jab into her husband's side. "You just mixed him up, Ed."

"Happens all the time." Stone hated deceiving these good people or anyone else.

"I ain't mixed up—he's *him*! I voted for him and he threw it away!"

"I'll throw *you* away if you ruin our vacation, Ed Blanton." She offered up another shaky smile to Stone. "We did vote for Governor Metcalfe. He was such a good, honest Christian. And handsome to boot." Despite her soft voice, she had a sharp gaze that narrowed on him, likely trying to see past the beard. "Terrible what happened to him. So sad to lose a man of character like that."

Stone managed a nod.

"Anyway, sorry Ed's giving you trouble—I told him to leave it alone. Lord knows you've been through enough. I mean, what the governor's been through. And you, since you look like him and all." She took her husband's arm and tugged him toward the front vestibule. "Now, come on. We need to get going for that caves tour."

Eating his pride and failure in one lumpy swallow as they left, Stone tried to haul his thoughts back into line. Thump down the words that had bludgeoned him for the past year. But he couldn't. He'd failed—failed the Blantons, failed Baltimore, failed himself …

He looked to Oscar. "How long are they booked?"

"All week."

Great.

So, he'd need to keep his presence minimal until they were gone. He stuffed his disappointment as he donned his black Cattle Baron. "I'll get my mom settled, but then I'll stay in my office or cabin during their booking. You good for a while?"

"Always," Oscar said with a little too much cheer.

"Let Rowe know what happened, so he can fill in." Grateful for the way his hat shielded his eyes, Stone ducked through the vestibule out onto the parking lot, eying the long, curving drive for the Beamer. Eighty-two degrees wasn't hot, but it somehow felt smothering today. Wind teased his senses, rustling the branches—along with Grief, who was sniffing out something. At least he wasn't eating another shoe.

Sunlight spat in his eyes as Brooke's black BMW swung around the final turn into the parking lot. Hour of reckoning. He steeled himself. Having not spoken to his mom in person since resigning office, he knew the verbal beating she'd unleash. They'd always had a good relationship, but after that mess, he just couldn't face her. He'd take Dad's belt any day over Mom's "look." Clara Mulroney Metcalfe had raised six kids while his father chased terrorists and his next rank. The Metcalfes were who they were because of her.

The SUV rolled to a stop beneath the overhang.

Now or never, Metcalfe.

Not one to shy from a challenge, Stone moved to the passenger-side door and opened it. Saw exactly what he'd expected: Hands resting on her beige slacks, Mom stared out the front windshield. Didn't move. Didn't speak. Words weren't necessary—the hurt was clear on her aged features.

"Hey, Mom." Guilt tugged at his conscience and pushed him into a crouch, his knees against the car's undercarriage. "Good to see you."

"Hmph." Her chin lifted as she maintained a fixed gaze straight ahead, her eyebrow arched. "You haven't visited in over a year. Haven't called in nine months."

"Yes, ma'am." He hadn't been ready. Still wasn't. But he was braced for the hours alone, ample lectures, and a ream of Bible verses. "I'm sorry."

Her gaze slid over him, and somehow, despite the way she made him feel like a punk kid all over again, there was nothing condemning in her expression or tone. She sniffed and tipped his hat. "Lord, have mercy! *What* is all over your face?"

Yeah. Called that. "Couldn't find my razor." Though he teased, Stone sobered, taking in the face lined with years of seeing her loved ones through storms. He'd caused more than a few of those wrinkles, and while she gave him what-for, his mom was as true as they came. "I'm glad you're here." It surprised how much he meant it.

"Are you?" She narrowed her blue eyes at him. "Nine months makes me wonder. I just wanted to be there for you."

"I know …" But he'd needed time to himself. "C'mon. Let's get you into your condo." He straightened and offered his hand, catching sight of his sister over the hood of her SUV.

Dark-haired Brooke arched an eyebrow and shrugged as if he had it coming, then moved to the rear without a word.

He cupped his mom's elbow as she shifted out of the vehicle. Once she was on her feet, he started for the rear hatch to grab her suitcase.

"Where do you think you're going? You didn't hug me."

He turned back. "Wasn't sure you'd want one." Bending in, he grinned.

She tiptoed up to wrap her arms around his neck. "You're my flesh and blood. You'll always be my boy, though I might still want to take you over my knee a time or two."

"Pretty sure you'd break your back again if you tried."

"That won't stop me."

"No doubt," Stone laughed. From the back of the SUV, he pulled out two wheeled suitcases, passed them to Brooke, then lifted another suitcase and two boxes. Juggling them, he led them into the lodge. As they passed the desk, he nodded to Oscar, who was already coming out from behind the counter with a ready smile and a luggage cart.

"Welcome, ma'am," he said as he extended his hand. "I'm Oscar and you can find me here most days. If you need anything, just ask."

Mom beamed. "Thank you."

Stone tossed his chin at his employee. "Please ask one of the staff to bring up a trolley and get her things from the car for us."

"On it, boss!" Oscar wheeled back around to his station.

Guiding Mom on, Stone nodded to the left. "That's the dining hall. Your condo has a full kitchen, but feel free to eat there as often as you'd like, no charge." He hesitated on the next part because he protected his privacy and downtime. "And you're welcome to join me up at the cabin."

"That's your home," she countered as they moved into the private hall. "I don't want to intrude."

"We're family—intruding is part of the gig." He indicated to the keypad. "The code is your birthday."

"Fancy." She grinned at Brooke, then pressed the access pad.

He toed open the door and shifted inside, holding it as his mom and sister entered.

"Oh my gracious." Mom cupped her hand over her mouth, shaking her head as she took in the home. "This is too much." Eying the living room with its fireplace, sofa, chaise, and large ottoman grounding the space, she smiled broadly. "This reminds me of our house, only much nicer."

Since she was giving up some independence, he'd wanted her to be as comfortable here and worked to replicate "home" here. The large square island with quartz counters, the industrial stove, and high-end appliances were personal favorites he'd duplicated when he'd built the cabin. Though not a chef, cooking relaxed him.

He set the boxes along the wall and moved further in. "Phone lines are private—not connected to the lodge. However, you can access the lodge by dialing the code on this card."

Brooke sauntered around the open-concept kitchen-dining area. "I'm a little jealous, big brother."

"No, you're not." Especially considering the New York City penthouse Brooke had and the insane amount she'd paid for it, far surpassing what he had here. Besides, it was too weird to hear Brooke paying a compliment. That alone told him she wasn't jealous.

He motioned to the other side of the kitchen. "Laundry room back there has a nook with desk and chair." He shifted and pointed to another door. "Bedroom is there with full bath and shower, walk-in closet."

"This is wonderful," Mom called from the laundry room.

One of the knots in his shoulders eased a little.

"She seems to like it." Brooke went to the fireplace, pulled out a framed picture from her purse the size of a feed bag.

Something in him twisted, seeing the last Metcalfe family photo she set on the mantel at Mom's home. Taken when he'd won the governor's race, when Marie at least acknowledged he existed. He eyed his siblings in the photo—Willow, Range, Canyon with Dani and their children. Leif had missed it, being on mission tracking down the woman who eventually became his wife. But the face that was a sucker punch ... his own son.

He still couldn't believe Marie had let Jack come that weekend. He hadn't seen him since. A raw burn started in his chest.

"How're you?"

What surprised Stone wasn't the question but that Brooke almost sounded like she really wanted to know. But she didn't. Her M.O. was small talk until she got to the real point.

"Fine." He knew how to get her off topic. "What about you? Staying for the night?"

She shifted her long, dark hair over her shoulder. "I ... " Out of the six siblings, she and Range had the darkest hair, though Brooke colored hers even darker. Anything to separate herself from the Metcalfe legacy, he guessed. She took in the condo. "Yes, I might stay a few days." She shrugged. "If that's okay."

Stone started. "Seriously?"

"What? Is it too much to ask?"

His sister never wanted to stick around, acting like the rest of them had the plague. Or that she was better than them, more enlightened. "I didn't mean that."

"I'll pay for my own room," her voice pitched. "I'm not asking for charity!"

"Whoa, hold up. Chill. I'm just surprised. You never have time—"

"Yeah, well, I'm handling the closing on Mom's house and ... a few other things. And she's been a bit distressed leaving the house and seemed like she could use some help adjusting." Her words tumbled out on top of each, as if trying to flee the truth that hovered at the back of her throat—the truth, because Mom was a grown woman used to handling life without her kids doing it for her. As if reading his thoughts, she crossed her arms and shrugged. "But if it's a problem ..."

"It's not." Whatever was going on had to be serious for Brooke to suggest spending more than a few hours with family. "We have plenty of rooms."

The front door bopped open and in trotted Grief, come to

own the place as he inspected boxes, no doubt wondering what happened to his home.

Brooke drew back at his dog as if he were a demon. "Cannot believe you have that thing here!"

"*Thing?*" He scruffed Grief's broad skull. "This is my best friend."

"Which is saying something."

"At least I have one." *Man, sibling rivalry never ended, did it?*

"I love the little desk nook!" Mom exclaimed as she reappeared, glowing. "And what a great idea to have a sink and built-in ironing board in the laundry room, too."

"Unless you'd rather housekeeping do it." Stone grinned, anticipating her response.

"I will not have strangers laundering my unmentionables!"

He laughed. "Thought you'd say that."

Her soft, blue eyes settled on him. She drew in a long breath and slowly let it out. "I like this." She nodded, hesitation and wariness falling away. "I like it a lot—even more because we'll be close again." She lifted her hands. "And don't worry. I have no desire to be in your business, as I'm sure you don't have any to be in mine. But this ... this is good."

Her words were ominous because Clara Mulroney Metcalfe had that gleam in her eye, that certain twist to her mouth, that said she was planning exactly what she said she wouldn't do— get in his business.

CHAPTER
TWO

AUSTIN, *Texas*

Every client took a piece of her soul.

Though she'd showered before leaving the hotel room, Brighton Buchanan would never again feel clean. She strode out and stepped into the elevator, Finch behind her. She turned, her back against the mirrored surface, and watched him press the button for the lobby. When the car slowed to a stop on the fifth floor and the doors slid open, he blocked the way but said nothing.

A man with a high-and-tight scowled. "Public elevator, dude." But then he seemed to see something—probably the weapon holstered beneath Finch's jacket—and palmed the air, shifting backward. "Easy, easy, Big Guy." His gaze struck hers.

His expression gauged her—was she okay?—but she shook her head, warning him to leave it alone. Confrontation with Finch never ended well for the other person. Besides, it just wasn't worth it. Nobody could help her. She was here because of what she was and what she'd done. There was no out. She'd accepted that long ago.

The elevator descended to the parking garage. Her heels clipped on the concrete as she moved to the waiting SUV. Finch opened the door and she climbed in, nodding at the driver in the front, then she slumped against the leather and exhaled.

The driver glanced at her. "Rough again?"

Every time is rough. "Nothing I can't handle." After all, she'd survived being a supermodel, hadn't she? Sometimes, she wondered which life had been harder.

Brighton buckled her seatbelt, blocking out the client she'd just left. He paid a lot, and that's what mattered to Ladomer. She watched the nightlife slide by as they made their way to the house. Let the motion of the vehicle lull her into a daze. Fingers curled around the charm on her bracelet, she closed her eyes. Tried to remember better times, a better man …

"Boss has a client for you tomorrow."

Brighton lifted her head to look at him in the front passenger seat. "I'm off tomorrow. It's my on—"

"Car will pick you up at eight."

"Finch, c'mon—that's my day. My only day."

He held out the phone to her. "Want to call him and tell him that?"

She swallowed and dropped back. Looked back out the window. At least she wasn't on the streets anymore with several clients an hour. She should be grateful. Again, her fingers curled around the blue charm.

They pulled to a stop at the office. She slid out and used the fob to unlock her Audi Q7. Behind the wheel, she started the car and let her phone sync. Eyed the SUV. They wouldn't leave until she did. Just one more measure of Ladomer protecting his property. And that's all she was.

The Lord of the Rings soundtrack emanating through the vehicle, Brighton put the car in gear, dreaming of an adventure with a good ending. She identified with the orcs and Steward of Gondor, controlled by the wizard. Driven by him. She just wished there really was some magical ring to throw in the fire and make all this go away.

Instead, she must settle for getting home and depositing her bone-weary self into a steaming lavender-scented bath with a glass of wine and some silence.

Mari would be there. *Okay, forget silence.* It was still weird sharing her home with someone, but she refused to let Ladomer put the girl anywhere else. It was stupid, really, thinking she could protect the fifteen year old from anything, but ... she was trying.

Brighton pulled into the garage and hit the button to lower the door. She ended the soundtrack, unsynced her phone, tossed it in her purse, and killed the engine. Once street light vanished behind the closed door, she stepped out.

The paranoia was real—and crazy, she knew. Nothing had ever happened. She'd expected him to go public with her name, destroy her. But he hadn't.

Which made zero sense since she had destroyed him.

Yet ... that was Stone, wasn't it? Honorable, higher-road Stone Metcalfe.

Pausing with her key in the lock of the door, she shut out that memory. "Leave it at the door, Brigh," she whispered and let herself into the house, keyed the security panel, then called, "It's me! I'm home." Setting her purse at the drop station, she kicked off her heels. "How was your day, Mari?" After retrieving the mail from the kitchen island, she riffled through it. Bills, junk, ads ... She glanced to the side, down the hall toward the front door. "Mari?"

Silence dripped through the darkness. Why was the house so dark? Internal alarm triggered, her pulse spiraled. She slid back to the keypad, entered a code, then crept back to where the hall to the front door diverged back toward the den. There was no reason to panic. They were home. Safe. But Mari should be answering.

Maybe she was asleep.

With me yelling?

She could've walked to the store for something.

Brighton tripped over something—Mari's sneakers. *The store two miles away ... without shoes?*

So Mari was here, but not answering. Brighton tried to conjure a reason for that. Cold travertine beneath her feet, she slipped toward the rear of the house. She swallowed, her mouth dry.

Scant light scampered out from the den.

Breath in her throat, she sneaked around the corner. Expelled a breath when she saw only a laptop. No Mari.

Glancing back toward the hall, she strained to hear anything coming from the front of the house. Brighton started in that direction. Nerves swarming, she wanted to call out, but that didn't end well in movies. In fact, it was pretty foolish giving away your location when instinct screamed something was amiss. Her heart now pounded, making it hard to hear anything over the blood rushing through her ears.

She eased into the front room. Curtains were drawn but a gap allowed street light to invade. Empty sofa and ottoman—a shadow shifted.

Heart in her throat, she flicked her gaze to the corner.

Mari sat in the armchair, unmoving, silent.

"What are you—"

A hand slid around Brighton's mouth. Pulled her back hard. "Quiet," the deep voice hissed in warning.

She slammed her elbow back, right into the soft part of his gut. Only it wasn't soft. It was hard. Solid. The grip on her mouth tightened, muscles crushing her against him.

"Lizzy. Stop."

She stilled, recognizing the voice. Cord. One of the rescue underground operatives. The reason she'd only used her working name.

"You with me?"

Still held captive, she nodded beneath his hand, and he

released her. She whirled away, reaching for Mari. The girl caught her hand—her arm, then snugged in close as they considered the two men lurking in the house. "What're you doing here?"

"You know why I'm here."

Her gut churned, wrapping Mari in a comforting hug. "I can't."

"You said you wouldn't leave without the girl—she's here. Let's go."

Her heart hammered, knowing this whole house was rigged with listening devices and cameras. Even if she managed to leave without tipping them off, they'd find her. "You idiot. They—"

The corner of his mouth lifted as he pointed to something he held. "It's disrupting any signal into or out of this house."

She looked at it. Felt the blood drain from her face. "Oh no." She shoved her hair back, thinking fast. Through what was about to happen. "You have to go. Leave." Squalling tires in the distance warned time was up. "Now. Get out!"

Cord cursed. "You sent a panic code?"

Guilt harangued her. "I knew someone was in the house— Mari wasn't answering."

His urgency returned. "Come with us!"

"No way. We wouldn't get halfway down the street before they'd be on us. I'm not risking my life or hers." Brighton worked to collect herself, calm down. Take control. "I'm staying here where I'm safe here."

"*This* isn't safe."

She pushed him toward the back door. "Go! Please."

"Come with us," Cord said, moving toward the door. "We're operators—this is what we're trained for. We know how to fight these guys. I can get you out of here. Both of you. I swear."

"You said you only go through the front door. This isn't the front door." She shoved him toward the rear of the house, the double meaning to her words almost made her laugh. But how could she laugh when Death knocked? "Go. You won't be able to help anyone if you stay."

"Think about it," he begged. "Promise—next time."

She hesitated, that thread before her beautiful and golden. The thought of leaving, not having to lose a piece of her soul every day …

Who was she kidding? There wasn't anything left of her to save.

That thread was fool's gold.

No, it was a noose!

"It's too late for me." She pushed them out, then closed and locked the door. Spun to Mari.

"Why'd you do that?" Mari shrieked.

Anger and grief were understandable—the girl was new to this gig—but right now … "Finch is coming. Forget those men were here. Not a single word or we're both dead." She hurried through the house, turning on lights, knocking over some lamps, a chair.

"Why couldn't we go with them?" Mari cried. "They wanted to help us."

"No, they wanted to help their consciences. Nobody can help and nobody cares, Mari." She hated the cruel words as soon as they left her mouth. "Men don't care about me or you, except what they can buy from us. This is me making sure when you do get free, you never come back."

Mari's expression brightened. "Really?"

"No." She charged at her, waving her arms. "What'd I just say—there's *no hope* for us. Think like that and you're dead. If Finch doesn't kill you, Drex will. Ladomer will make sure of it. Got it? We're nothing but inventory, *property*." Her pulse roared. "We're stuck here. Forever. Get used to it!"

"Why're you being so mean?" Mari buried her face in her hands.

"Because—"

Crack! The front door splintered. Flew off its hinge. Night and debris spilled in as Finch and Drex rammed their way into the house, weapons drawn and aimed.

Heart skipping a couple of beats, Brighton spun Mari behind her and glowered at the men. "What took you so long?"

After clearing the house, Finch stalked toward her. "What happened?"

She had to buy some time, be sure Cord was gone. "We thought … " Trying to calm herself was no act. She was terrified. Hated herself for what she'd said to Mari. The danger she'd foolishly introduced into their lives. Danger she'd just turned away along with their only chance of salvation. "We were scared."

"Where'd they go?"

She hoped enough time had passed. "Out back." When Ladomer's men rushed in that direction, she yanked Mari into a hug, whispering, "I'm sorry. I needed you to cry. If they saw you smiling, they'd know something was wrong and then …"

"We'd both be dead."

"She ratted us out—told them we went out the back."

With a heavy exhale, Cord watched from the king-cab truck as Ladomer Horvath's muscle rushed from around the back of the house, weapons out, scanning the street. Ready to engage if necessary, Cord held his weapon low and out of sight. "For her own safety."

The men split up and patrolled the street, gratefully never heading toward Cord. When they started back for the house, Cord let out a captive breath.

"Got there in under two minutes," Low muttered. "They must have a base nearby to get here so fast."

Cord knuckled his lower lip as he monitored the activity happening at the house a block down the lamp-lit street as a realization hit. "They surveil her 24/7." He shook his head. "That's why she went ballistic. She knew disrupting the cameras would bring them."

It wasn't unusual for captors to tightly control the movement and locations of their girls. But this … this was unusual. Not only was Brighton kept in an upscale home on her own, but Horvath supplied whatever it took for Brighton's other self, "Lizzy," to service high-end or high-profile clients. She was important. And while she seemed to have a lot of freedoms, tonight was proof that freedom was an illusion. All combined, this had to be Cord's most complicated and dangerous extraction to date.

"I say we bring in the Feds."

"Not yet." Cord gritted his teeth. "If we convince her to come out on her own, we don't need them, plus it gives us more time to plan and have protections in place. Later, she can file charges when she's ready." If she was ever ready. Her Tier 1 clients increased the risk exponentially that she'd have a price on her head. "We need to do this right and quiet. Convince her to come out."

"I've never doubted a mission, but after what she did to Metcalfe—"

"C'mon, Low. You saw it—she's terrified."

Lowell grunted. "Guess going up against Horvath and whoever's holding his leash warrants that terror, but … Metcalfe didn't deserve that."

"None of them do—not even her."

Another grunt from Low. "I say either yank her now or walk away."

"No—to both. Because I'm not giving up on her and I haven't found the head of this ring yet. Besides, we don't have anyone covering our sixes if we have to go in hot."

Ops were always done in cooperation with local authorities, but this girl...she'd hit his radar when she'd been implicated in a scandal that destroyed a close buddy. After all the news and focus on Stone's inappropriate conduct—which, for many politicians, was just another day on the job—Cord had dug into the facts. Read everything he could get his hands on and slowly a picture started forming that he didn't like. It pointed to trafficking.

And if her captors used her to take down a political power-hitter like Metcalfe, who else had they strung up the proverbial flagpole? That's when he'd made it his mission to learn everything he could about her. Unearthed her identity. Followed her, proving the trafficking theory. She had gotten trapped in an industry that was sickeningly lucrative.

"Listen. If we do anything tonight, and it goes south ..."

"Yeah, yeah. I know." Lowell shifted, palming his weapon as they continued to watch. "We burn bridges with the local LEOs and Feds that it's taken years to build."

"We're already on a short rope with the alphabet soup."

"Probably because their higher-ups are using rings just like Horvath's for their weekend getaways."

Cord clenched his teeth, focused on that white stucco house worth an easy mill. "We need a new plan."

"No spit," Lowell snapped. "But she gave us up. Maybe ... maybe this is a lost cause. I mean, I want to help Metcalfe as much as you do, but this ain't the way, man. We've seen it before—the girl gets scared and burns us. We can't afford that here."

Cord thumped a hand at the windshield. "Horvath has a leash around her neck and a claw in her chest. She gave us up out of self-preservation, but I think she also bought us time."

Lowell sat for a few minutes before cracking his knuckles.

"The kid wanted to leave."

Cord noticed, too. "She's young, desperate." Unlike their

objective who'd been in chains so long the weight of them had become a part of her identity. Maybe they *should* break their M.O. Snatch the girl and her self-proclaimed protector to safety.

Lowell hissed another curse as the men returned to the house. "They're going back in."

Back inside? Why? Cord tensed at the unfolding scene. Brighton stood just inside the front door, doing her best not to let the goons pass. He wasn't really worried about them trying to get favors from Brighton. All the earmarks of this girl said Horvath would kill anyone who tried anything with her. But he sure didn't like the way they were bullying their way back into the house.

A shot cracked the night.

Cord pitched himself out of the truck. Weapon in hand, he sprinted down the street toward the house. Even as he slid into the well of the front porch, he heard Lowell thundering behind him as more screams split the chaos. Glock up, he advanced.

Pain exploded across her cheek from the butt of the gun. Sent Brighton flying backward. Aware of the glass coffee table, she tried to avoid it, but the blow was too sharp, too fast. Her hip connected with it. Slammed down. The rain of glass formed a jagged cushion, cutting into her thigh and hands. Brighton cried out but saw Finch coming in for another blow.

"He'll kill you for this," she growled.

"No, he'll thank me for reminding you of your place. Now, get up." He grabbed her by the hair and rammed her head into the side table.

Dizzy but focused, Brighton had enough wherewithal to not fight these men. Yeah, she'd had classes on how to protect herself from drunk clients—but these men weren't drunk. And she'd learned the hard, painful way to never use those skills against Ladomer's men.

A blur of rage called Mari swept past her as the girl vaulted at the brawny thug.

"Mari, no!" Glass from the coffee table sliced Brighton's arms and wrist as she struggled to her feet. The cuts stung but weren't bad.

Drex was big—much bigger than the spritely fifteen year old. He backhanded Mari, sending her sprawling into the corner of the entry. Her head hit the corner with a sickening thud. Air gusted from her lungs and she collapsed.

"No!" Brighton screamed and lunged to intervene.

Finch manifested between her and Mari, shoulders squared. He leered. "You want more? Maybe you need to be reminded of what you are."

His insinuation nauseated her. "You know Ladomer will kill you." Her voice quaked.

"Not after he finds out you've been trying to escape."

"I would never do that," Brighton lied, knowing all bets would be off about her safety and appearance since he felt she needed reminders.

"Oh, I know that. And I'm going to make sure." He tugged at his belt buckle.

Brighton shoved at him.

But he was prepared. Blocked—and caught her arm. Twisted it down and around, behind her. Pitched her forward, dropping her to the carpet as a blood-curdling scream pierced her ears. His weight pinned her hard, her head bouncing off the floor. She stiffened. Tried to think. Tried to figure out how to—

A shot rang out.

Brighton jerked up, confused. Vision blurred from the blow, she couldn't make sense of what she was seeing. But she was freed from Finch's bulk. She scrambled aside and saw Mari hurrying toward her. Had she shot someone? What happened? Why weren't the men—

Wait. No.

More shapes moving.

Still debilitated by that blow, Brighton shook her head. Her gaze fumbled to where Finch lay groaning.

Hands pulled her up. "C'mon."

"Get off me!" She kicked and bucked.

"Easy, easy. It's okay."

"What ...?" She could hardly think around the pain but recognized that the voice didn't belong to Finch or Drex. Even as she came to her feet and moved toward the front door, glass crunching under her feet, she realized it was Cord. He'd come back, stopped the men—had he killed them? She strained to look over her shoulder as he led her from the house.

Clarity rang like a gong. If she let him take her, Ladomer would find out. Then he'd hunt her down. She jerked to a stop. "No. I can't."

"You must," Cord said, catching her by the arms. "They'll kill you."

"Not if I stay—"

"They're down."

His words stilled her. The body at her feet—Finch wasn't moving. Neither was Drex. How? "Oh my gosh—he'll *murder* me!" Panic drummed at the core of her being. "You don't understand." She searched for Mari. "I can't ... She's ..."

"My partner took the girl out to the truck. We have to go now!"

Ears ringing, head woozy, and arms still stinging, Brighton struggled to think, to see. "Why's it so dark?" She felt herself falling ... then rising suddenly. Flinging out a hand to balance herself, she stiffened.

"Easy. I've got you."

He was carrying her. Across the yard. She felt the muggy

Virginia air. Heard the *cree-up* of frogs in the nearby community pond. Heard a car roar toward them.

"Ladomer!" She wriggled, reaching back toward the house, oddly dark. "I have—"

Tires screeched. So did Brighton.

Hands turned her. Nudged her into a vehicle.

She flailed, panicked. Terrified. Ladomer would eviscerate her for killing his men. For escaping. He'd punish others. Her brother! "No. Stop!!" Her temple knocked against something metal.

Hand on her crown, Cord firmly guided her back into the truck. "In. Hurry."

She tried to leap back out. "I have to find Mari!"

"I'm here! I'm here, Lizzy," Mari said, arms and breath skating around her, pulling her back into the truck.

Surprised to find the girl smiling at her, tears glossing those big eyes, Brighton relaxed. Relief swept across her chest as she hugged the girl, even as the door thudded closed, and the truck lurched away from the house, the engine roaring.

Numb, she tried to wade through the disorientation, the panic, pain …

"Belts!" Cord shouted from the front.

She and Mari separated, scrambling for seatbelts. Once buckled in, they grabbed hands and held on tight. Brighton almost looked back but decided she didn't want to do that and see her pursuers. For a moment, longer than two heartbeats, she'd let herself remain in the delusion of freedom.

CHAPTER
THREE

BEXAR-WOLFE LODGE, *Northern Virginia*

It seemed all he was doing these days was paying through the nose for one thing or another. Stone confirmed the money transfer, then nodded to the contractor. "Done."

"Much obliged," Harry Darkin said. "And I think your dog approves of the café. Probably should put dog treats on the counter."

"He gets enough of those from Oscar." Stone glanced at Grief sprawled over tiled floor that had once been part of the hotel coat closet. It now was a trendy coffee bar with seating for a dozen, thanks to Darkin. "Thanks again. Your work is top-notch."

"Appreciate it, Mr. Mulroney. When your boss figures out your next project, gimme a holler." Darkin lifted his tool kit. "I appreciate the business—and a customer who pays on time."

Chuckling, Stone walked the contractor to the lobby, scanning to be sure the Blantons weren't around. He hated that most people here didn't know the lodge was his, but it just made things easier to be a nobody in a backwater town. "I know there are a couple more projects planned before the year's out."

"We've all benefited from the fresh business coming to the lodge under the new ownership."

"Not sure everyone agrees with you."

"I'm going to guess you mean Inspector Pellet." He bobbed his head as he locked his tool kit into the back of his dualie. "She's ... special."

"That's a word for it." Stone shook Harry's hand. "Take care." He strode inside and past the front desk, heading to his mom's apartment, when his phone rang. "Hello." After the scandal, he'd learned to never answer with his name.

"Stone?"

The voice was ... familiar. He slowed, waiting for the person to say more so he could put the voice with a name.

"It's Taggart."

Grief at his heels, Stone eyed his mom's apartment door, then backed up and turned toward the floor-to-ceiling fireplace anchoring the waiting area. "Hey." He hadn't seen Cord Taggart since Balad. "How's it goin', man?"

"Good, good."

"Been a while." He slid a hand down the back of his neck, then tucked it under his arm, getting the sixth sense that this wasn't a social call.

"Yeah, it has."

There was a hesitation, a pitch to his voice that told Stone to take cover, brace for impact. His old buddy wanted something. As the knots in his shoulders tightened again, he squared his stance. "So, what's going on?"

Not everyone is out to destroy you.

Night had fallen and the ambience of the courtyard was serene yet ominous in light of this phone call. He ducked into his office with Grief and shut the door, sitting on the corner of his desk in the darkened space.

"Look, I'll be straight—I need a favor."

Up here in the mountains, running a lodge, there wasn't

much he could do in terms of a favor, but he also wouldn't say no to this man. "Name it."

"Seriously? We haven't talked in years and you're willing—"

"I owe you. Cough it up."

There came a breathy, nervous laugh. "With you there were always two things: cut it straight and have a plan."

"He who fails to plan is pl—"

"'Planning to fail.' Yeah, yeah. I know—McArthur."

Stone snorted. "Churchill." Pretty sure Cord made that mistake on purpose. "So, the favor?"

"I've got a friend who needs a place to crash for a few days, and I hear you have an extra bed or two." Taggart had always been one to help others.

How had Cord Taggart known he owned the lodge? Pinching the bridge of his nose, Stone worried what kind of "friend" they were bringing. But he wasn't going to renege on his willingness to help. "Sure, no problem. When?"

"I'm about two hours out."

Stone blinked and twitched straight, alerting Grief. "Now? Uh … okay." He started for the lobby to make the reservation, trying to grasp what was going on that his buddy would reach out unexpectedly like this. "What're you doing up this way? Weren't you at Bragg?"

"Contract work now. More money."

That's what they all said.

At the front desk, he logged in and scanned bookings. "Okay, we have a conference group coming in next week, so nothing long-term I'm afraid, but we can do a couple of nights."

"That dog'll hunt."

"So, your friend and you?"

"Ya know, yeah—I'd take a bed and shower, if you can spare it."

Something about this nagged at Stone but he entered Taggart

into the booking for the first room. "Okay, let me get the information on your friend for the res—"

"Gotta run. See you soon."

Emptiness gaped through the line. He hung up on me? Stone frowned and shook his head.

"Problem?" Oscar asked as he ran daily receipts before closing out for the night and handing off to the nightshift.

"Nah," Stone said. "When's Olivia get in?"

Oscar indicated to the back. "Here now, grabbing a late dinner before she clocks in."

"Good. In a couple hours, a man named Taggart will be here for two rooms. Bill's on me." Maybe Stone wouldn't have to come out and get caught up in whatever mess Taggart was bringing. Besides, last thing he wanted was to explain to his battle buddy how he'd so colossally screwed himself over. "I've logged it in, so everything should be set up."

"Understood," Oscar said.

"If they need me, I'll be in the condo."

"Sounds good."

With a whistle to Grief, Stone headed to his mom's place. Over dinner last night, Mom had told him not to worry about her, that she and Brooke would spend the day setting up the place. Even the best of people would want a break after a day with his sister.

Rapping on the door, he paused as it wheezed open. Grief nosed in without a lick of shame. "Mom?" Most of the boxes were already broken down, several more stacked shoulder high formed a path to the kitchen, where he spotted his mom, sitting on a bar stool, face buried in her hands.

"Mom!" He hurried to her. "What's wrong?"

She looked up with a tired smile. "Not a thing. I'm just ..." Her gaze traveled the box-strewn condo. "I'm going to be busy for a few weeks. And it's kind of hard to get used to the idea that *this* is home." Grief twisted her features. "And if I'm honest, I miss our big house."

"I hear you. You've had a rough few years, but … honestly? I'm glad you're here, Mom."

"I'm *glad* to be here. With you, Stone." She patted his arm. "Really glad."

He wanted to redirect her mood. "Have you eaten?"

"Not yet," she said around a yawn. "Thought I'd grab a bite around six or so."

"Mom, it's seven."

Her weary eyes traveled to the digital clock on the microwave. "So it is. Maybe that's why I feel so drained and emotional."

He toyed with inviting her to the cabin, where he'd whip up something, but he wasn't up for an interrogation tonight. Speaking of— "Where's Brooke?"

"She needed some things, so she went into town. We agreed to take a break for the rest of the night and pick up after breakfast in the morning." She smiled. "It was so nice of you to give her a room—she could've slept on the couch in here."

"Not necessary when we have vacancy."

"It's so strange to think you own all this. I had no idea you wanted to do this with your life."

Neither had he. Not until everything else had been ripped from his hands. "So, dinner?"

With a laugh, she glanced at the boxes. "I have no idea where my pans and dishes are but—"

"Let's head to the cabin. I'll cook tonight."

"Oh, I'd love that. Best meal is the one you don't have to make." When Grief nosed her hand, she laughed again. "You are a monstrous thing."

"So is his appetite. C'mon. I'll make chicken marsala."

"My favorite."

Stone smirked. "Me or the food?"

"Like you have to ask." She clucked her tongue with typical Metcalfe mischief in her blue eyes. "The marsala of course."

Virginia Rest Stop

Cord sat in the motorcoach, scarfing down a burger while the girls were in the back, showering and being tended by an aftercare specialist.

Lowell sat in a swivel rocker on the other side, slurping a milkshake. "Horvath's going to come after us hard and fast."

Noting the door to the back room opening, Cord arched an eyebrow. "Quiet," he said as a willowy blond emerged. She closed the door and strolled to the front of the motorcoach, cracking open a bottled water as she joined them at the table.

"How're they?" he asked.

"Shaken, cut up, bruised mentally and physically." She sipped the water. "I think Brighton might have a concussion. I put a butterfly stitch on her cheek, but the wounds she carries inside will take longer to heal."

Brighton Buchanan had been trapped in the trafficking nightmare for six years as "Lizzy," quickly became a Horvath favorite, serviced powerful and rich clients ... meaning, she lost parts of her soul every time. That was a lot to come back from. "And Mari?"

She stole a French fry from him and ate it. "She's relieved to be safe. While Brighton was showering, Mari and I called her parents. They're going to meet us tonight."

Cord rapped his knuckles on the table. "That's good." For the girl. But it might mess with Lizzy's head to lose the one place she'd had to focus her energy over the last six months. He motioned to the silver and blue SUV parked across from the motorcoach. "Trooper is here. He'll escort you both." He swiped his tongue over his teeth.

"That'd be appreciated. I'll stay down there for a couple of days to make sure she starts counseling and gets back into school, whether online or in person."

"I've already reached out to Banning down there," Cord said.

Lowell grunted. "He's one tough son of a gun. That's the kind of legal representation she'll need if she files charges."

Admittedly, Cord was a little reticent for that ball to get rolling, thinking how it could complicate her plight.

She shrugged. "Whatever she's up to, but she'll need time. Like Brighton."

"As always, we don't rush them. We've been working to pinpoint Horvath's boss, so anything we can do to stop this from going sideways is great." Cord finished off the burger. "I'll get Brighton to safety as soon as she's cleaned up and ready."

The aftercare specialist speared him with her blue eyes.

"Don't say it," Cord groused, knowing what she was thinking. "It's nothing I haven't said to myself, but we have no options."

"Taking her to him is a *mistake*. Put her in a safehouse."

"No way. Horvath is too well connected around here to tuck her in one of our known safehouses. No." He shook his head and sat back, drinking his soda. "While I know Stone won't be happy to see her, I also know he's too decent of a guy to turn her out."

"Won't be happy? To him, she destroyed his career and life—that's like a massive firestorm waiting to happen!"

"Maybe, but I stand by my belief that he's too good of a man to turn her out."

"You are not really that dumb, Cord!"

He appreciated the way his team challenged him. Even if they resorted to name-calling. "There's logic behind it. Trust me. I wouldn't put her or this organization in jeopardy."

She shoved back her long blond strands, hemp bracelets

hugging her wrists. "When was the last time you talked to him?"

"An hour ago."

"Before that?"

Man, she had laser accuracy, didn't she? "A few years."

"Exactly," she said, her lips tight and anger brightening her features. "He's not the same guy since 'Lizzy' happened. This won't be good—for either of them." As an aftercare specialist, she knew people and counseling. Knew how to get right to the heart of a situation, and he hated arguing with her, but logistics and tactics were *his* specialty.

She flared her nostrils. "She's been through too much to be thrown to the Panther of the Potomac when he's ticked and territorial."

Cord snorted. "That's a stupid moniker."

"But accurate. Stone broods, plans, stalks. That's not what she needs right now. She needs safety, security, and the belief that she's going to be okay. We have to help her—"

"I have nowhere else that they can't track," Cord argued, sitting forward, done with the grilling. "Most important thing right now is to get her out of this state and somewhere they can't locate. The lodge isn't in his name, and he's the last person they'd expect to hide her."

She frowned, crossing her arms on the table. "How do you know the lodge isn't in his name?"

Smirking, Cord snagged back his fries. "I know a guy," he said in his best Italian mobster accent.

"Yeah, and I know *that* guy. He's my brother!"

"Willow, chill. I got this. Trust me."

"Stone's your brother?"

Willow whirled around, coming up out of her seat with a slow smile. "Hey ..."

Brighton stood in sweatpants and a Virginia Tech t-shirt from a travel stop. Her cheek was swollen and sporting the start of a wicked bruise. White bandage cuffed her forearm. Even with her hair in a wet knot atop her head, she was a stunner. It didn't surprise him that she'd managed to distract Stone Metcalfe.

"He is," Willow said softly.

Brighton's large brown eyes dipped low. "You must hate me."

Ever Willow, she pulled the girl into a hug. "Actually, I think you're amazing." She squeezed then released her. "You've been through a lot and you're still fighting. Not giving up." She hugged her again, then stepped back. "And I hate to do this, but Mari and I need to head out. Her parents are expecting us."

Brighton started. "Oh … I … She's leaving?"

"I'm afraid so, and the sooner the better."

She swallowed, looking at the teen who rushed into her arms.

"Thank you, thank you so much," Mari said around tears. "You saved me. I wouldn't have survived if it weren't for you."

Though Brighton said nothing, the struggle was all over her expression and stiff posture. "Go home, live your best life," she whispered to the girl. "Promise me. Stay with them. Love life."

"I will," Mari cried. "I promise."

After a few more tearful good-byes between the ladies, Cord stepped out of the motorcoach, verified the coast was clear, then waved Brighton out.

She exited and let him hurry her to the dark blue F-250. Once she climbed in, he handed her a burger meal and took the front passenger seat.

Behind the wheel, Lowell grinned back at her. "My truck ain't as spotless as Cord's, but it'll get us where we're going."

Cord hated surrendering driving control to Lowell—mostly for his own safety—but it made sense to switch vehicles. As they regained the highway, he glanced back, the fast-food bag untouched. "Doing okay?"

"Brilliant," she snarked, but the bravado crumbled and there sat a raw, frightened woman, staring out the truck window. "I can't believe you did this. You realize he's just going to find me, right? Then I'll get the beating of a lifetime, lose any privileges I've earned and—"

"Hey."

She blinked, meeting his gaze firmly. Daring him to tell her it'd be okay. She'd heard the lie before, he bet.

"*Privileges?*" He raised his eyebrows. "Privileges shouldn't be a home and feeling safe. You shouldn't have to lay down your soul for that." He told himself to calm down. "Besides, don't worry—I'll make sure he never touches you again."

"Easy words, harder to make good on them." She deflated with a huff, leaning back against the headrest. "Idiots."

He didn't take the words personally. She'd been to Hell and back, endured the worst of men. Experienced a lot of broken promises and executed threats. There was so much to process and plenty to warrant her roiling anger.

A while later, her voice carried through the quiet of the truck cabin. "I heard you and that woman. Why were you talking about ... *him*?"

The unexpected softening of her words and her inability to say Stone's name surprised him. She sounded ... small. Wounded. Her auburn hair, olive complexion, and wide brown eyes were nothing compared to the size of the fight in her. Evidenced by the split cheek. Big fight in a very small package, especially for the power player he'd tagged at the house.

"How's the cheek?"

She scowled at him for not answering her question, then pushed her gaze out the window. "It hurts—a lot. Like being ignored." Quiet for several minutes, she asked, "Where are we going?"

"Trip's a little over an hour, if you want to grab some Zs."

With another huff, she burrowed into the corner of the door, whether brooding or sleeping, he couldn't tell. She'd been powerless for a long time, he guessed, and while he didn't want to exacerbate that sense, he also didn't want her trying to bail on the highway if she decided going to Metcalfe was the wrong move.

This was going to be his most ballistic placement, but it'd work, and she'd be safe because he was counting on the guy's warrior ethos that was shaped by godly values. Stone Metcalfe didn't do anything halfway. That's probably how he'd careened down that slippery slope right into the arms of this beautiful woman.

"Look, I'm going to know in what—fifty minutes?" She really wasn't one to surrender control easily, was she? "Why not tell me now?"

"Why not snag some rest so you're not irritable when we get there?"

"Wow. Harsh much?"

"All the time," Lowell chimed in.

"What is this? Throw Cord under the bus hour?" He sniffed and adjusted his seatbelt. "We never give out information on placement before arrival. Do we?"

Lowell lifted a hand. "This is different."

"*Every* case is different."

"That's a bunch of bul—"

"Okay, okay," Lizzy groaned. "Forget I asked."

CHAPTER
FOUR

BEXAR-WOLFE LODGE, *Northern Virginia*

"What a fabulous meal. Where did you learn to cook like that?"

"Spent months not being able to sleep. Cooking show reruns kept me company."

His mom eyed him, sympathy there and he just prayed she didn't start in on him already. "Sometimes," she said quietly, "it's hard to remember you're my *adult* son, not the teenager running around the house in his swim trunks and Hawaiian shirt trying to be like those TV shows."

"That was over twenty-five years ago."

"To you, but to me it was yesterday. All your life, you never failed to impress me." She smiled as they walked the property for an after-dinner tour of the renovations he'd made since she'd been here for his campaign launch and victory celebration. "I confess, after so many months of silence, I'm surprised to find you doing so well."

Scent of chlorine hitting him as they navigated around the updated pool, Stone thought that through for a few seconds. "I am." He ran a hand over his beard as he peered out at the mountains basking in the glow of a summer moon. "Honestly didn't think I could come back from …" He drew in the reins on that swell of memories.

"From what happened," she supplied gently.

"From what I *did*." But he did not want to go there. "Being here, owning and renovating the lodge"—he motioned inside to where a family sat by the hearth, playing a board game—"has given me purpose, a reason to get up each day, to … live."

Concern twisted her brow. "Was it really that bad?" Blue eyes searched his. "So bad that you didn't want to live?" She touched his arm, slowing their progress. "I guess that's a dumb question, considering you wouldn't come see or talk to me. We'd been close before."

He'd ruined a lot with one stupid decision. Not ready for the heavy dialogue, he focused on what he could stomach. "The lodge has been a godsend."

Mom eyed the sun setting behind the mountain. "I can see why you like it here. It's so peaceful."

"I appreciate its solitude and going by Jackson Mulroney also affords me the anonymity I didn't know I'd wanted." He shrugged. "There's no pressure here, except to be the manager for the lodge."

Her gaze strayed to him, but then she looked down, and he could feel her disappointment again, the lingering questions he'd deftly avoided for the last year. No matter where he turned, this nightmare wasn't releasing him from its razor-sharp talons.

Might as well get it out of the way. "Go ahead. Ask."

She eyed him, those blues so familiar—he and four of his six siblings inherited them. "I'd hoped you would tell me, so I wouldn't have to ask." But then she sighed with a small smile. "What happened, Stone?"

"I screwed up. Made a bad decision and it ruined everything," he said with a shrug.

Her face softened. "It's hard for me to believe—"

He sniffed.

"—because you were always the straight shooter."

"*Was* being the operative word." He rubbed his knuckles.

"But that's what I don't get," she said, her voice pitching with concern. "This *isn't* you—you're the businessman, the loyalist, the planner crossing every jot and tittle. I could believe something like this of Canyon, maybe Leif, but *you*?" She gave an airy laugh. "Never."

He wasn't the same man anymore. Wasn't the perfect soldier, sheriff, governor, or … son. "Well, it was me, my fault." He met her gaze. "Best you accept that or living here will get miserable real fast." He regretted his tone, but not the truth of his words.

"There's a lot of anger in your words."

He hated it—that her perfect little son had fallen off his pedestal. Hated what he'd done to himself, to others. "What do you want me to say, Mom?" He felt the creeping edge of that anger rising around his collar. "I lost my way. Got high on power. Threw it away—all of it. And with an escort!" His chest tightened, the torrent desperate to overtake him. "Sorry for tarnishing Dad's name. For shaming you. Sorry!"

"Shaming *me*?" She tsk'ed, looking aghast. "Every one of us makes mistakes we'd rather bury."

The words struck a mark, vaulted him back to his teen years. To Dad's conversation he'd overheard. The one that rocked his world. Just like he was doing to hers as well. Apple sure didn't fall far from the tree, did it? "Yeah, but not all of us end up on the six o'clock news across the country." Running a hand down the back of his neck, he could still hear those reports running 24/7.

"And tonight in the latest on the scandal that has rocked Maryland's gubernatorial mansion, Stone Metcalfe has resigned. In a statement delivered with his resignation, Governor Metcalfe said—and I quote—'I took this office on a ticket promising to defend our laws and its people, but I have broken both promises. My actions were reprehensible and

indefensible. I appreciate the trust placed in me and apologize that I have let you down. I am confident Allen Kovacs will continue the work we campaigned on and started during my time in office.'" The reporter turned to her colleague. *"I'm shocked, Rick. This is the last thing I expected from Stone Metcalfe."*

Mom touched his hand with her small, leathery one. "I couldn't care less what people think or what they *think* they know." Still holding his hand, she eased onto a nearby chair at one of the outdoor dining tables. "Can you tell me *why*? What happened that you would walk away from everything that has so resolutely defined you, your character, and your actions for your entire life? That is what confounds me." Her silver brows furrowed over pale irises. "Never would I believe you'd lose your bearings over a *woman!*"

"You mean an escort." He didn't want her to have any illusions, any way to exonerate him. He didn't deserve it. He dropped into a chair across from her and leaned forward, sloughing his palms.

"Even with Marie," Mom went on, "you were absolutely insistent upon treating her right, getting married, having a family—all in that order. You said it was the honorable route."

Marie was a different story. That was high school. He was cocky, a Metcalfe, and hadn't yet discovered Dad's secret. How else could he explain this without bringing all that up?

"So you can see why it's so difficult to believe you and ... an *escort*?!"

"She wasn't ... *that* to me." He pinched the bridge of his nose. "I didn't even know she was one." He thought of her brown eyes, lilting laugh ... "In my position, there was no way I could date without intense media scrutiny, so I gave up on the idea. Then the dinner parties started and there were ... ladies. I was appalled, of course. Disgusted. Told them I wouldn't show up if they continued that. They swore it wouldn't happen again, and I focused on my causes and agenda. Ya know, working the crowd, garnering financial backing and political support. That's how I met her."

. . . . .

"Here." She wagged her hand at his phone, and before he could sort out what she meant, she'd taken the phone and was tapping quickly on the screen. Her nails were her own—not those fakes a lot of women wore. "If you change your settings," she said, her brown eyes brightened by the screen in the dim lighting of the event, "like this …"—she kept working—"then people can't randomly send you photos or texts." She straightened and spun his phone back to him. "There you go."

Stone glanced down at the phone, bewildered. "I …" He thumbed his eyebrow. "Thank you." He smiled at her. Found himself ensnared in her smile and the audacity of taking the governor's phone from his hands.

She cocked her eyes, suddenly shy. "Yeah. Sure." Suddenly, she diverted her gaze to the floor. Ah, there it was. She finally realized who he was. "I know devices—they sort of control my life."

He sniffed. "I hate the things. They're shackles."

"Same." Their gazes locked and Stone willed his brain to work, to find something to say.

"Sir."

The stiff tone of his bodyguard pivoted Stone toward him.

Geary glanced past him with an assessing gaze on the woman as he said, "Mr. Kovacs asked for you."

"Right." Stone turned to her—only to find her gone. He scanned the room to no avail.

"Sir. This way." Geary touched Stone's elbow in urging.

"Back into the mouth of the lion." Stone couldn't help one more visual sweep of the room for the woman who'd treated him like a person, not the governor. The woman he'd noticed almost as soon as he'd entered the ballroom.

. . . . .

Bexar-Wolfe Lodge, Northern Virginia

He swiped a hand over his mouth and beard. "We got along, seemed to have a lot in common. She was young, smart, funny—reminded me of Willow."

"Ahh," Mom said warmly. "You always had a soft spot for your younger sister." They sat in the quiet of the evening, sounds of familial laughter drifting from inside. "So, you had a lot in common ..."

"I thought we did." He straightened, a hand propped on his leg as he watched Grief inspect a critter. "They said she was an administrative assistant to a cabinet member. She showed up at a few more parties, and I always looked forward to seeing her. We'd talk, laugh, connect." He rubbed his chin against his shoulder trying to shrug off the sound of her laughter and the way it infested his mind. "The world didn't seem so cold and impossible when she was around."

"And you never knew?"

He shook his head. "I mean—the evidence was there, I guess. If I'd looked hard enough, I would've put it together."

"But you didn't?"

"I just wanted more time with her. Thought that's what she wanted. Obviously, she did—because they paid her to set me up." Rawness coated his chest and throat. "At first, we just bumped into each other. Though, I've wondered if that was set up, too. But I'd grab coffee and she'd be there. I'd eat out, and she'd walk in with a woman friend. We made the most of the times, talking, laughing. Then I asked her out. But because of my position, we met at a hotel in the hopes of avoiding media scrutiny. Stupid, really. It had a kitchen, so I made dinner. We'd eat, watch movies, sometimes attend a fundraiser party."

"You kept things platonic?"

Stone pushed to his feet. Shoved his fingers into the pockets of his jeans. He hated this. Hated himself. *Just get it over with.*

He balled his fists. "In the beginning, yeah." His mind flung back to her, her laughter … kisses. Her passion. "I was stupid. Listened to the wrong voices. The job was hard, the pressure unreal, and I just wanted one thing for me." He sat again and growled. "It's stupid and selfish now that I hear myself say it. Fact is, I just didn't *think*." He folded his arms over his chest. "Maybe I didn't care. I don't know. It all got to me—the position, the power." Ashamed, he shook his head. "Thought, heck yeah—I deserve the attention of a beautiful woman." What a fool. "I ignored the signs and the consequences."

"So, you *were* intimate with her?"

"No." His word bounced off the walls back to him. "We never … got that far." He was glad for the dark hour so she couldn't see the heat climbing his face.

She tilted her head. "You didn't have sex with her?"

"Might as well have." What guy talked about this stuff with his mom? Sure could use a drink. A stiff one, but he'd sworn that off since the scandal, too. "Weren't far from it. I had every intention …"

"What stopped you?"

"Canyon."

Her brows winged up in surprise.

"Yeah. Role reversal, right? I was the one always straightening out his sorry butt." He snorted. "She and I … there was no lack of passion between us. We were in bed when my phone started ringing. It was Canyon's ring tone."

"You set a ringtone for your brother?"

With a snort, Stone adjusted his hat. "No, *he* did. Some TV show theme song. He thought it was hilarious." He welcomed

Grief ambling over for a belly rub. "If he hadn't called ..." He closed off the memories, powerful and present. "The people she was working with to take me down had more than enough evidence to make it the sex scandal of the year—recordings of our talks, photos of us kissing, of us in the bed ..."

"Oh, Stone. I am so sorry."

He wasn't sure if he appreciated or resented her sympathy.

"But you said you didn't have sex with her, so why didn't you fight it? Instead, you walked away from your career, your—"

"Is that what you care about? A *career*?" He gritted his teeth. Stood.

It felt like a demon was trying to crawl out of his chest.

"I care about you, Stone. We haven't talked in months, and that's not like you. And this story, what you went through ..." She rose as well, then let out a long sigh. "I am sorry. I never meant to push, but I care. You're my son and—"

"Just better if we bury it."

"I want to understand."

"Understand what, Mom?" Strain ached through his chest. "I did it—I was in bed with an escort. Walked straight into their trap. Ruined my life, my career. Lost my ever-loving mind thinking this pretty, vibrant girl really had a thing for me." He snatched off his hat. "Instead, I found out I'm just a dirty old man."

"Stone—"

"Don't!" He held up a hand. "Don't say it." It hurt to breathe. "Please."

"Sorry, but I have too much Irish in me to stop now." She covered his hand with hers. "You're a good, decent man. And you're certainly not the first man to have his head turned by a pretty woman."

The similarities to his father never ended, did they? Still ... "You can't make this into something positive, Mom."

She glanced down, and it killed him to see her so desperate to make things right, to help him find his way back.

"I screwed up, and *nothing* will change what I did." He drew in a long breath, then exhaled with a huff. "I know that. Paid the price." After another sniff, he couldn't help but recall Scripture. "If I'd just respected and honored her, the way you raised me to, the way the Bible guides, none of this would've happened." He scratched his beard and grunted. "Anyway. Yeah. Now I'm starting over. With a painful serving of humble pie and this lodge." He nodded, scanning the hills, the building with its garden lighting that provided a dull glow along the path. "C'mon. I'll walk you back to the condo and tell you the plans I have for some upgrades around here."

Though she gave him a hurt look, his mom stood.

Inside the lodge, he removed his Cattle Baron.

"Speaking of children—"

"Who was?"

"—have you seen Jack? How is he?"

"Not since I came here, but I've talked to him. He's doing well."

"Why on earth haven't you see him?"

He couldn't believe she asked that. "Marie—rightly—felt I wasn't a good influence for him right now in light of the scandal."

She shook her head. "I do miss that young man. Hard to believe he's a teenager already."

"Just barely." Stone hated that his son was entering manhood without him. "I'm sorry I cut you out. I just had to remember how to live ... breathe."

His mom stopped at the juncture to her condo and tugged his sleeve. "Thank you, for the meal and for being honest with me. I'm still proud of you."

He gaped.

"After all that, you got back up after and you're firmer in your convictions and faith."

He wasn't so sure, but … "I'm trying."

"That's all we can do." She nodded, then planted a kiss on his cheek. "See you tomorrow." She laughed. "I love that I can say that now. Night, son."

"Night." He saw her into the condo, then rounded the corner and saw a man standing by the front desk.

Wearing khakis and a black shirt, revealing his sleeve of tattoos, none other than— "Taggart."

His buddy turned, grinning. "Big Guy!" He pulled him into a shoulder hug and patted his back. "Look at you. What's with the ten-gallon hat and face fur?"

"You can talk." Nudging his brim up, Stone scruffed the guy's shaved head. "You had more hair than a camel last time I saw you."

"I was mistaken for one many times, too." Taggart laughed but it sounded … empty. "Thanks for letting us come."

Us. Stone glanced around the empty foyer. "Your friend?"

Taggart thumbed toward the restrooms. "Long trip and bladders needed emptying." He pursed his lips. "If it's a'right, Low and I will crash then head out first thing."

"Lowell's here, too?" What was this? A reunion?

Taggart's laugh sounded hollow as he shifted.

Warning claxons blared in Stone's mind as he glanced toward the restrooms, then his friend. "What's going on?"

Someone exited the restrooms—a woman, who was now hugging the water fountain between the two doors. Her clothes were baggy, her hair strangely haloed beneath the dome light. Yet, she was … familiar.

Taggart glanced at him, the woman, then back to him. Like he was worried.

"What—?"

She turned.

Stone's breath punched from his lungs. A stinging wash of ice shocked his veins. He took a step back. "No," he growled, turning to Cord. "No! You did not—You piece of—"

"Listen—"

"*No.*" Hands fisted, he could not believe this.

It wasn't happening. He'd left office. Left her. Did everything they asked. No, he wasn't retreating.

Stone shifted and surged toward her. "Get out." No way she was ruining his life a second time. "*Get out!*"

She recoiled, angling toward the burly mass of muscle called Lowell, who cradled her in place as her complexion went white, panicked.

Taggart hurried forward. "Please, Stone. She needs a place."

"No! She can buy her way into someplace else." Stone shoved his friend away. "You sorry—" His pulled back his fist, aimed it at Taggart. Heard a shout. Caught himself. Cursed his friend. Shoved him again. Stepped back, his mind operating in slow-mo.

Hearing the roar of his heart, the rage coursing through his system, Stone looked at her. Glowered, but then exulted. At least this time, *she* was the one cowering. He pivoted on his heels, storming away from the lobby. "Get her out of here!"

CHAPTER
FIVE

BEXAR-WOLFE LODGE, *Northern Virginia*

Every rejection he shouted bludgeoned her. He was still larger than life. So handsome. So powerful. So … livid. Daggers flew from his eyes.

Brighton staggered beneath his rebuke. Humiliated at the way he yelled for her to leave. A jolt of heat hit her, then bottomed out, and sent a chill through the foyer. Her stomach roiled, tossing the empty contents of her stomach up into her throat. She stumbled and bumped into Lowell.

"Get her out of here!"

She flinched at the roar of his voice.

His gaze slammed into her and his lips thinned. Those blue eyes turned thunderous. "Son of a—" He stabbed a finger to the host at the desk. "No rooms! They're leaving. And if they don't, call the sheriff!" With that, he stormed away.

Stricken by his utter rejection, Brighton gnawed the inside of her lip, biting back the tears. It wasn't a surprise the way he reacted. Yet his vitriol pierced her heart. Unable to move, unable to process, she watched him go, drowning in his seething hatred. His rage had been so raw. Vicious.

Chin bouncing as she fought the burning tears, she noticed

the stunned curiosity of the hotel guests. Noticed the way forks and glasses in the dining hall stopped clinking. The way the host behind the desk stared at her, gap-jawed. With a dart of pain a metallic taste glanced across her tongue as she bit too hard on her lower lip. She deserved his fury, his hatred. That and so much more.

Something cold and wet nudged her fingers. She pulled her hand away and glanced down, startled to find a huge black dog sniffing her.

"Grief, come!" Stone commanded as he stalked toward a large fireplace.

The dog whimpered and bumped his shoulder against her thigh, demanding attention.

"*Grief!*" Stone yelled as he waited at a juncture to another hall. "Come!"

Big Black Beast whined but fell into a lope after his owner.

"Metcalfe!" Cord started after the bigger-than-life man, but spun to Lowell. "Get her checked in."

She was too paralyzed to shriek at him, too stunned to believe *this* was where he'd brought her. Never in all her life would she have let him bring her here, if she'd known.

Lowell drew her toward the desk with him. "Two rooms—"

"No, I—"

"Sorry." The clerk shrugged, lifting his hands. "The boss said no room." He eyed Brighton as if she had the plague. "Sorry, I do what he says. That includes calling the authorities." He reached toward the phone docked nearby. "If necessary ..."

Lowell's meaty paw rested on the worker's. "Don't."

She caught Lowell's log-thick bicep. "Please." Her words were quieter than she meant them to be, her courage nonexistent. "Let's just leave."

But Big Guy wasn't paying attention. "Two rooms. Now!"

"I do not answer to—"

"Please. Let's just go," Brighton pleaded. "I don't want to stay h—"

"Do it!"

"I will not! He said—"

"Give her a room," intruded an authoritative, feminine voice that belonged to a dark-haired woman. She strode across the lobby in smart navy slacks, a white silk blouse, and confidence like armor.

Red colored the host's face. "Ms. Holloway. But … Mr. Stone—"

"*I* will deal with him," she asserted. "Let's stop making a spectacle and get her into a room."

"I could lose my job—"

"Not at all." She handed him a credit card. "Here. A room."

"They wanted two."

Her eyebrow arched. "Are you going to make this whole process difficult, or are you going to get it done?"

He tucked his chin, the clacking of keys evidence he was doing as told though his hard-set jaw warned he was not happy about defying his boss.

Who was this woman? She clearly knew Stone. Brighton just wanted to crawl into a hole as she looked in the direction Stone had vanished. It'd stolen her breath to turn around and see him relaxed and smiling at his friend. Her shocked brain had frozen her, made it impossible to do anything other than being a punching bag for his angry words.

She'd never forget those first few seconds when he didn't realize a traitor was in his midst. Glorious. He was still breathtaking and gorgeous. Muscular and—bearded! What was that about? The hat—he'd started wearing those when they were dating. To hide his identity, but she'd tried to explain that a man like him in a cowboy hat did anything but blend in. He drew the eye, the heart, the will—*everything*! The stinging cuts and throbbing headache fell away. She was enraptured in those blue eyes.

Then, that moment snapped like a sonic boom when he'd seen her. His expression had morphed. He recoiled as if he'd been burned by acid. It'd ripped out what little she had left of her soul.

Wanting to shoot Cord for this fiasco, Brighton jerked toward Lowell. "Did he know?" she hissed at the towering oaf. "Did Cord know about this—*him?*"

"Later," he said in a low voice.

"No, there will be no *later*. I want to leave." Brighton shoved loose strands from her face and shifted, looking toward the revolving door. "I can't do this. It's ... I can't be here. *Please.*" Her pulse pounded like war drums, which was exactly what she'd stepped into. A war. With Stone.

"Just hang on," Lowell said.

"This was stupid-cruel," she hissed around stinging eyes. "I cannot believe—"

"Here we are." Ms. Holloway was at their side, handing over keycards. "Two rooms."

Brighton ducked and tried to hide her tears and humiliation.

Lowell hovered protectively at her side. "Thank you."

Ms. Holloway faced Brighton with a discerning gaze. "You're in a safe place," she said firmly, directly. "Do you understand me?"

Safe place? There was no such thing. Still, Brighton hesitated, glanced at Lowell, who seemed just as confused that this woman could possibly know ...

"Do you understand that you're safe?"

The question felt like a trap. Brighton tried to smile. Tried to think of something to say, but her mind could not remove itself from Stone's fury. It hurt. Like an oil driller burrowing down past the concrete reinforcements around her heart.

"Since she's too scared to talk," the woman snapped, "how

about you explain her bruises and cuts, the butterfly stitch on her cheek? Is this your doing?"

Lowell twitched. "No, ma'am."

"No!" Brighton yelped. "He—they ..." She couldn't say they'd rescued her, because the woman would want to know from what. "They're good men. They're—"

"Good men do not do that to a woman," she said, pointing to Brighton's injuries.

"You're right," she said, her throat feeling swollen and raw. "And they didn't."

"Brooke?" An older woman came toward them, lifting her hands in bewilderment. She was petite with silver-blond hair styled into a chic cut as she glanced toward the large fireplace at the far end of the lobby. "What on earth was that all about? I've never seen him in an uproar like that."

"I know. It's okay." Ms. Holloway focused on Brighton. "Management will take care of you, and if they do not, I'm in room 109. Please let me know if I can help you." With one more long look at Brighton, then a glower to Lowell, she hooked her arm through the older lady's and moved into a side corridor.

"C'mon." Lowell headed toward a wing of rooms in the opposite direction.

"I want to leave."

"We stay here tonight. No other options." He gave her a sheepish look. "Besides, we can't do anything until Cord returns. It's not smart to stay in the open with all the attention we've drawn."

Awareness spread through her as she noticed an older man with a Vietnam Veteran hat sitting by the fire with his wife, both giving her disapproving glares. She felt like the hoodie she wore didn't sport a team logo but rather the letter A for Adulteress.

How in the name of all that was holy had she ended up here?

Breathe ... Breathe ... Breathe ...

Rage vibrated through Stone, defiant of the command. Why couldn't God just let him find some peace? Where was this grace Mom always talked about? He'd screwed up and paid for his mistakes ten times over. When would it be enough? How did he keep ending up on the wrong end of love, being betrayed. First Dad, then Marie, and now—*her*!

The door to his office jiggled and he straightened—so did Grief, who let out a low warning growl. Not in the mood for conversation, Stone headed out the rear door with Grief on his heels. He gritted his teeth when he didn't hear the door shut.

"Stone. Wait!"

Brisk mountain air smacked him as he stomped up the path, ignoring Taggart thudding after him. "Go back if you know what's good for you."

"C'mon, man. Please."

He rounded on Taggart, grabbed him by the collar, and slammed him up against the brick wall. When pain ricocheted through his fist and red bloomed at the corner of Cord's mouth, he realized he'd punched him.

Rattled, he shifted. Wasn't letting the guy off the hook. "A 'friend'?! You knew!" His pulse hammered amid Grief's angry barks that mirrored his own. "You *knew* about her. About me!" He shoved him again, thumping the guy's bald head on the brick. "That's why you hung up when I asked for name and information. You knew I'd say no!"

Taggart wiped blood from his lip. "You're right. I knew. Everything. About you. Her."

"You're done." Stone stabbed a finger at him. "I don't want to hear anything else from you—ever. She goes. You go. Now!" Stone spun toward the cabin.

Cord caught his arm.

Grief slid in, snarling. Forcing Taggart back.

"Hear me out. Please." He palmed his hands. "I beg you."

Stone struggled for a breath that wasn't choked with rage or adrenaline. He cursed again, shaking his head, hauling in breaths around the rubble of his life.

"I know this might make me scum, but … you owe me."

"You low—"

"If you hear me out, no matter your decision, I'll respect it and call us even."

Hand on his belt, Stone huffed through several thick breaths. Closed his eyes and shook his head. Told himself to walk away before Cord used those operator skills to talk down an unfriendly.

If he listened to whatever bull the guy wanted to dish and still refused, the debt would be paid. Good, because Stone never wanted to see this guy again. "Talk."

Taggart stood several inches shorter than him, but what he lacked in height, he more than made up for in tactical expertise. "First—I *am* sorry for ambushing you with this, her. But I honest-to-God had no choice."

His respect for Cord dropped another notch. "There's *always* a choice." Stone had made many bad ones in the course of the nightmare that led to this moment but always owned them.

"You're right."

"You're ticking me off." Stone looked out at the mountain, wanting to escape.

"She needs a place to lie low for a few days. I don't trust anyone else with her."

"Not my problem. There is no way on God's green earth she stays here. She already ruined me once. I'm not going to hand her the RPG launcher to do it again—this time, taking the lodge with her."

"Please. I know—"

"You *don't* know!" he barked, shoulders squared. "I heard you out—now I'm refusing. And she goes." He stared his buddy down. "That's what you said, isn't it? That the debt would be paid?"

Taggart stared back, his jaw muscle jouncing. "You're one cold-hearted—"

"Me?" Raising his eyebrows, Stone stepped forward. "*I'm* cold-hearted? Who just waltzed into a man's home and livelihood with the very person who destroyed him, then asked him to invite her in for food and bed?" He cringed at that last word.

"And this is the best you can think of me? Of her?"

"Her?" Stone cocked his head. "I can think of a lot worse."

"She was trafficked."

"I don't ca—" He snapped his gaze to his buddy. Stilled. "What do you mean?"

Taggart didn't flinch. "You were a sheriff. You know what it means."

"Bullspit."

He smirked. "It's easier to believe she was a selfish, wanton prostitute, isn't it? That you're the only one affected by what happened."

"You dare stand there and say she's innocent after what she did to me?"

"No. I can't say that." His friend's bravado dulled. "I will protect her, even defend her to an extent—but I can't lie. She knew what she was doing, but she hasn't had a choice in six years."

Stone studied his friend, tried to wrap his mind around the heinous situation Taggart suggested. But then he thought of the way they'd gone straight to the press ... "Not buying it. You're saying this to—"

"*Why* would I do that?" Cord growled, his eyes darkening. "She's been trafficked for six years."

Trafficked. Somehow, the word hammered past his rage. Jaw clenched, Stone glanced down as the full meaning of that horrific crime struggled into full meaning. Tried to think through that. The possibility. Wrestle his own guilt—fighting human trafficking had been one of his administration's platforms. He felt sick. And livid.

"What she did to you was wrong. No way around that. And I wish there was time to lay out the whole story, but I won't do that without her permission. Besides that, it's late and I'm dead tired. The bald truth is that while I'm out of country, she needs to be safe."

Why did that word—safe—twist up his gut? "Out of country?"

"Fly out tomorrow." Cord flashed his palms at him again. "Pulling her out tonight wasn't planned. Just ... happened, but I want her kept safe."

"Safe from what?" Stone fought to restrain the fury knifing his chest.

"Some serious crap." His buddy tucked his chin and peered through a thick brow at him. "I came to you not to rub this in your face but because I know what type of man you are. It's why you left the Army for law enforcement, then shifted into politics—to be a difference. Make a difference for those who can't fight or protect themselves."

Protect her. The woman who destroyed his life? Stone turned and grabbed the nearest table. Upended it. Paced, hands on his belt, trying to breathe.

"I know ..." Cord sighed and shook his head. "Please. Just ... let her stay. For a few days."

Let her stay. At the lodge. In his line of sight every freaking day. His failure gloating at him. Invading his sanctuary. He wanted to throw Cord out on his backside and slam the door behind him. But if this story about trafficking was true ... "It doesn't add up," he muttered, his honor wrestling with the horrific truth of that crime. "They ambushed me. She got me into bed, and they had photos of us in that room! Blackmailed me out of office. I can't buy that she didn't have a choice. I can't let her stay. Sorry. Just can't."

Cord hesitated for a moment, eying him. That's when Stone realized he'd delivered info on the scandal that nobody knew. What did his buddy think of him? Probably disgusted—thinking he'd hired an escort.

"Tonight," Cord said evenly, "I seized an opportunity to extract her. We had no time to plan or prepare. If they find her … she's dead. As much as it sucks to think about, you are not the only one she's been used to take down. No justice can come to you or anyone else—including her—if they get to her."

Trafficked. Sickening! His gut cinched. "Son of a biscuit …"

"And I know Stone Metcalfe won't let that happen." He angled in, his expression sobering. "Look, man. I'm sorry for what happened to you. I don't know what went down between you two, but you've *never* been a player, never slept around even when Marie did."

Stone bared his teeth at the guy.

"So I know you had feelings for her, and I need you to dig into that and *think*. They will kill her. She wronged you—yes. But it's not a cut-and-dried scenario."

He eyed his buddy, breathing through flared nostrils. "Tell me you're not messing with me."

"Scout's honor." Cord held up his hands again. "I don't work for Uncle Sam anymore. *This* is what I do now, combat human trafficking. My organization has global reach." He pointed toward the doors. "She needs help and shelter. I swear that's all I'm asking."

"I've worked too hard to eke out a life after the nightmare that woman caused."

"A good life," Cord conceded, and they both knew Stone had already lost this fight. It's why Cord stayed put. Didn't push. Didn't move.

God had a sick sense of humor.

Stone should walk away. Tell them to drive off a cliff. Crap it all—this wasn't fair. "How long?"

Cord considered him, relief in his dark eyes. "Unknown."

In other words, indefinitely.

Stone turned away. Snatched off his Cattle Baron. Shoved a hand through his hair. Replaced the hat. He couldn't do this. See her every day. The heated moments with her raced through his mind even now. "No."

"Okay, then just a couple days, maybe a week." Cord shuffled forward. "Two at the most. I don't know what I'm going to be facing once I leave, but that should be more than enough time."

"You realize how hard I've worked to get on my feet again? What it was like to start my *entire life* over?" His words bounced off the walls. "All because of her, and you want me to willingly let her back into my life."

"Not your life, the lodge."

"The lodge *is* my life!" He dropped back against the rock ledge. Scrubbed his beard as he growled. Two terrible words forced him to reconsider: human trafficking. Curse it all.

"I need her hidden until we can get her legend built and sort who's at the top of that org chart above her captor." Cord lifted his shoulder in a shrug. "You're the last place they'd look for her after what happened."

"Yeah, because only an idiot would let her back into their life!" While he might be angry and resent Brighton Buchanan, he wasn't cold-hearted.

No. Maybe he was, because he couldn't do this. "I'm sorry. I can't ..." It felt like that day he resigned all over again. The day he read that letter. Saw those pictures.

Yet ... he knew more than enough about the skin trade. It repulsed him to know he'd been unwittingly caught up in it. Defying everything he believed in, fought for. "My whole career I hated the perverts who did this to people. But admitting even these slimeballs are smarter than me ..."

They'd targeted him, shredded his life, and he'd never seen it coming.

Man, he felt sick. "This sucks."

Cord started, his gaze lit with hope. "You'll let her stay."

"No, I didn't ..." Stone looked to his cabin, then to the lodge. If she didn't come out of her room and he kept to his place or office, he could avoid her. "If she stays, *you* owe me—big."

Cord gave a relieved shake of his head. "Absolutely."

"Who holds her leash?"

"Ladomer Horvath trafficked her to some high-ranking VIPs. He's the tip of a very vicious, multi-headed org with branches all over the world that we've been trying to dismantle for over a year. It's insane. We've made big headway in the last two months."

"I want all intel on threats against her, or this ends here. And your promise it'll be no longer than a week."

"A week." Cord nodded, but he hesitated.

"No more," Stone warned. "Seven days, then she's gone. I'll drive her to Dulles myself, if I have to."

"O-of course. Deal."

He was really going to regret this.

CHAPTER
SIX

"We good?"

Cord locked the door, his head splitting like his lip. "Yeah. Bought us a week."

"A week? That's not—" Lowell frowned. "What happened to your mouth?"

"Stone happened." He raked a hand through his hair. "And at least we have a week. It's more than I thought we'd get out of him." He glanced through the open door to the other room, where Brighton was curled up in an armchair, staring at the curtained windows.

"She's been like that since we got in here." Lowell shifted around in front of him. "Seeing him really rattled her, then she got mad at me that I wouldn't get her out of here." He widened his gray eyes. "I think I agree with Willow—this is a bad idea."

"It is, but it's all we have right now." Cord checked his phone and the messages piling up. "I need to make some calls." Hearing sniffling, he glanced at her again and felt his heart twist. "Did she eat?"

Lowell pointed to the dresser where two trays of food sat. "The woman who paid for our rooms showed up with that."

"The pretty brunette?"

Smirking, Low laughed. "Thought you might notice her."

"Hard not to." He'd always had a thing for the power-hitters. Skirts and dolls he had no interest in, but women with fire and intelligence knocked him to his knees every day of the week. Maybe he could find her and thank her personally.

"How could you do this?" Brighton's voice was shrill as she stood from the chair, the clothes hanging off her. Later, she could buy something that fit better using the allowance the organization provided by donations.

"I hear you." Cord nodded. "It's just for a short time and the only option we have."

"He *hates* me," she strained out, her veins in her neck popping and tears streaming down her face. She batted them away. "And he has every right." Her voice was thick and raw with emotion. "I never wanted to see him again."

"I'm sorry—"

"No!" Brighton stormed over, her brows tangled in anger. "No, you're not going to apologize and think this is okay. You've pulled me from one nightmare into another. You seriously want me to stay here? With a man who'd rather see me dead than breathe the same air?"

"Stone would never want you dead. I think you know that, but this ... this situation is tricky. I get that. He and I talked, worked things out."

Her chin trembled with restrained tears as her gaze flittered to the carpet, and she looked so very lost. "I can't be here. I have to leave. Now."

"You have to—"

"No!" She slapped at him. "No, I don't. I want to leave."

"We can't." It was impossible for her to understand all that went into getting her here, away from Horvath—the operators, the RV, the specialists. "I know this ... isn't ideal. But I need you to stay for a while."

"I can't." Her voice cracked and her brown eyes pooled with more tears. "I cannot see him every day knowing he hates me, that I … ruined him."

"It's in the past now. We're fighting for your future. Got it?" He felt his phone buzzing. "Look, it's late—why don't you get some rest. You'll feel better. Lock the door to your room. You're safe here."

"You're stupid if you think it's that easy! I'll never be safe. Ladomer proved that to me."

"You're right. It's not easy. None of it is. Not what you've been through, not what it will take for you to stay free. But it will be worth it."

"Says you." Defeat pushed her through the door joining the two rooms. She hesitated. Her gaze bounced to his, then back to the wood floor. "I … the door … I don't want it shut."

He appreciated the unexpected trust she'd just handed him, feeling safer with the door open than closed. She might not believe she was safe, but she felt safer being able to see them. "We'll keep it ajar," he agreed. "Low'll be here. I'm going to make some calls, grab some food, then I'll be back."

Without responding, she drifted into the other room and curled onto the bed, facing the door.

Cord held up his phone in explanation to Lowell and headed out. In the lounge area, a couple sat enjoying a fire, so he moved out by the pool. Dialing, he sat at a stone table and bench to talk with his partner back in Maryland.

"How's it going?" Marriott asked.

"Rough but workable."

"Got some pretty hot potatoes back here."

"Not surprised." Cord's gut tightened, hating the ramifications for those left behind after Brighton's extraction. "We knew this would hit him where it hurt. Keep eyes on it."

"Yep. Arrangements are in place for the next meetings."

Nigeria, then Kabul. It was going to be long haul, but should net them some significant headway. "Good. Thanks."

After that, he connected with another operator in Nigeria and the buddy of a friend with Igbo connections. L.A. next. His phone pinged with a text from Willow, saying the reunion for Mari went well. *Thank God something went right.* Head hurting, he rubbed his eyes. Leaving Brighton here was risky, but the location was too perfect—remote enough to be safe, but close enough to Dulles to relocate her once the paperwork came through. Stone might hate her, but he'd keep her safe. Risk was the name of this game—a long game. But he'd find the head of the dragon that took Cicely.

Promise you, Cissy …

He ran a hand over his shaved skull and thick beard. Hung his head, elbows resting on the table, hands hooked up over his shoulders. Some days just took it out of him. What he saw. The daily bureaucratic fights. The surprising difficulty of even working with other charities. It shouldn't be this hard to rescue and re-establish survivors.

"Mind if I intrude?"

At the sultry voice, Cord straightened. On the other side of the table stood the pretty brunette who'd intervened at the front desk. "I was just about to give up on this day, but I think the sun just came out."

With a wry smile, she slid onto the stone bench and folded her hands on the table between them. "Can we be direct?"

Wow. The lady had chutzpah. "As long as we start with names."

She leaned to the side, her long black hair sliding over her shoulder. "You're military—likely former. Maybe now contract or black ops."

He grinned. "That's a really long name."

She drew her chin up. "That girl—"

"Sorry." His amusement bottomed out. He keyed up the

flirting to get her to chill or off-kilter. Either would work. "No name, no game," he said with a shrug.

Her nostrils flared, and God forgive him, but she was hot. A spitfire. "Brooke." It sounded like it hurt her to give in. She wasn't used to providing information—she was used to taking it. Commanding the scene.

She folded her arms. "Now, why did you bring her here?"

He'd dealt with people like her before and wondered if he could annoy her as much as he'd annoyed all the others. He switched to the other side, sitting next to her. Extended his hand. "I'm Cord."

"I really don't care."

"Ah, but you should." He gave her a lazy grin. "You want information from me."

"I know your kind."

"Sounds promising."

Pale irises hid beneath dark bangs. "Look, would you just ..." Her confidence wavered and she looked down, picking at the sleeve of her blouse that added a lot of femininity to her already-amped beauty. Head angled, she squinted at him. "The woman you brought to the lodge—I know who she is. Tell me why she's here."

Well, crap. He really hoped she didn't know who Brighton was. There was an intensity to her words and expression that he had to redirect. "I thought you knew my kind—isn't that enough?"

"No, it's not—"

"And who are you that you injected yourself, paid for the rooms, paid for food."

"You know my brother and knew full well what that woman would do to him."

Brother? Double crap.

"Is this ... are you trying to destroy him again?"

Her words sucker punched, struck at the core of who he was.

"No." He wasn't really at liberty to discuss this, but he wanted to explain to her that Stone was his buddy. That he knew Stone's kind. Yet, he couldn't. The information was too sensitive. And while the eyes might agree that she was related to Stone, he didn't know that for sure, and no way would he compromise this operation. No matter how bad he wanted to know this woman better.

She considered him for a long while. "Is this about trafficking?"

Wasn't he supposed to be getting *her* off-kilter? Not many people surprised him. Cord shifted and straddled the bench, facing her, his knee bumping hers. "Now why would someone like you ask a question like that?"

She cocked her head. "Someone like me? What does that mean?"

"You're attractive, intelligent, successful—"

"I'm a partner in a New York City law firm."

"—and arrogant."

Shock rippled through features that then went crimson. "Look—"

"Oh, I am."

She stomped to her feet and started away.

Cord launched after her and caught her hand. "Whoa, hey." He swiped a hand over his beard to hide his smile. She'd been too easy to rile. "Sorry."

Fire sparked in her gaze. But then her expression shifted and her defensive posture grew relaxed, confident once more. "You were playing me." The anger returned, and her left eye pinched. "To distract me."

Cord could not help but smile appreciatively. "You are *very* distracting," he said, erasing most of the distance between them, not disappointed when she didn't remove herself. "So I thought it only fair."

"Trafficking." Brooke arched an eyebrow. "Is that what this—what *she* is about?"

"You seem really intent on that. How d'you know I'm not her john?"

Her gaze swept his face, and he could bask in that for a long time. Thought to slip a hand around her waist, but she'd probably deck him.

"You're not."

Yeah, definitely need to get to know her. "How else would I have her or bring her here?"

Again, she studied him. There was definitely something alluring about having those pale blue eyes trail over his eyes, nose, and mouth. "First, he'd *kill* you if that was true."

Why was she so focused on trafficking? Cord inched closer, surprised when she still didn't back away. "And second?"

Her defiance flared. "This isn't really difficult. I just want to know if it's—"

"Why? Why are you so interested?"

She blanched and he could tell she was about to withdraw. That was the last thing he wanted, even though he was playing with fire. That look in her eyes? He'd seen it enough in this line of work to be bothered by it. A *lot*. Especially, especially coming from her.

Holding her gaze, he eased in, liking the way she watched him—daring him yet … hesitant—and reached behind her, plucking her phone from her back pocket.

She drew up, lips parting in surprise. "What—"

He opened his phone and paired the two, then returned hers. "Now you have my number."

She rolled her eyes again. "You think this is about you?"

He let his gaze linger on her features a little longer than appropriate until she shifted. "Isn't it?"

"You're military, therefore a definitive no." She stepped back.

"And if you do anything to harm my brother, I will be sure you never breathe clean air again."

Cord couldn't help but grin. "So this means I'll see you again?"

She stalked off. Smarts. Fire. Sass. She had it all going on. And he *really*—

A solid thwack against his chest thumped the air from his lungs. Coughing, he caught the hand and nearly broke the wrist before he registered the face. "Stone." He stepped off.

"Get your eyes back in your head, Taggart, or I'll shoot skeet with them." Stone planted his hands on his belt. "You're really ticking me off tonight. Shouldn't have let you through that door."

His friend had always been a tough guy, but seeing his rage flare again, Cord eased back. "Sorry. Just some things she said to me—"

"I don't care what she said. There are two conditions to her staying here."

"Your sister?"

Stone glowered.

Right. Brighton.

"One—no more than a week. Dead serious. You don't come back, she'll be walking the roads." He had a mean streak as woolly as his beard. "Two—she stays in that room. Nobody sees or talks to her. Meals will be delivered and housekeeping will take care of laundry, but she's responsible for upkeep. Clear?"

Cord nodded. "Crystal." There was no way the bona fides would be ready that fast, and no way Horvath would stop looking for her so soon. Which meant Cord had to figure out how to buy her more time before Stone tossed her onto the street.

CHAPTER
SEVEN

BEXAR-WOLFE LODGE, *Northern Virginia*

Being locked up by Stone Metcalfe was no different than being held by Ladomer Horvath.

Okay, not true at all, but the thought appeased some of the resentment running through Brighton.

"Do you understand?" Cord stood just inside her room. "Don't leave the room. Everything will be provided—meals delivered and anything else you need."

"I've just changed one form of captivity for another." Again, not entirely fair. This wasn't captivity, not by a long shot, but she wasn't one to sit in a room all day. That's part of what got her in trouble in the first place.

Hm, so maybe a little contrition was in order. She'd tried to escape once a long time ago and made some fatal mistakes. So this time around, she wasn't going to do that. Even if it meant being trapped here with Stone.

Cord's beard twitched. "I know this isn't ideal, but he's right—you can't be seen. If Horvath gets wind of your location—"

"Believe you me, I get it more than any of you." Strangely—stupidly?—it wasn't Horvath she was worried about. Brighton deflated. "But I ruined him. Knew what they intended, and ... I let it happen." Not at first.

. . . . .

BALTIMORE, MARYLAND

"No way. I'm not doing it." How had they figured out she'd fallen for the governor anyway? That she'd even talked with him.

Idiotic question, considering they tracked her every move. Even the measures she'd taken with her phone weren't foolproof.

Ladomer slid his hand along her cheek, traced her jaw, slipped his fingers behind her neck. In one fell swoop, he slammed her face into the wall.

Pain exploded across her nose and mouth. Cupping her face, she felt warm blood between her fingers. She gaped. He'd never assaulted her face. Only her body. The face had to be pristine—even in modeling, her face had been a commodity. Still was, just now for their clients. But Stone wasn't a client, and she vowed to never let him become that to her. He was so much better. She'd spent time with him. Admired him. Loved him.

"Want to try that again?" Ladomer asked, standing over her.

Brighton pushed off the wall. Felt her knees quavering, but letting them destroy him ... through her. "No. I can't do it. He wouldn't believe me. He—"

His fist connected with her face. Sent her spiraling. Something clipped her legs. She hit the floor hard. Scared—truly scared for the first time in a long time—she looked up at him. Wondered how far he'd go. Did it matter?

"We thought you'd be a witch about this." He dug his phone from his pocket. Swiped a few times. Nodded at someone, then turned the screen to her.

A blurry, grainy image bounced through what seemed to be a live feed or call, someone was in a park of some kind.

Wiping the blood from her mouth, she asked, "What is—"

A voice too filled the feed—family, precious.

"No …"

The camera panned and landed on a teen in line for a concert.

Her heart sank—she'd paid for Aston to attend his favorite band at Central Park. "Oh no."

The angle shifted and unbeknownst to Aston, a man stood behind him with a gun pointed at his back.

"No!" Brighton whipped to Ladomer. Saw Leon. "You swore you'd leave him alone. You promised if I stayed—you can't do this!"

. . . . .

Bexar-Wolfe Lodge, Northern Virginia

"Hey." Cord crouched at her knees, drawing her back to the present. "You have to put that behind you, okay? I know, he knows. It's done. Over."

"It'll never be over." Her eyes burned as she fought the tumult eating at her soul. "I can't believe you brought me here."

"It's a waystation," he said. "For now, bide your time and you're home free."

"I have no home." Besides, this wasn't a waystation. It was torture.

"You will. It starts here, now. Remember when we first talked about pulling you out?" His tone was soft, encouraging. "I warned the first few months would be rough. You'll make it." He stepped toward the door. "I need to get moving. You have the burner—my number is in there. Use it only when absolutely necessary and only once. I've told Stone I'll cover any costs, so get whatever necessities you need. You'll have supplies coming from Aftercare soon."

She shrugged. "I don't need anything." Clothes were the least of her worries.

"We should have your paperwork soon, and I think you'd like to know that Mari has been returned to her family."

Relief washed through her, yet— "She has guards, still. Right?"

He nodded. "Plain-clothes operators will watch her for a while." He flicked open the door and Lowell was there waiting. "Close and lock the door. Take care."

Considering them with wide eyes, Brighton did as instructed, then glanced around the room, reality crashing in on her. For now, she was free of Horvath and had nothing to her name except too-big clothes, a bag of convenience store toiletries ... and loneliness. Isolation. Holed up in a hotel with the one man who *didn't* want her.

Hugging herself, she felt lost, unsure what she was supposed to do all day. For the last six years, she'd been tied to a phone, told where to go, what to wear, and who to meet. Before that— the same with her agent and modeling gigs. Today? She sat on a lumpy chair watching TV. Flipped through channels for a bit. Already felt bored, so she wandered to the large window, slid open the sliding glass door, and stepped onto the small concrete patio. Brisk air wafted around her as the morning sun climbed into the sky. Eying the sloping mountain in the distance and the trees and lush vegetation, she could almost believe a fresh start was possible.

But ... why here?

To face my accuser.

They hadn't spoken since Ladomer sent the photos. Warned they'd go public if he didn't immediately resign. She'd tried to stop Ladomer, begged him not to do that to her or Stone. He'd been shrewd, though, protecting *her*—his property. Though nothing happened—well, not in the truest sense, which had both angered and shamed her—he'd taken down the most honorable man she'd ever known. A set-up that destroyed his career, publicly humiliated him, and ruined him.

It'd gutted her that she'd been part of it. All her life, she'd been full of fanciful ideas and dreams. Gifted with beauty—that's how Mama had put it—Brighton had bought into the measuring tape everyone used to assess her life and sought a modeling career. She quickly realized it gave her control of her life, something she'd never really had as pastor's kid. She was on the cusp of going international when one stupid choice dismantled all control, or illusion thereof.

Then years later ... God blessedly dropped Stone Metcalfe into her life. She'd tried to hide their connection, afraid Ladomer would find out and do exactly what he'd done. Stone had so stood out like a beacon, a lighthouse in the dark storm that had seized her life. He was strong, powerful—not just in position but his physical strength. He wasn't handsome in a rakish way, but refined. Distinguished. A man who belonged in a suit. And his character said he was a man who also belonged in power.

That night, when he'd turned those blue eyes in her direction, she hadn't believed her fortune. They'd played the coy game, stealing glances at each other. She'd intercepted trouble from him three times that night, and he'd noticed. Said she'd rescued him ... But really, he'd rescued her—from despair. From believing nothing good would ever come her way. Believing there was no hope.

A whistle snapped her gaze to the left, down the sidewalk to the pool and rear doors of the great foyer. And there he was in all his six-two glory. That black cowboy hat, jeans, a button-down ... So much like the day they met in the capitol. She'd been struck mute at the sight of him, and her heart—well, he did things to her heart that shouldn't be allowed.

And wouldn't.

Because he hated her.

Before he spotted her, Brighton slipped inside. Silently, heart thumping, she locked the sliding door and turned.

Pounding assaulted the door to her room.

No way that could be him. He couldn't reach that door in that short of time. Could he? Then who was knocking at her door? Had Cord come back?

What if Ladomer had already found her?

Terrorized by the thought, she could not move. She jolted when the knock repeated. Whoever it was, they weren't going away. Which meant they knew she was in here. Quietly, she crossed the room and slid up to the peep hole, her mind wreaking havoc and pointing out that someone with a gun could kill her right now. She braved a glance.

On the other side stood the woman from last night. She'd been so nice. Caring. Even stood up to Lowell. The woman hadn't known heartache if she had that kind of confidence.

Brighton flicked the locks and removed the security bolt, then eased open the door.

The woman smiled in her smart slacks and blouse, hair expertly styled. "Hi. I'm Brooke Holloway. We met last night."

"I remember." But why was she here? "I'm Brighton."

Brooke held up a reusable grocery bag. "We look like the same size, so I thought you could use these."

Stunned, Brighton took the bag and checked the contents. A couple of blouses and lounge pants. And they weren't cheap knockoffs but all brand names. "I couldn't—"

"You can. And will." Brooke pushed the bag back to her. "Have you had breakfast?" She nodded toward the main lobby. "I'm about to eat with my mom."

"Oh, I can't. I have to stay—"

"Mom has a private condo at the back of the hotel. Nobody will see you."

"I … shouldn't." Admittedly, though she was an introvert, there was something suffocating about knowing she couldn't leave the room.

With a huffy smile, Brooke took her hand. "Come."

"Oh, please—no." Though she dragged her feet, Brighton wasn't going to have an all-out brawl with her and draw attention. She slipped into a steady gait, as her training demanded, and heard the door click shut behind them.

Please, please do not let Stone see me out here …

Brooke laced their arms and led her down the carpeted corridor toward the front. "I know you think I'm being rude, but I also know I'll only be here a couple more days, and if they're making you stay in there …"

"Oh, I'm not—"

"—I thought you could use some company."

How on earth did this woman know so much? Brighton was more than a little mortified that she seemed to understand the situation. "How do you …?" And exactly how much did she know? Why wasn't she disgusted?

"I had a chat with Mr. Taggart in the dining hall."

Ah. Well, that was infuriating. She didn't need people knowing her business. Especially not *that* business.

As they swept past the main lobby, Brighton frantically scanned for any sign of Stone—the fireplace, seating area, the closed café, the front desk, and dining hall. If he saw her …

Nerves thrumming, she expected at any second to hear him, hear that roar of his, demanding she leave. *"Get out of here!"* Involuntarily, she hunched her shoulders, hoping to shield herself from the memory of those words, which she still felt along her nape. She nearly crumpled in relief when they entered a narrow hall with one door.

Brooke entered and held the door for Brighton. "Mom, we're here."

Hesitantly, Brighton stepped inside, taking in the cozy living room with fireplace and just beyond it, a narrow wood dining table.

"In here," a woman called, "pulling the quiche from the oven."

Moving ahead of her, Brooke tossed a glance over her shoulder. "If there's anything my mom is good at, it's fattening people up." She strode into the open kitchen-dining area where a huge island seemed to cozy up to a gas cooktop and oven. "Mom, this is Brighton."

"Hello, dear," the woman said as she came around and extended a delicate hand. She was several inches shorter than Brighton's five-nine height. "I'm Clara Metcalfe."

"Nice"—Brighton twitched at the name—"to meet you." Clara. *Metcalfe.*

Mom.

There was no way this was a coincidence.

Breathe, idiot! She forced a smile across her face as her mental gears struggled to turn the cogs. Her gaze bounced to Brooke, who'd said her name was Holloway—and she wasn't wearing a wedding ring. But those blue eyes were unmistakable. Were these two women his family? His *mom and sister?* That would explain a condo at a hotel.

Hello, numbskull!

Had she entered her own living version of Dante's *Inferno?* Could the last twenty-four hours get any worse?

That would be a *no-thank-you-exit-stage-right.* "You know," she said, her voice quiet, her stomach roiling, "I think I should go. I'm feeling a little … lightheaded."

"You're probably famished," Mrs. Clara said. "A good breakfast will fix you right up."

Brighton's stomach rumbled as she sat on the counter-height bar stool.

"See?" Mrs. Clara laughed. "What'd I tell you?" She returned to her cast-iron skillet filled with a spinach quiche. "With all that bellowing from Stone last night, I bet he frightened the energy right out of you."

"He was acting like a buffoon." Brooke poured orange juice into three glasses, then flicked her gaze to Brighton. "Don't take him personally. That's how he is—not the loud thing, but the buffoon part."

"Well, I wouldn't say that, but yes, he is ... strong, a leader," Mrs. Clara agreed. "He has always taken his role very seriously as big brother to his brothers and sisters."

Plural. On both. "How many siblings?" Her mouth went dry, wondering what they'd think of her if they knew she was the reason their loved one had been ruined.

"There's six of us," Brooke said, handing her a glass of OJ. "Not that you'll remember all our names, but there's Stone, then me, Canyon, Willow, Range, and Leif."

Six. She couldn't imagine such a big family. Brighton sipped the juice, her mind connecting yet another cog. Willow ... Her Aftercare specialist ... "Wow."

You've got *to be kidding me.*

Definitely an inferno.

Serving slices of quiche, Mrs. Clara laughed. "You can say that again, but I've loved every minute of being their mother." She joined her at the island. "Now, tell me," she said, her voice perpetually jovial, "what on earth was all that ruckus last night?"

"Mom," Brooke admonished, taking the stool on the far end.

"I'm just saying, he was bellowing awfully loud and *that* is not like Stone." Mrs. Clara lifted her fork. "He's quiet, formidable."

No kidding. The first time she'd met him, Brighton had been so intimated she couldn't talk, so she'd feigned distraction with his phone. Didn't help that he was drop-dead gorgeous with that debonair persona. Not Chris Hemsworth, but more old-school like Pierce Brosnan or Sean Connery. "The hat doesn't help."

"Agreed!" Mrs. Clara and Brooke said in unison.

"He's just started that up in the last year or so, though I don't know why," Mrs. Clara said, shaking her head. "I mean, we're Southern, but not *that* much."

Brooke cut off a piece of quiche. "He needs something to hide that big head."

"You talking about me again?" Stone's deep voice resonated through the apartment, pouring molten dread down Brighton's spine, freezing her fork midair.

He was here, and he'd see her. Know she broke the rule about staying in the room. Then he'd be livid and start yelling again. And then his mom and sister would know she was the one—

"Ah, there you are!" Mrs. Clara opened her arms wide for a hug. Which worked well to hide Brighton. "Come give your mother a kiss!"

Wanting to die, Brighton shrank to conceal herself. In the space of one day she'd gone from thinking she'd never see him to never wanting to see him and feeling his scorn like a torch blower.

His thudding boots sounded closer—as did the clicking of dog's nails. That big black beast trotted around the island and lifted on his hind legs to counter surf.

When Stone planted a hand on the back of his mom's stool, his gaze on his dog, her heart did the Macarena—just as that traitorous organ always did around him. "Off," Stone commanded.

Brighton sank lower just as the dog did. Miraculously, he still hadn't spotted her, but it'd happen. There was no escape. She couldn't look. Couldn't face the oncoming rage.

"Morning, Mom," he said, his voice deep and resonant. Gorgeous like the rest of him.

Her gaze slid in his direction as he doffed his hat and bent to kiss his mom—those stormy eyes speared a lightning bolt straight into her heart.

His skin seemed to literally dance as he recoiled. That ridge between his eyes tightened. Fury superheated the air.

CHAPTER
EIGHT

"Unbelievable! What're you doing here?" He could kill her. And Cord. "I told him." He thrust a finger at her. "Number one rule—you stay in that room! If you can't do that one simple thing, it's time for you to leave. Now!"

Brooke slid into his path. "I invited her to have breakfast with Mom and me. The dining hall wasn't safe—"

"Her *room* is safe!" He'd waded into a rip-current of betrayal. Granted, nobody here knew what was going on with Brighton, but he wouldn't let her use that to her benefit and destroy more of his life.

Recalling Cord's warning that Horvath would be looking for her, he bit back a curse. Knew she shouldn't be alone, so he'd have to escort her back. "Let's go. I'll take you—"

"You will not!" His mother came up in all her five-two indignant glory. "She is my guest."

Stone fisted his hands. Tightened his lips. While he'd told his mom about the scandal, she didn't know the woman in her condo was the responsible party, so he needed to temper his rage. "Mom—"

"I don't care what bad blood exists here, but rudeness is

not—"

"You have no idea—"

"What is wrong with you, Stone?" His mom scowled her disappointment. "How can—"

"Please." Voice soft, Brighton scooted around them. Man, she played that dejected card to the hilt. "It's okay. I'm … I'm sorry. I shouldn't have—"

"That's right!" Stone barked, turning straight into her. Towering over her. "You shouldn't have. Do what you're told."

She snapped her chin down, but not before he saw shock and hurt in those caramel irises that had always turned his knees to putty. Quickly, she made for the door.

He glowered at his sister, then turned to follow Brighton. His arm caught and he jerked around.

Brooke's age-old defiance flared. "I'll go with—"

"No." He flipped her hold and drew her back. "She and I need to talk."

"You're being a bully. A mean, abusive bully, Stone! Stop—"

"Leave it."

"She's traumatized."

"Not near enough," he hissed, hating himself for those words, but he wouldn't take them back. He stalked across the foyer, seeing the way her short legs hurried her toward the room. She reached the door before he was halfway there and swiped the card. The access light flickered red. Struggling to swipe the card again, she shot him a frantic look.

What he saw hauled him back: Fear—of him. It slowed Stone, told him to release the anger tightening his lungs. Then again, hadn't she ruined enough of his life?

She tried again—dropped the keycard and whimpered.

Forcing himself to calm down, Stone reached her as she retrieved it.

"It's not working." Her voice shook as she shuffled back a

step but kept swiping the card. She was so stressed she nearly dropped it again.

He put a hand over hers.

She froze.

So did he. The touch was a mistake. Reminded him of how small she was compared to him. How she had fit in his arms. Felt against him. The softness of her murmurs and kisses.

Step off, Metcalfe.

"It's upside down." He took the card and unlocked the door, which swung inward as if shoved open by their expelled breaths.

Brighton rushed in.

Stone stood in the hall, unwilling to cross that line. To be alone with her. Yet, he had to make her understand a few things and that couldn't be done out here.

He stepped in far enough to shut the door, and twinged when she scurried across the room to stand behind the chair, gripping the oversized shirt tightly in her hand. Her hair was piled atop her head in a wild, carefree way. On the dresser was a grocery bag filled with clothes. For some reason, that hit him crossways.

Focus, Metcalfe. He folded his arms. She needed to understand and comply with the rules. "I agreed to let you stay at my lodge—"

"*Your* lodge?" Those molten eyes came up.

"—with the understanding you remain in this room." Stone tightened the slipping control on his temper. "Meals will be delivered here. Laundry handled via housekeeping."

Her gaze went to the curtains. As if she wanted to escape.

"Cord agreed to the terms, so by default, you do as well. If you can't abide by them, then you know where the front door is."

She chewed her lower lip but said nothing.

Seeing her with Mom and Brooke ... "What'd you say to them?"

"Who?"

"My family."

She scowled. "I didn't say anything."

He tightened his jaw, refusing to fall for more of her lies.

She sniffed. "Of course you don't believe me."

"I have every reason to believe you'd damage what's left of my life."

Her head dipped, but even from six feet away, he could see the way her chin bounced beneath restrained tears.

Nope. Not falling for that. "Oscar has the front desk during the day, and Olivia at night. If you need anything, dial zero." He turned and gripped the knob, calling Grief, who trotted over. "Otherwise, do not leave this room."

"Stone."

He hesitated, taking in a breath, letting it out, then faced her.

Brighton Buchanan had always been confidence balled into a five-nine package of spunk, but now … standing there, shifting awkwardly, she reeked of vulnerability. "I am sorry."

He snorted. Yanked open the door and left. No way he'd believe that. Not after the way she'd worked him, seduced him so her cohorts could photograph them and take him down. Roughing a hand over his beard, he made his way back toward the front desk.

Brooke was waiting in the foyer, arms crossed.

He sure didn't need a lecture. "Hey," he said with a clear voice. "The trail's cleared. Want to go for a hike later?"

She startled. Then rolled her eyes. "You're not putting me off that easy."

He stepped into her personal space. "What is this, Brooke? You haven't given an iota about me or Mom—or any of us—in years." He jutted his jaw at her. "What're you doing here? Why're you in my business now?"

Hurt flashed through her expression, but that classic,

indifference that defined Brooke slid right over like a mask. "Not everyone is your enemy, Stone. I want to help."

"Help what?"

"*What* is wrong with you?" she demanded. "You're the big brother, the one with all the answers, the one looking out for everyone. Yet this sweet woman—"

"That woman destroyed my life!"

She lifted her chin. "So it *is* her."

He could not believe he'd just done that. "I have work to do." Signaling Grief to come, he started for his office.

"Is that offer for a hike still on the table? So we can talk. You sound like you need it."

Just like his sister, trying to take the high road, instruct and correct him.

"I've never seen you behave so poorly, Big Brother. The man yelling at a woman, the man raging like a wild beast—that wasn't the brother I've always looked up to."

"You never looked up to anyone in your life, Brooke. You've always looked down on us."

She startled. "That ..." She sighed. "What you did, how you treated her—that's abuse, Stone. The sheriff in you knows that."

"You're operating with one-tenth the information and making assumptions."

"Abuse is abuse, Stone. No matter what color you shade it with."

"Enough." He brushed past her into his office, tossed his hat on his desk, and dropped into the chair. Head buried in his hands, he let out a long breath. Leaned back in the chair and stared out the window overlooking the pool. He'd bought the Bexar-Wolfe Lodge for peace, to start over. Got a pretty good lead on both. Now ... Brighton was back and everything upended.

He stared at his computer, knew he'd never get any work

done today, so he grabbed his hat and went out the rear door—only to realize Grief wasn't there.

He glanced back at the door. Recalled signaling him to follow. But he'd been so frustrated with Brooke, he hadn't noticed his dog hadn't obeyed. He crossed his office to the lounge area. Gave the low whistle that never failed to bring the black Malinois to heel.

Nothing.

He strode to the front desk. "Seen Grief?"

Oscar looked up from his work. "No, Boss."

Where on earth was that mongrel?

An idea hit him. He recalled Grief sniffing at a door. "No," he groaned. But with the way his day had started … Stone stalked across the lobby toward the rooms. Something in his gut tightened when he saw Brighton standing in the door. Irritation slashed what little restraint he had on his temper.

"He was scratching," she explained. "When I opened it, he darted inside."

"Why're you opening the door? Stay inside! Is that too hard to comprehend?" He nailed his dog with a glower, Brooke's chastisement strangling his temper. "Grief, come!"

The Malinois lifted his head from his perch on the bed and thumped his tail.

"Come!"

"Sorry," Brighton said, "I would've brought him, but you told me to stay—"

"Grief! Heel!"

"I see why you named him that." Her words were soft, nervous.

"It's all I've had since you." His words came out as pointed as he meant them. "C'mon, boy." But his dog stayed on the bed, tail thumping the coverlet. He knew better than to let his frustration into his voice with his dog, but he'd had enough. "Grief!"

"Come on, buddy," Brighton said cheerily, nodding to the hall. She stepped out and Grief leapt off the bed to follow her.

Unbelievable. "Traitor."

"Me or your dog?"

Stone didn't trust himself to answer. There was too much edge churning through him, so he made himself walk away. He had a bad feeling this would be the longest week of his life.

CHAPTER
NINE

She could not stay here and deal with his scorn day after day. Last night, she'd cried herself to sleep. Heaped condemnation on her stupid self for destroying the only man she'd ever wanted to talk about "forever" with. But that forever had become *forever hated*. Forever detested, reviled.

Granted, he had every right to feel that way but … she could not bear his complete rejection *and* face him day in and out. When his dog scratched at the door, she'd known better than to let the sweet beast in, but she'd wanted to apologize to Stone, explain everything. She'd never had that chance. And while it might not erase her guilt, it might …

Yeah, she had no idea. She just wanted to voice her side of it.

Yet, the minute she spotted Stone storming toward her room—as if he'd known Grief was with her—courage fled and fear took up residence. There was no apology she could offer that would give him back what had been stolen. She knew that. But if he just understood that she really hadn't had a choice …

. . . . .

BALTIMORE, MARYLAND

Water rushed over her hair and face. She let it. Tried to wash away the filth. The shame. The stain on her heart. Curled in the corner of the shower, she hugged herself with one hand and shielded her head with other. Let the tears come. Reached up and turned the water to full hot. She hated herself, hated her life. Didn't want to live.

But living kept Aston alive. Safe.

Emptiness. An existence that was just that—existing. Making it through one day, one client appointment after another.

"Be grateful you have a roof over your head—a very nice one—and a luxury SUV. You have it good, Lizzy. Don't ever forget that."

Good. Strange how that word could have so many different meanings and levels.

But it never would apply to her or anything in her life.

Except … him.

But he would find out who she was. What she was. What she did. And the only truly good thing in her life would be gone.

So just let it go before it hurts too bad.

A song drifted through the steamy shower. She shouldered it out, but then it registered—his ring tone.

Brighton lifted her head. Just let it go to voicemail. Dull that interest before the pain became too sharp, and she ruined him as they'd ruined her. When quiet reigned again, she choked off a sob, only then realizing how much she wanted to be a part of his honorable, normal life. To be loved. To know that yeah, he saw a pretty face, but he saw more. He saw her. Not the supermodel, nor escort. He'd never tried anything. Never slept with her. Hadn't even kissed her.

Why hadn't he kissed her?

The ringtone erupted again.

Brighton stood and cut off the water. Wrapped herself in a towel and snatched her phone. "Hello?"

"Lizzy, hey. It's Stone."

Tears came unbidden. His voice just set her world right. "Hi," she said, her throat raw and soft.

"You okay?"

"I am now," she admitted, then cleared her throat. "So, tonight?"

"Same time?"

"Same bat channel?" she said with a laugh, repeating their routine. She shouldn't go. She should cut it off. Before they found out about him. Who was she kidding? They had to know. They knew everything about her.

"Looking forward to it. Manicotti?"

"Mm," she agreed. "And tiramisu."

"Tiramisu it is." His smile came through the phone. The same smile he'd delivered when he showed up with groceries and flowers.

In the kitchen now, he went to work on dinner while she sat at the island watching him. He cocked his head, those pale blue eyes puncturing the dark cloud around her. "What's going on, Lizzy?"

"Sorry?"

"You're sad."

She wasn't sad. Her *life* was sad—it was sad he didn't know her real name. "Because dinner isn't ready yet." She didn't want her mood to ruin this, the one bright spot in her life, so she moved around the island to get the dishes.

Stone reached back and caught her fingers with his. Laced them. Lifted her hand to his lips and kissed them.

Breath stolen, she peered up him. A towel over his shoulder, he had no idea how gorgeous he looked.

"Talk to me, beautiful."

Her heart pittered. Then pattered. "Why haven't you kissed me?"

He considered her for a long moment, little space between them, his hand slipping to her waist.

"It's just a kiss," she said, a line she'd fed herself for the last five years.

"No," he said huskily, his gaze on her mouth. He drew his thumb gently over her lower lip. "It's not just a kiss. It means a lot more. It's promise, a beginning."

Her heart was about to thrash its way between her ribs. She caught his arm and held on, the room canting in a dizzying concoction of attraction.

"If I begin something … I finish it."

"And you don't want to do that," she supplied, trying not to show how much that hurt. "Not with me."

He shifted, his expression heavy with intent, with attraction. "Wrong again." He smirked in a way that melted her knees. "I very much want to begin *and* end it." He angled closer, those blue eyes taking her in. His breath whispered over her mouth seconds before his warm lips teased hers. "But I want to do it right. Perfection shouldn't be rushed."

. . . . .

Bexar-Wolfe Lodge, Northern Virginia

He had been so perfect. All those evenings of laughing, cooking, talking. Nothing sensual or inappropriate.

At first.

After the scandal went live, Brighton focused on work, clients. Anything to numb herself to what she'd done, violating his trust. Seeing his face, watching him on the news as he was ushered into a waiting SUV to leave the governor's mansion for the last time, his head down in shame.

A choked sob rose in her throat. And here, in the lodge,

there was no fear of Ladomer or his men hearing and condemning her "emotional outbursts," so she let the tears come. Praying to a God she'd shelved that fateful night with Leon that had changed everything. It was too much to hope for Stone's forgiveness, but maybe ... maybe God could help him not hate her.

She woke up sometime later to find the sun no longer glaring at her, and she rolled onto her back. Head aching, eyes puffy from crying, she cringed at the grumble of her stomach. Her first thought was to head out and run to the local bagel shop, but reality gave her habit a swift kick into reality. There was no bagel shop here. Only the four walls of this hotel room. Not even a coffee shop. Groan. That could possibly be the cruelest thing here.

No. No, that was a lie. Seeing Stone and experiencing his wrath—those were the cruelest.

Brighton slipped off the bed, ordered a tray of food—which was promised to arrive within a half hour—and decided to shower. She dug through the clothes from Brooke, then got cleaned up. Hair wrapped in a towel, she emerged, determined to somehow find better shampoo that did not leave her hair feeling like cardboard.

A knock came at the door with the pronouncement of "Room Service."

Still expecting Ladomer or his men to find her, Brighton checked the peep hole before opening the door.

A short, burly Latino with a goatee grinned at her. "*Hola, bella dama!*" Happy and gregarious, he nodded. "I see now why he yell. I also would yell!"

Brighton blinked, then came the flush of embarrassment. She was used to having men flirt with her, but it was somehow unexpected here—after all, the desk clerk clearly sided with his boss. Job security, she guessed.

He passed her the tray of food.

"Thank you," she said, backing into the room.

"No matter what ju want, dial three-five, and Alvaro"—he thumped his chest—"make it, jes?"

Brighton smiled. "Okay. Thank you." She doubted Stone would appreciate his chef being commandeered.

A voice boomed near the foyer—not loud, just … strong. Stone. Afraid he'd be angry again, she stepped back and nodded to Alvaro. "Thank you." Letting the door close behind her, she aimed the tray toward the table.

"What was that?"

His deep voice snapped her around. The glass of water tumbled off the tray and clattered to the floor. "Augh!" Thank goodness it wasn't actually made of glass, but her leg was wet now. She hurriedly set the tray down and rushed to grab a towel from the bathroom.

How had Stone gotten into her room so fast? What, had he run to intercept?

"What were you doing talking to Alvaro?"

On her knees—likely a position of abject humility he preferred from her—she glowered up at him. "I was thanking him for my lunch."

"It's two!"

"Look." She couldn't hide her sarcasm. "I know you always have your plan and schedule to keep, but I … I …" Brighton wilted. She had no fight, so she resumed blotting the water from the carpet.

"I told you to stay in your room!"

She stamped to her feet—and the towel wobbled off her head, wet hair tumbling down her back and face. She shoved it back. "I did! It's not my fault the chef delivers the food to see who you enjoy yelling at!"

Stone drew up, his hands fisted. That blue gaze blazed at her, then skidded to the floor. His jaw muscle jounced violently as he turned to the door, all but ripped it off the hinges, left, and slammed it behind him.

Pulling in a jagged breath, Brighton felt adrenaline crash through her system, leaving her shaky. She wilted onto the bed and buried her face in her hands. She couldn't do this. She could *not* stay here and have that happen every time he saw her. She wasn't sure what was worse—his hatred or the fact that she still wanted to find the sweet spot they'd had in Rockville.

If only Stone would hear her out, know that they'd given her no choice …

It wouldn't matter. She'd ruined his life, and he would never look at her as he had that last night when passion had been high and that stupid phone call thwarted what she'd wanted most— Stone's love.

Enough. She would not survive a week like this.

One way or another, she had to get out of here. Brighton eyed the door—no, too obvious. The glass door to the patio … That might work. Stalking to the doors, she plotted her escape. Hilary, another of Ladomer's girls, had taught her all she'd need to do to escape. But Brighton didn't have survival skills that would see her across a mountain. And that's what stood in her way—a beautiful, forbidding mountain.

But the route Cord had brought her hadn't been mountainous. So she'd have to find that route. Brighton reached for the phone, determining to get answers now, so she could be gone at the first opportunity.

It'd been two days, and Stone couldn't shake the memory of how she'd yelled at him. Or that scaredy-cat look in her eyes that hit him sideways, as if she were some wounded creature …

Bullspit. *He'd* been the victim, words he'd never voice to

anyone else. She'd worked her wiles and gotten him into a compromising situation ... then destroyed him.

You let it happen. Too enamored with the beautiful young woman paying attention to him. His conscience always had been louder than his mouth, keeping him in check.

Except that it hadn't. Not with Tizzy.

He groaned at the nickname. It'd been a slip of the tongue during one of their more passionate moments. Afterward, she'd admitted Lizzy wasn't her name. It'd taken her a while longer to offer up her real identity. He couldn't believe her real name was the same as his mom's favorite specialty shop, the one from which he'd bought many a birthday and Christmas gift.

Mom ... She'd had Brighton in her apartment. Laughing, eating, talking ...

His gut roiled. What had Brighton told them about him, about them? Mom was disappointed enough in him without all the sordid details.

For cryin' out loud! Why was he still thinking about her?

Jerking back to his desk and the work waiting, he ran a hand over his beard. The darn thing was irritating him now. Just like the occupant in 107.

His phone rang and he saw it was the front desk. "Hello."

"Mr. Mulroney, Chandra Pellet is here for your appointment."

Thirty minutes late. But he had to play nice. Pinching the bridge of his nose—how had he forgotten about the meeting with the inspector?—he sighed. "I'll be right up."

Stone secured Grief in his private dog run attached to the office, then made his way down the hall. He spotted the inspector in a gray business suit and skirt, sitting ramrod straight near the fire. Her dyed-brown hair did little to hide she was well into her sixties and her prejudices. All poise and arrogance.

He groaned inwardly. She was so much like Brooke—knew

how the world and everyone else should function and had no compunction against telling them, too. Pellet—yeah, he'd had too much fun with that name, though she pronounced it as pay-lay—had been set against him from day one, even though nobody here knew who he really was. Still, the only way to win her over was to prove his character and not give her a reason to doubt him or connect him to the scandalized governor.

"Inspector."

She stood, lifting her briefcase effortlessly. "Mr. Mulroney." She gave him a tight-lipped smile as her shoes tapped over the tiles toward him. "I wondered if I'd have to wait all day." She was trying to get the upper hand.

"Only if you were any later." Okay, he shouldn't have said that, but the woman had it coming, since she was a half hour late. "This way." He started for his office.

"I think not."

Stone stopped and glanced back with a frown. "Pardon?"

"I prefer to sit in the open with w—others."

Witnesses. Was that what she'd been about to say?

Stone frowned. There was no way she knew the truth. Was there? He was so close—just had to toe the line a little longer, get the permits approved by this inspector, who also chaired the county planning committee.

He indicated toward the front of the lodge. "We can find a table in the restaurant."

Nose in the air, she pivoted in a move that made him wonder if she'd ever served. Nah. The military would've knocked that arrogance out of her.

With his back to the wall—in more ways than one—Stone sat in the restaurant with the inspector, enduring her recitation of previously denied permits: the hunting license, which she found noisy and violent; the overnight trail ride, which she found dangerous and irresponsible; the zipline, which she declared a lawsuit risk and unsightly. Then she tackled his request to build an indoor athletic arena and a small daycare to draw more families.

"I must confess, Mr. Mulroney," she said, drawing the glasses from her nose with that superior air, "I am a bit alarmed that … you are so focused on families—*children*. A man like you should have other … interests."

"A man like me." Warmth trickled across his neck and shoulders.

She knows.

Not possible. How could she?

"Well, yes." She shifted on the chair, and he found himself hoping she'd sat in the lumpy one. "I mean … It was no secret—it was all over the news."

"I'm sorry …?"

"Oh come. You don't think the beard and hiding up here changes the fact your real name is Stone—"

"Ma'am."

"—Metcalfe."

Hand fisting on his leg, he gritted his teeth. "I'm not hiding."

"Then why the pretense?"

"To protect this lodge and avoid journalists hunting me down. You may have decided my guilt, but *nobody* knows what happened there exc—"

"Except you and that woman."

Stone gritted his teeth. When he'd left office, he'd vowed to never speak of it with anyone.

She stretched her neck as if he'd victimized her. "It was … inappropriate and with you trying to bring people up here to be in their swimsuits—"

Heat charged down his neck at her insinuation. "Fine." He heard the bark and realized Brooke had a point. He was turning into a bully. "Forget the athletic center. But I we'll never get anywhere until you rid yourself of the idea that I'm a predator."

"I never said—"

"Let's skip the games, Inspector. All I want is for this lodge to be viable and bring business to the area." He had no patience for her or her accusations. Knew that, in her mind, nothing would clear his name. "So. Moving on to the café." Anger churned through him. "It's built, inspected, and now—"

"Perhaps"—condescension oozed through her tone—"if you had actually waited for me to sign off on it before opening it, I could've handed you the approval right here, but since you didn't—"

"It's *not* open." Stone fought the urge to laugh at the absurdity of her claim. "I haven't even found someone to work or manage it."

She nodded out the door. "Then what do you call that?"

Fed up with this woman and the mountains he had to scale to get her approval on the stupidest things, he glanced over his shoulder. What he saw wouldn't process, and yet it yanked an oath from his lips. His sister sat at the café counter being served a steaming latte by none other than Brighton.

"What the ...?"

"I suppose you thought to hide that from me." Mrs. Pellet gathered her papers and briefcase from the table.

"I had no such intention. But I do have an intention to let everyone who passes through know that Mrs. *Pay-lay* would rather make assumptions and infer intent rather than follow the law. After all, the café passed fire and food inspections, but she wants to hurt the people visiting her county rather than allow them to enjoy it." An idea hit him, one he told himself to ignore. Not to speak. "Or is this about something else? I mean—are you failing me so you have more opportunity to come and talk to me?"

Pellet went white. And Stone regretted his words but couldn't take them back. She snatched a paper from her folder and slapped it against his chest. "Just try to get any of your other permits approved!" With a harrumph, she clipped her way out of the lodge.

Stone wanted to ball up the permit and throw it at her vanishing form. But there was someone else he needed to deal with first. Permit in hand, he stormed toward the coffee bar.

CHAPTER
TEN

"Well, that looks like a Category Five."

Brighton looked up from rinsing the frothing cup. "What?"

"A Category Five—hurricane." Brooke bobbed her head toward the restaurant, then sipped her quad-shot with hazelnut.

Brighton followed her gaze and slammed right into Stone's. "Oh no." Jerking back to the counter, she didn't even have to guess why he was angry. "You said he went to town!"

Brooke flicked a hand and slipped from her stool. "I'll handle him."

"Please, don't—"

A wall of chest slammed up against her periphery. "Haven't you done enough damage to me already?" Stone's razor-sharp words minced nothing.

"I needed espresso." Brooke inserted herself between them, cutting off his glower. "So when I found out Brighton used to be a barista, I begged her to make me one."

Uncertainty flashed through his blue eyes as he again looked to Brighton. "I didn't have a permit for this café to be operational, and the inspector—who just left—threatened to reject it because, when she saw you in here, she thought I'd opened it."

A swarm of nervous jellies struck. She saw the inspector getting into her white Lexus and swallowed hard. "I–I'm sorry."

"What, are you trying to ruin *everything* in my life? Destroying my gubernatorial career wasn't enough, you have to go after this one, too?"

Had he thrown acid on her, it wouldn't have burned so deeply or painfully. She hadn't ... Never ... Brighton hurried out of the coffee bar.

He gestured with his hands. "Why are you even out here? You're supposed to stay in your room. How is that hard to understand?"

"Stone!" Brooke's tone sliced right back at her brother. "You buffoon. Only caged animals stay locked up."

He pivoted toward her. "Thought you were leaving. You never want to stick around the family. Why's it different this time? Like seeing me openly ruined?"

Tears burning, Brighton rushed around the counter and hurried to her room. Every step hammering his words— destroying my career wasn't enough?—further into her soul. Enough. He didn't want her here and she didn't want to be here. Common ground. The only one they'd ever have, apparently. And she sure wasn't going to walk on eggshells for however long it took Cord to return. He'd said a week, but it already felt like a year. Between her own guilty conscience and Stone's constant berating ...

She was done. Out of here.

"You are a beast!"

"You always say that." Stone glanced around the coffee bar

counter. He turned off the machine and put the frother and spoon—both clean now—back where they belonged.

"Do you really expect her to sit alone in a musty hotel room for two weeks?"

"*One* week." He planted his hands on his belt. "And yes, I do expect her to stay there. And be grateful I didn't throw her out when they showed up."

"Grateful? You overgrown ape! She's a broken woman—"

He huffed and started for his office. Hearing his sister's assertive steps pacing him, he gritted his teeth.

"You have no idea what she's going through."

He rounded on her. "What *she's* going through?" Man, it hurt to breathe past the roiling fury in his chest. "She—" His mind lit on guests sitting in the nearby waiting area, watching them, and he resumed course.

Though Brooke followed, at least she had the common sense not to air any more dirty laundry in the open. "I do not understand you." In his office, she closed the door.

Stone dropped into his chair. "I don't have time for this, Brooke. I'm running a lodge." He grunted. "More like trying to salvage it now." He dragged a hand over his beard. "Salvage my whole life."

"And that's *her* fault?"

"Yes! She used her wiles and worked me. Cost me my career because that's what her handler wanted."

His dark-haired sister actually managed to show him sympathy right then. "Stone ... I—"

"No." He did not need this from her. That was as twisted and wrong as it was even having Brighton in the lodge. "I thought you were closing Mom's house and heading back to New York."

Arms folded, she slid into a chair. "I'm ... working on some things." She tilted her head and squinted at him. "You *really* like her, don't you?"

"Where the heck did you get that idea?" He dropped his gaze to the paperwork littering the desk. "When are you leaving?"

Brooke smirked. "Wow, I really hit a nerve."

Not in the mood for this sisterly antagonism, he leaned forward. "Do you realize how close I came to the lodge getting shut down out there?"

Her amusement faded. "What do you mean?"

"That inspector who just walked out of here has denied multiple building and program permits, failed every project at least twice—and now I find out she knows who I really am." He let out a long breath, remembering that look in Pellet's eyes. "She thinks I'm some pervert out to exploit women and children. Wouldn't even sit in this office with me to discuss the outstanding permits and future projects. She has tried several times to get this place shut down. Couldn't ever understand it." He huffed a breath. "Now, I know why."

He shook his head, a raw burn at the back of his throat. Hated himself because, really, he had no one to blame but himself, did he? "Last time she was here, she said I was unfit to run Bexar-Wolfe." He narrowed his eyes, remembering how she'd watched the café … "If she realizes who Brighton is …"

Understanding slid across his sister's face. "You can't let that happen."

"All the more reason she needs to stay in her room—"

"Dig into that heroic complex that has always defined you and our brothers and *protect* her!"

Stone exhaled heavily. "Look, I didn't ask for this. Cord shows up with her in tow, begs me to let her stay, and suddenly I'm standing on a cliff's edge being battered by the elements and about to give way."

Brooke watched him for several minutes, then finally edged forward. "Listen." She threaded her hands together. "I see several things here."

"Is this your official analysis?" Through the windows, he

spotted Rowe coming from the trailhead. Though the guy interacted with the guests as the manager, Rowe was better suited for the more physical aspects like trail rides, etc.

"First—you let her stay when your friend asked you to."

"Not like I had much choice."

"But you did," Brooke said quietly, confused. "You've *always* said everyone has a choice. You could've sent them packing, turned them out. And of late, that's the big brother I know. Second—I've *never* seen you as angry or as volatile around anyone as you are around her."

Again, he dropped his gaze.

"Which tells me you might be appropriately ticked off her at her, but you like her. A lot."

"I—"

"No." She silenced him with a hand. "Even when Marie took Jack and left, you were never like this. Never raised your voice. Never erupted. You've done exactly that on three occasions in just as many days with this girl. I don't know how, but she's gotten under your skin. For you to have slept with her, risked your career—"

"I never slept with her."

Brooke hesitated, questions dancing in her blue eyes.

"We didn't." He cocked his eyebrow.

"Regardless," she said, apparently deciding her point was still valid, "she drew you out, engaged your heart. I'm not even sure Marie really ever did that."

"You saying I was heartless with my wife?"

"I'm saying you've always had the plan, the goals. Your wife and one-point-two kids. Marie filled that plan. It was something you could control, something you could line up. A plan that helped you create order in the chaos of life." She thumbed over her shoulder. "Brighton? She's an unexpected element. Unpredictable. Beautiful and vibrant. But I have to be honest—"

"Do you?"

"—I do not like how ... *small* she acts when you're around."

"That's what happens with a guilty conscience."

"Then *you* should be cowering," she chastised, settling on the chair. "I believe with Brighton it's more than simply a guilty conscience. I think she truly feels terrible for what she did, and that's because she's crazy about you and hates that she can't find a way back into your favor." She smirked and shrugged. "And your arms."

"Never happening." Stone pushed his gaze to the window, refusing to entertain that.

"But you?" She got that devious look in her eyes. "I think you want it to happen. You really care about her or you wouldn't have this anger. It's all over your face."

He stood and motioned her toward the door. "I need to get some work done."

"Start with the much-needed work on your heart, big brother. Because I have a feeling *that* problem isn't going away anytime soon." She came to her feet. "And I swear if you do not stop yelling at her—"

"When did you start caring?" The words were sharper than he'd intended. "That's right—you don't. You just like to tell everyone how to live their lives when yours is a nuked mess."

Hurt rippled through her olive complexion ... something most people probably wouldn't have noticed, but being siblings, there was little they could hide from each other.

With a sad smile, she started for the door. "That you attempt to redirect tells me I'm right." She twisted the knob. "Tread carefully. Mr. Taggart said her pimp was one of the worst he'd encountered. You have a chance to help her. Don't regret ignoring that." She left and closed the door behind her.

Pimp. The word plunked in his gut.

But wait—when had Cord and Brooke talked enough for him to tell her that?

Rowe tapped on the glass door and let himself in, an urgency in his expression. "Hey, Boss."

"What's up?"

"Thought I should mention it, but maybe it's not my business."

Stone waited.

"That girl you brought up here a couple nights ago?"

His gut clenched. "Yeah?"

"Saw her hoofing it down the western slope toward the main gate."

CHAPTER
ELEVEN

Plunging through the dense overgrowth of the treed hillside, Brighton had to get as far from Stone Metcalfe as possible before he noticed her absence. She'd have to call Cord, tell him she needed somewhere else to stay. Anywhere else. *What* had he been thinking bringing her here? How had he ever thought Stone would accept this, her?

"What, are you trying to ruin everything in my life?"

His feral words made her stumble. Her foot caught on a fallen branch. Twisted her leg. Sent her sprawling. Hands shoved into a soggy spot, mud splashing her face as pain corkscrewed through her muscle. With a yelp, she stayed on all fours. Cried. Dug her fingers into the mud and strangled a shriek. This wasn't the life she'd wanted—men using her, losing a piece of her soul every time. To be thrown at the mercy of the one she'd thought different. The one man she'd started to …

"No," she gritted out. She wouldn't say it. And crying wouldn't do any good. She pushed to her feet and felt a sharp pain tear through her ankle. Wincing, she guessed she'd sprained—or strained—it. Maybe fractured. But she wasn't quitting. And she wasn't staying here. She couldn't. Not anymore.

He would never forgive her. Any doubt about that had been erased in the last week. At least she didn't have to wonder anymore. Or dream.

Wiping muddy hands on her jeans, she hobbled a few steps more. But each attempt to move on only sent painful daggers up her leg. Using a tree for stability, she beat the heel of her hand against it, giving vent to her fury.

Why? Why couldn't just one thing in her life go right? Why couldn't she catch a break? She hated herself for her part in Ladomer's scheme, but even more, she hated herself for foolishly thinking Stone would turn out different from the other men. That what they'd had wasn't him just being another client.

Fool!! Fool fool fool!

She had to get out of here. She'd make Cord understand this was the worst possible scenario. Brighton dug through her backpack and found the burner phone. One-time use. If she called, asked for a new place, that was it. She couldn't use it again.

Which was fine. She wouldn't need to use it again.

She turned it on and opened the contacts to the single number stored there. But her mind took a winding path—what if she made this call and … somehow Ladomer traced it … came here …

Oh, if he found her here with Stone … there'd be no mercy. From either man. Ladomer would punish her in cruel ways for going to another man—not that she'd done that, but he'd see it that way. And Stone would be in danger and livid that she brought Ladomer to the lodge.

Haven't you done enough already?

Either way, she lost. And she'd end up back in Baltimore … working …

Thumping the phone against her forehead, she tried to figure out what to do. Staying here wasn't an option. She needed out. She'd rather go back to work than meet Stone's fury every day.

She slid to the ground, hugging her pack, and peered up at the tree limbs and sky. Tears blurred the greens and blue. Would she ever be happy? She snorted. Forget happy. She just wanted to be safe. Not wondering what would happen when she met clients. Not running scared. Was "safe" possible? Would she ever be loved after all she'd done, all the men …?

This was Stone's fault. He'd done this—given her that false hope. Tricked her into believing happily ever after might actually be a real thing that happened in life. It just proved she was an idiot. Tears, scalding and furious, raced down her cheeks.

God, where are you?

She sniffed, her nose starting to run from her crying. Where had God been all these years when Ladomer sold her body to men?

Donning his hat as he strode up the hill to his truck, Stone called the front desk and told Oscar he'd be back in a few. With Grief, Stone hurried to his truck parked behind the cabin and all but ran into Brooke strolling down the trail.

"What's going on?" Brooke called.

"She took off." Stone banked left toward his driveway, pulling the keys from his pocket.

"What're you going to do to her?"

He skated his sister a glower. "What do you think? Remember, I'm a buffoon."

She rolled her eyes. "Bring her back and be nice. She's fragile."

Nice was the last thing he'd be. Brighton had been nothing but trouble since she'd arrived. No—since he'd met her a year ago. Rankled, he opened the truck door. "Hup." He waited until

Grief sailed into the cab and parked himself on the passenger seat before climbing in behind him. Even as he pulled out, he was struck by Brooke's comments. Strange that she was showing more concern over Tizzy.

Gotta stop calling her that.

Windows down, he drove around the cabin and onto the far side of the parking lot. As he hit the mile-long driveway, his phone rang. "Yeah."

"Hey," Rowe said. "I'm at my desk. Gate security hasn't been tripped and neither have any of the perimeter sensors."

They'd set those up to track bear and wildlife intrusion onto the property, since guests often walked the trails. And if the sensors hadn't been tripped, then Brighton was still on the property.

"Okay, thanks." He slowed the truck, probing the trees and open stretches for sign of her. He recalled the pink shirt she'd had on. Should be easy to spot.

Grief stuck his nose out the window, pulling hard draughts of air while Stone scanned the trees on both sides of the drive. He'd give her a piece of his mind. What was she thinking, running off like this? Did she want to get caught? Was she that anxious to get back to her work?

Grief bolted out the window and tore off. Had he found Brighton? Stone parked to the side, grabbed his hat, and climbed out. As he donned his hat, he caught a flash of pink in the opposite direction from Grief's trajectory. Squinting, he peered down the slope.

About a hundred yards from the perimeter fence and county road, Brighton sat at the base of a tree, hugging her knees. He wasn't close enough to tell for sure, but it seemed she was crying.

Crap. Stone swallowed. They'd come a long way from nights of movies and laughter. Her in his arms, the music sultry and low ...

But then, none of that had been real. All that time, she'd been working him.

After double-checking for Grief—what had he torn off after?—Stone started toward Brighton, his sister's admonishment to be nice, that Brighton was broken, echoing in his thick skull. He had thirty paces to wrestle his antagonism into line.

Only when she glanced up and scrambled to her feet, shifting away from him—pain contorting her face—did he realize he'd stopped. "Leave me alone!"

"Easy."

"Don't! Don't yell at me again." Tears smeared rivulets down her muddied face as she protected her left foot. Was she injured? "I am not staying. I'm leaving. I've called Cord."

Stone started at that. "You did what?" He stomped forward.

Brighton shuffled back. "Stop! Leave me—" She stepped wrong, tried to catch her footing, but her feet slipped out from under her, sending her crashing down in a puddled heap.

He started forward but she let out a shriek that stilled him.

Auburn hair stringy and flecked with mud, she pounded the ground, creating a slurping noise in the muck. "I didn't want this!" Words scraped and strained from her throat. "I don't want to be here. Don't want to hear or see every day what I did to you, that you hate me. It wasn't me—I didn't want to hurt you! It was the last thing I wanted. I was happy. *We* were happy." She choked back a sob. Literally growled. "Just ... leave me alone. I'm going. Trying. Don't tell me again that you hate me. I can't stand to hear it again. *Please ...*" She shook her head. "No more."

Eyes closed, Stone swallowed the rawness of the words she'd howled. He roughed a hand over his face and hung his head. Looked at her.

Muddy hands to her face, she sobbed.

He might hate himself, but he didn't hate her. As much as

he'd tried to convince himself of that since he'd left Baltimore, he didn't. Couldn't. Brooke was right—Brighton had gotten under his skin. Bad.

Regret nudged him closer, quietly, carefully, then he crouched. Couldn't bring himself to look into those brown eyes. He had no idea where to start. Until he noticed her gripping her ankle. "What happened to your leg?"

"Tripped," she said around a sniffle.

"Is it broken?"

"No … I—" She shrugged. "Don't think so."

He nodded, not sure what to do next. There was no plan to consult. "Let's get you back to the lodge."

"No." Defiant brown eyes snapped to him. "I'm not staying locked in a room for another week. I can't take that or you yelling at me every time I make a move or even breathe wrong. Please … Just … Go. I'll find a way … out."

Feeling every bit the buffoon his sister had called him, Stone stared at the ground, then back in the direction Grief had taken off. "You can't walk, and you're covered in mud. So, let's get you cleaned up and … we'll talk. Think we both need to get a few things off our chests."

Wariness parked at the edges of eyes that had melted his willpower more than once. But now, the brightness was replaced by a fear that soured the food in his gut. He considered the leg she still held off the ground. "Can you make it to the truck?"

She eyed him and the driveway, then finally nodded. Stubbornly independent, she struggled to her feet. Slipped. When Stone reached for her, she gritted out a "no." Took a step and jerked violently. Dropped her pack and fell back against the tree.

Stone snatched it up, slung it over his shoulder, then moved in and lifted her off the ground.

"No!" She stiffened as he hoisted her into a better hold. "I just need a stick."

"If you slip, you risk injuring it further." He slogged up the mossy undergrowth back to the drive.

"Put me down. I can—"

"Open the door is what you can do."

She huffed and caught the door handle, then pried it open. When he aimed her into it, she arched her spine and cried out, "Wait!"

"What now?"

"I'll get your truck dirty."

"For the love of Pete." He popped her onto the seat. "You won't do anything Grief hasn't." He drew the seatbelt out and passed it to her. "Well, I'd appreciate it if you didn't puke like he does. Hard to get that smell out of the leather." On the other side, he climbed in. For a second, he thought to pull up to the front, but they didn't need anyone seeing him carrying her in. That'd draw attention. People remembered that kind of thing. Great way to get himself in trouble again.

He opted for his cabin. Which felt a lot like inviting the devil to dinner.

CHAPTER
TWELVE

BEXAR-WOLFE LODGE, *Northern Virginia*

"Holy ... wow." Propped against a door frame, Brighton gaped at the place Stone had delivered her to. She'd seen some swanky, modern places, but this ... this was glorious. Rugged. Rustic with clear modern touches. Classy. A wall of windows offered an unhindered view of the mountains, and to the far right and down the hill, the lodge.

"What is this place?" Afraid to move and leave mud slicks, she tried to keep her imprint small.

"My place. Hang tight." He strode across the living room and disappeared around a corner.

His place? She'd assumed he lived in the lodge in a private residence or something like his mom. The living room was nicely appointed with a leather sofa and two recliners. A dog bed lay by the unlit fireplace. "Where's your dog?"

"Took off when I was looking for you. He'll find his way back." He reappeared. "I only moved up here a few weeks ago, so the guest bath doesn't have a shower curtain or supplies. You'll have to clean up ... back here."

"Okay." Wondering at his hesitation, she stepped forward and winced.

He strode toward her.

"N-no." Brighton held up a hand, not ready to be in his arms again, at least … not like that. "I got it." She hopped to the first chair, then to the massive island that set off a wall of cabinets and a really large gas cooktop. She couldn't help but smile, remembering how much he'd loved cooking. Surfing the counter, she made it a few more hops to the door jamb. And saw what made him hesitate—the bathroom he'd instructed her to use was part of the master bedroom. *His* bedroom.

It was strange—everywhere they'd met for their time together had a bed, but he'd never taken her to it, except that last night … when the warmth of his kisses on her neck, the urgency and power of his touch …

"Back here." His voice was gruff and startling as he moved past her and pointed to another door. "Shower's there, towel's in the closet here. Use what you need."

This felt like a trap. Or a danger. Likely both. "And why am I cleaning up here, not in my room at the lodge?"

"Besides the fact everyone would wonder why you're covered in mud, injured people stand out and are remembered. We don't need or want anyone remembering you."

"Right."

"Shout if you need anything."

Her stomach squirmed as he brushed past her again, his hand making the barest of contact with her arm. She'd always had the nervous jellies around him—the man's presence was powerful. And she'd been part of his electrical circuit for a while. Until she'd ruined it. He'd never take her back but … maybe when they talked later, she could make him understand, see that she wasn't evil personified.

Grateful for the toiletries from the lodge that she'd stuffed in her backpack, Brighton showered, then donned the only articles of clothing that weren't muddied—a frilly white, sleeveless shell, and a pair of yoga pants. "At least my agent will never see me in this." Not that her contract was good anymore, thanks to Leon.

After towel-drying her hair, she looked around for a comb. Opened a drawer—shaving gear. Ironic considering the beard, but who was she to judge? The cabinet below the sink had cleaning supplies and ... a travel kit. Surely the man had a comb somewhere. She spotted another drawer and opened it. Aha! She lifted the comb ... and stilled.

Beneath it lay a picture. Of her and Stone. "What ...?" she whispered and picked it up, heart pounding. He still had it. She remembered being with him in that little village in Virginia. Looking at antiques. Simply enjoying being together. Alone— well, mostly.

As governor, he wasn't ever alone, but his security detail did a good job keeping their distance. He had his hat and her heart. She'd begged for a selfie, and he'd finally relented. Stood behind her, his chest her pillow, and wrapped a muscular arm around her, engulfing her in his strength as he lifted the phone. Holding onto him as he snapped the selfie, she felt the scrape of his scruffies. Even now, she felt them against her cheek, a realization that made her heart stutter and ache. It'd been complicated seeing him, dating him, but it seemed so simple compared to now.

Voices in the living room snapped her out of the reverie. She slid the photo back into the drawer, wondering that he still had it, and gathered her things.

A soft knock on the door startled her out of her reverie. "Hello?"

Brighton stilled at the jovial voice. "Yes?"

"It's Clara, dear. Stone asked me to look at your ankle. I was a nurse."

Brighton hobbled over and unlocked the door, sheepishly peering out at the older woman.

His mom stood back and gaped. "Oh, you can't wear that. It's too thin."

Hugging her things closer, she cringed and shivered at the cool mountain air that swirled through the cabin. "I … I don't have anything else that's clean."

Mrs. Clara angled her head toward the front of the cabin. "Stone, do you have a sweater or hoodie she can borrow?"

"Wardrobe, lower right drawer."

Nodding, his mother went to the large black furniture piece and opened it. She returned with a sweatshirt. "Here you go."

When Brighton saw the design, she felt her insides seize. "Oh, I can't—"

"Sure you can. He said so. He won't mind."

But he would. A lot. Because that sweatshirt was one she'd bought him from the place where they always started their evenings—Manny's Crab Shack. "Honest. I'm goo—"

"Put it on before you freeze and end up with pneumonia." Mrs. Clara wagged her hands at Brighton, shooing her back into the bathroom. "Go on, dear, so I can get a look at that ankle."

Reluctantly, Brighton closed the door and stared at the sweatshirt. Traced the embroidered logo. Why did he even have it still? Between this and the picture …

Don't think about it. Just put it on. Clearly, he'd forgotten about the memento. Bottom drawer meant least-used, right? She slipped into the sweatshirt. True, she was warmer, but Stone … he'd think this was her idea. He'd get mad. Accuse her of trying to rub it in his face.

The photo … the sweatshirt … Reminders of their time together. The best six months of her life. Had he wanted to remember those times just as much she had?

"Get her out of here!"

"Haven't you done enough damage?"

Yeah, no desire to remember. And when he saw her wearing

this sweatshirt, he'd likely burn it—with her in it! Maybe she should get a different one from the—

"C'mon, dear!"

Reluctantly, she moved into the living room as quietly as possible, doing her best not to draw his attention from where he was cooking in the kitchen.

But he turned. And like a hawk, his gaze homed in on the sweatshirt. A shadow spirited across beard-roughened features.

And somehow, locked in that moment, she knew he was recalling their dinners, conversations, laughter. Holding hands. Kisses.

Dreading his anger again, she scrambled to explain. "I—your mom—it was in the drawer." She chewed the inside of her lip. "I can change—"

"Don't be daft, dear." Mrs. Clara motioned her into to the living where she was sitting. "Come. We'll get you into the recliner and put that leg up." She motioned to Stone. "Help her over."

Before he could refuse or—worse—comply, Brighton hobbled to the chair and plopped down. "See? I'm good."

Mrs. Clara gave her son a severe glare as she sat on the leather ottoman that served as a table. Her blue gaze returned to Brighton as she lifted her leg. "This one?"

Brighton nodded, ears trained on the kitchen where something sizzled and crackled. The wafting aroma of fajita meat—one of his favorite dishes—made her stomach rumble. Self-conscious, she gave his mom a sheepish grin. Which quickly vanished at the older woman's manipulation of her ankle, eliciting a yelp and hiss from Brighton.

"Sorry about that, dear. Indeed likely a strain or sprain." She went to the kitchen and returned with a baggie of ice. "I prescribe RICE."

So much like her own mom had been. Brighton nodded. "Rest, ice, compression, and elevation."

"Indeed. Three down and one to go."

"I'll ask Alvaro to pick up a bandage when he heads into town tonight for supplies," Stone said.

"Perfect." Mrs. Clara then provided some ibuprofen and water. "Take these and stay off it for a while. This chair is great for elevating it." She smiled down at her as Brighton took the proffered medication. "I think your ankle is not the only part of you that needs some healing TLC."

Mind reader much?

"And in light of that, I suggest we eat dinner in here with you."

"Oh, no. You don't have—"

"Yes, we do. I heard your stomach. And he's made a fine meal. Just sit and rest that leg."

She was treating Brighton like a victim, not an escapist. Not the woman who'd ruined her son's career. Then again, it was hard to even think of the rugged, larger-than-life Stone Metcalfe as "son" to this diminutive woman.

Sitting and staring at the TV with some sitcom playing as he and his mom whispered less than ten feet away, Brighton couldn't help but wonder about that "we'll talk" he'd gruffed against her ear. When he'd said that, it seemed he might not have been quite as angry as before. Or maybe it was just another deflection. His words had sounded like a warning, though. And it terrified her. Because it meant honesty. A lot of it. And a lot of it from her.

During their months together, he'd laughed and kissed her because he hadn't known what she was. Every day it'd killed her, being with him, enjoying their time together, his laugh, his character. It made her want to tell him the truth. To be a better person. She'd even started believing he might understand that she'd been forced to entertain men.

Stone was all about the choice, about the will. No, he

wouldn't understand. He'd just tell her she had a choice and she'd made hers.

But now, she was here. With him. And they were going to talk. That couldn't be just some cruel twist of fate. It had to mean something, right?

Yes, that you're a naïve idiot.

He'd so looked forward to fajitas alone with the news, but it was strange and borderline disturbing to be eating with Brighton. In his home. Sitting in his chair. All through dinner there'd been a frustrating, awkward silence that he let his mother fill with small talk and questions about Brighton.

"How're your parents?"

Brighton wasn't sure—they hadn't seen each other in a while, though her mom died years ago. Her dad was a megachurch pastor but she refused to watch his streaming services.

Do you have any siblings?

A younger brother, Aston.

All things he'd known about her. Things she'd shared with him in Baltimore. There had been other questions, but Stone had gotten lost in his own thoughts about how they'd gotten here, what he was supposed to do with all this. When he took the dishes from them both and loaded them in the dishwasher, Mom came to his side.

"I don't think it's right for me to leave."

Stone frowned at her. "She and I need to talk."

"She's afraid of you," his mom said, her eyes wide. "Why—"

"It's not me she's afraid of—it's the truth." He tightened his jaw. "Please. We just need time to talk."

"Why? What do you hope to accomplish?"

He shoved a hand through his hair and huffed. "Maybe not

to hate her so much." He felt miserable saying that, but it was true.

"You don't hate her—you're angry with her. There's a difference."

"Not right now."

"It may seem—"

"Mom." He caught her shoulders. "I'm forty-three. I don't need a lecture or instructions, not after serving in the public sector in one form or another for most of my adult life." And she didn't know who Brighton really was. Or … did she? Had Brooke told her?

She skewered him with a disapproving look. "I'm not sure about that lecture …" But she gave a hesitant nod. "Fine. If you or she need anything, you know where I am."

He almost laughed. "I do. Thank you." He walked her out and watched her slip into the private rear entrance to her apartment, then headed back inside to find Brighton struggling to her feet. "What're you doing?"

"Leaving." There was more defeat than defiance in her tone.

He thought about letting her do that, about reclaiming his peaceful evening, but truth was, there would be no peace till he got this out of the way. "I said we need to talk."

"It's pointless, Stone. You'll still hate me, even if it's not as much." Her voice sounded off. "This won't change anything, except maybe to alleviate your conscience about having tried."

He cursed himself for not being quieter when he'd talked with Mom. "That's unfair, but I hear you. And we won't know what good it'll do until we try to hear each other out."

"Will you?" Her eyes narrowed. "Will you hear me out?"

He wanted to spit out a retort along the lines of "of course I will," but he wouldn't lie. So he took a second to shift his attitude. "I will." Even if it killed him. Pointing to the chair, he moved toward the sofa. "Sit and elevate that leg."

"Always were bossy," she muttered as she eased into the

chair and reclined. Relief loosened the knot between her eyebrows.

He sat on the edge of the coffee table, elbows on his knees, fingers threaded. "When's Cord coming for you?"

"I thought you worked that out with him."

"You said you called him …"

"Oh." Brighton blanched, then looked down. "I … I never made the call."

Really, he shouldn't be surprised. "Why lie about that?"

Her face reddened but then she wilted. "I didn't want you to think … I mean—" She sighed and drew herself up. "I knew you didn't want me here, so when I saw you, I just wanted to make it clear I was leaving." She did this limp-shouldered shrug that annoyed him. "Before you got angry again."

"Nearest town is more than twenty klicks. You would've been walking way past dark." His conscience packed a punch it wanted to deliver that the way he'd treated her left her feeling like her only option was to run away. And that wasn't all his conscience was chattering about—it also said he should give her reassurance that the lodge was a safe place, that she was safe … here. But letting her stay felt like a betrayal and there'd been enough of that in his life.

"I can't do this, Stone," she whispered, her eyes large and liquid chocolate. "I can't stay here with you hating me, yelling at me …"

He ran a hand over his beard and exhaled. "Makes two of us."

Surprise leapt into those rich brown eyes that had drawn him across the room at that first charity event. "If you'll drive me into town, I'll catch a bus or cab—"

"No."

She winced. "Okay." She wet her lips. "If you'll let me rest tonight, I'll call an Uber or—"

"I said no." He rubbed his knuckles. "Cord entrusted you to my care."

"But you *don't* care and you don't want me here."

Stone stared at his hands. "No, I don't, but you're here." He met her gaze and straightened. "Let's not dance around this anymore." With the way his favorite chair swallowed her, she looked small and vulnerable. "Tell me." Heart ramming against his ribs, he wasn't sure he really wanted to know. "Lay it out for me, beginning to end, how you ended up working for Horvath."

Brighton caught her lower lip between her teeth, brown eyes going molten. She worried the tassel of the throw pillow she held like a shield against her chest. "I ..." She shifted. Cleared her throat. "When I was eighteen, I'd just signed a modeling contract with a big New York agency. Really thought I was going somewhere—they were trying to help me get European gigs— Paris and London. Success spiked my ego. I traded good friends for popular friends. I was ... terrible to my family." She sniffed. "They haven't spoken to me since a big falling out over my not going home for Thanksgiving when my mom fell ill."

Her voice sounded raw and sharing this clearly wasn't easy for her. "Instead, I spent time skiing with my model friends— and that's the holiday my mom died. They've never forgiven me. I was full of dreams and full of ... myself. Maybe too much like Mama, but thankfully, I was raised by my dad and his conservative, godly values. Raised me to know the Beatitudes, trust God for everything. Save myself for marriage ..."

Stone resisted the urge to pace. He'd been raised the same way. And he'd waited till marriage, then Marie had an affair and left him. Same as Dad.

"One night ..." The light in her eyes dimmed faded. "After a big show where I'd been scouted and chosen by a top Paris label to be their new face and work exclusively with a French designer, they threw this huge, blow-out party. Everyone was there. Big models and Hollywood stars. It was ... extreme. Leon

Mueller was there—I'd had a crush on him since his first movie. That night …" She tucked her hair behind her ear. "I … I thought I'd arrived. That I was enlightened, liberated, celebrated." Her eyes pooled with tears. "He roofied my drink and that night, I lost more than my arrogance." She gave him a thin, broken smile. "A week later, he emails me pictures of us … naked."

Pain pinched his neck. "Sounds familiar."

She chewed her lip again. "It's their M.O." Her face writhed as she tried to restrain the tears. "He threatened to go public, destroy not just me but my family—my father had just been made senior pastor at their church, and my brother was just trying to survive his freshman prom."

Stone refused to look away or feel sorry.

"Leon told me they'd delete the photos if I'd go out with a client. Just dinner, they said. So I went. Only he didn't give me the pictures. Said I had to do one more favor." She sniffled as she talked, her words thickened by the grief of what she'd been through. "Each time, there was one more and … *more*. Each time, unbeknownst to me, they were taking more pictures. Eventually, I caught on, knew that everything I did was being photographed or filmed. It was a way to control me and blackmail the men I met. I tried to stop, get out, but they'd beaten me. When that seemed to not have any effect, they started hurting others to force me."

He buried his face in his hands. Wrestled with what had happened to her. But there still came that truth … "So, when we met at the Adagio … you were sent to—"

"No." She growled answer. "I was there to have lunch with a friend, not to … work."

Unable to sit still any longer, Stone went to the window. Folded his arms and stared out at the mountains. If he believed her story, it meant they were both blackmailed. It forced the guilt off her shoulders and back onto his. He'd known better …

"I made a mistake when we met and forgot that they somehow *always* watch, looking for the next target. I thought— wanted to believe I knew enough to hide you and how I felt from them. I don't know how long they knew, but … they did." She sounded frustrated. "Remember that time we showed up at the same event, the golf charity one?"

Though Stone looked at the mountain ridgeline in the distance, he recalled the green dress she'd worn. The way she'd had her hair partially braided and in an updo. He also recalled how she'd treated him. He cast her a look over his shoulder. "You were rude to me." Which had surprised and annoyed him, because he'd liked her interest in him. And she'd looked amazing.

"Shortly before I spotted you, I also saw Finch—one of Ladomer's lackeys. That's when I realized they'd known about you—us—all along." She shuddered. "It terrified me. I was so afraid if I showed any interest in you, they'd go after you. I'd been on their chain long enough to know what they were capable of."

Hands tucked under his arms so he didn't ball his fists, he shifted back to the window. Didn't want her to see his anger over the scumbags ruining lives and interpret that toward herself. That night had been when he'd figured out how much he'd liked her—when he'd started entertaining *dating*. A risky prospect as governor. It'd put her under scrutiny. Make her a target.

"I told them no, Stone." He heard a commotion and saw in the reflection that she was on her feet, hobbling toward him. "I told Leon and Ladomer that I refused to work you."

He roughed a hand over his mouth. "Yet you did." Though he didn't turn, he caught the firelight that glowed over her face as she looked down.

"I realize to you, it's that simple, but it was the most difficult decision I've ever made. And it wasn't made lightly, but …" She shuddered a breath. "They'd threatened to go after my brother again. Not kill him—but drag him into that life. The thought of him being sold to men who got their jollies off young boys ..."

The thought nauseated Stone.

She fell quiet for several long seconds. "I had found one good thing, one thing that made me smile and willing to face each day, and they turned it against me. If I didn't keep the appointments with clients, if I didn't make them happy ..."

A buzzing started at the back of his brain.

"I had figured out how to survive, but I wasn't going to let them ruin my brother's life, too."

"But you let them ruin *my* life."

She hobbled closer and caught his arm. "I tried ... *tried* to protect you by varying where we went, what time, how I got there, but they still found out. I told them I wouldn't hurt you, wouldn't do that, and that's when they showed me a live feed of Aston with one of the lackeys right behind him. They were there, *right there*, poised to grab him."

Stomach churning, Stone rolled around her and grabbed the door handle. Stepped out. Felt the smack of cold air that did nothing to dispel the hot anger roiling through him. Rage drove him away from the lodge. Away from the fury of wanting to kill someone.

CHAPTER
THIRTEEN

"Have you found her?"

Finch tensed. "Not yet." He couldn't let that be his only answer or they'd find his body floating in the Potomac. "We're closing in. Traffic cams show them leaving the beltway, headed west."

Ladomer glowered. "Get. Her. Back. And whoever took her? Make them pay in a long, excruciating way. Bleed him for every cent he's cost me."

"We've got the stills from the footage, and I'm working on his identity. But sir?" Finch knew the boss didn't like to talk about it. "He's *targeting* your chain."

"I guess you better find him before he costs you more than a month's wages."

Month? He cursed. "We will."

"You'd better, or I'll put you on a permanent repayment plan."

In other words—death.

Bexar-Wolfe Lodge, Northern Virginia

So much for a talk.

Frustrated that he'd walked out, Brighton hobbled out of the cabin and searched the undulating terrain and tree line for Stone. She didn't know why she bothered—it was clear her story repulsed him. *She* repulsed him. She'd wondered even back then, when he was hers, what he'd say or do when he knew the truth. Now, she didn't have to wonder.

His dog—where had he come from?—nudged past her and trotted down to the pool. "Grief, no. Come here, boy." Wouldn't Stone just love it if she lost his dog? There was clearly a reason he named his dog that. "Grief! Please!"

Snout to the ground, the furry beast headed up a slope of steps and into the foliage.

"Grief!" Unwilling to negotiate stairs with her aching ankle, she took the wider path. Luck not only had *not* been on her side, it'd been set against her. If she tried the steps, she'd likely break something. "Grief, come back! Where did you go?"

"He's okay." The resonant voice came from behind.

Brighton shuffled around, surprised at the handsome guy coming her way. He didn't look like a lodge worker. In fact, he looked a lot like he'd stepped off a catwalk.

"Grief wanders all over the place but always comes back when he's ready." He shoved a hand at her. "Rowe Kincade. Bexar-Wolfe manager, trail guide, and all-around nice guy."

Unsure whether to believe Superman, Jr. about the dog, she accepted the handshake. "Brighton, though you might call me 'dead meat' if anything happens to Grief."

"Nah." He had a wicked grin that would bring most girls to their knees, but she'd had enough of his type to last several lifetimes. "Stone lets him wander the property for added security. Grief might ignore you, but one whistle from the boss and he rockets back."

Rowe extended something, and she glanced down, surprised

to find a small yellow-and-blue box. "Chef asked me to bring this up to the cabin. Considering your limp, I reckon it's for you."

She accepted the wrap. "Yeah, thanks."

"You seem a bit unsteady. Let me help wrap your ankle."

"No, it's alright. I …"

He took it back and unboxed the wrap.

"Uh …" Brighton glanced in the direction Stone had stalked off, searching for Grief or his grumpy owner. Instead, she saw only trees … trees. Oh, look! More trees. She really did not want Stone angrier at her, and this delay—

"Sit on the retaining wall." Rowe urged her back until she plopped against it. "This won't take a second." He went to a knee and slid her shoe off, then made quick work of wrapping the bandage like a helix.

It felt wrong to have him handling her leg, but he had a knack for it. Besides, it sure was a lot easier than trying to do it herself. "You seem familiar with doing this."

"Baseball. Never broke it, but I had some wicked sprains turning bases." He set the claw hooks to hold the bandage in place. "That'll work." He slid her shoe back on—and thank goodness she had a ballet flat on or it wouldn't have fit—and stood. "Give it a go."

Flashing him a smile, she saw shadows moving past him and up the hill. "Oh …" But when she searched the spot, she found it empty—well, except for the trees. Carefully, she came to her feet arms out for balance. "Wow, that helps. Thanks."

"Might do better with a crutch or cane." He held her hand to steady her. "D'you do this hiking out toward the road?"

She frowned. "How'd you—"

"I was out clearing brush when I saw you."

"Oh." So that's how Stone had known where she was.

"Should probably rest it for the next twenty-four."

"I was, but Grief—" Brighton caught sight of the beast

darting behind the cabin. And she wasn't sure, but it seemed to be chasing a six-two shadow.

"Boss has a workshop back there. Bet Grief found him."

"Well, I guess I should make sure he's okay." She cringed. "I mean Grief. Not Stone—the boss."

His knowing gaze skimmed over her, then he shrugged. "Yeah, wouldn't want to test his temper these days—either of them."

What did that mean? She hobbled a few steps, then threw over her shoulder, "Thanks for the bandage." Making her way up the hill, she wished sprained ankles were like muscles—the more you exercised them, the better they felt. Instead, she could feel it swelling and stretching the bandage with each step.

Rounding the corner, she slowed at the light spilling across the gravel path from an open door. Repetitive clanging from within warned that Rowe had been right about what—*who* Grief sought. Stone was in there. And from the sound of it, taking out his frustration on something with a vengeance.

This is stupid. Go back. You don't need him—or any man.

Brighton closed her eyes. She didn't *need* him. But she did *want* him—to understand. To know she wasn't the wretch he believed her to be.

But ... wasn't she? Chewing the inside of her cheek, she sagged against the side of the building. Took the weight off her leg. This was an impossible situation. He'd wouldn't accept her explanation. Because he was right—she had made a choice. To protect her brother. Not him. And that galled him. He'd never forgive her.

Frustration coiled through her. Tightened her chest. Gritting her teeth, she stemmed the dark emptiness that had swallowed her life. It'd been so unfair. All of it. She didn't ask for this. Made one mistake ...

Something wet flopped her hand.

She started and looked down. The black beast was there.

"Grief," she said, his name swallowed by the clanging inside. She slid down the wall and wrapped her arms around the dog who'd settled onto his haunches, his back to her as he squinted contentedly out over the terrain and panted a steady rhythm.

"Thanks," she whispered, as glad as he was for the company.

Hammering out the kink from where a tree had taken down the large swing gate that led to the trails, Stone swung and landed blow after blow against the iron. Every time reforging it. Exhaustion weighted his limbs, but he continued hammering until the bend was unnoticeable, so the gate could shut and lock. Satisfied, he turned and laid it across the worktable. Set down the hammer and gripped the edge of the worktable. Used his shoulder to wipe the sweat from his brow and closed his eyes.

God, why ...?

Mixed up a dozen ways from Sunday by her story, he couldn't decipher if she was blaming him for what happened to her or to himself, or both. Then there was the heaping pile of dung that smelled a lot like guilt—he'd known his actions with her weren't above reproach. If he'd behaved more in line with honor and godly values, they wouldn't be here. She wouldn't be here. She'd be ...

Yeah, he didn't like where that line could end.

But shoving her back into his life, when he'd moved to the lodge to get himself straightened out, back on the straight and narrow—*doing a fair job of it, too*—it just ...

Grief brushed against his left leg.

With a smirk, Stone dangled his hand, waiting for Grief to nudge it, and when he felt the cold snout, he rewarded him with some lovin'.

"What is it?"

Had lightning shot through him, the reaction wouldn't have been as shocking as hearing Brighton's voice in his workshop. He braced himself. Flinched inwardly. Squeezed his eyes.

"I remember you telling me you liked to work with iron." Her voice was soft. Uncertain. Scared.

He wanted to answer her, but hot dang, he didn't trust himself to move, to speak. He clenched his jaw tight and opened his eyes to the piece on the table.

In his periphery, she stood next to him. Facing him. Touching the iron gate. Quiet and delicate, her presence was a dichotomy in this workshop of sweat and iron. She shifted and hobbled, throwing in his face that his silence cost her time on a sprained ankle.

"Shouldn't be here," he ground out.

Brighton dipped her head, hobbled to shift and then lost her balance.

Stone reached out to steady her. Reflexively, he hoisted her up and set her on the table. Which was a mistake. Because now she was right in front of him. Eye to eye—hers wide. Her lips parted. Hands on his shoulders.

And that was too familiar. Weirdly intimate.

Yeah, didn't think that one through ... Gripping the worktable on either side of her, Stone snapped his head down. Willed himself to ... not. Not move. Not touch her. Not breathe.

Get out, idiot. Leave.

"I know you don't want me here, but ... I ..."

Stone moved his gaze around, trying to find a safe spot to land. Her legs and knees took up most of his visual field, so he stared at his hand. Couldn't help but notice how close it was to her thigh.

Stop stop stop.

"Do you hate me?"

The question was a sucker punch, especially when she asked in that broken whisper. "No." It surprised him how much force barreled into that answer. He wanted to hate her, but he couldn't. "I hate myself for …"

Everything.

Her fingers were on his beard, tracing it, touching.

Driving him mad.

"It's softer than I'd expected," she said quietly.

Now both hands teased his beard, sending charged volts of electricity into his gut, across his shoulders. Hollowing out his hearing and shutting down the part of his brain that said this was a *bad* idea.

He caught her wrists. "Don't."

"Please don't hate yourself," she whispered. "My time with you was a … gift. A haven. You were a refuge—my refuge in a very terrible storm that had taken my life."

Stone released her wrists. Grabbed the edges of the table again. But his thumb traced her jeans …

"I've never met a man like you." Her words were but a sweet fragrance across his face as she leaned in closer. Too close. It was familiar—this was familiar. She was familiar and warm. Sweet. Beautiful.

Her lips were there, offering themselves. As they always had. Less than a half inch to bridge the gap. All he had to do was take that kiss. And all his demons wanted it. Wanted her. They were right together, good together.

This is wrong.

"Tizzy …" He cursed himself for using that name. Groaned, hating how much he wanted to again taste her sweetness. Fall into that sweet spot. But he had to be strong. Didn't want her to think that he—

She stole the kiss he withheld.

Stone let her, savoring the softness of her kiss. Promised himself just one. Sweet mercies and relief rushed through him so strong he told himself not to move. Not to kiss her back or respond.

But she took another. This one more eager than the previous, one that tested his resolve.

Okay, enough. Step off, Metcalfe. Breathe.

But the kiss and her warm breath lingered over his mouth. Pleading, or maybe she was trying just as much to tame this. He cupped her face to hold her there, keep this from getting out of control. But the teasing way her lips danced on his was enough to break his slipping control. Tempted him to take a kiss of his own.

It was just a small kiss. Him, too aware of her uneven breathing. Just one. That's all. Couldn't hurt.

Until she released a soft moan and pressed in.

Restraint fled. Stone caught her mouth with his, remembered how they were together. How right she felt in his arms.

Her curves curled into him, hand sliding up over his back, inviting him deeper into the kiss, which he greedily accepted. Appreciated how she fit against him. The way her fingers dug into his hair.

Crap. Stand down, Metcalfe. Stinging awareness hit like liquid nitrogen, shocking cold sanity through his passion-drenched skull—she'd been trafficked. Used and abused.

This ... taking what she offered ... was what every other man had done.

Repulsed with himself, Stone gently caught her wrists again and unwound her arms from his neck and shoulders. Broke off the kiss. Swallowed around his jackhammering pulse.

This wasn't right. He'd known that before her kiss.

But he hadn't *understood.*

Even as he stepped back, he saw the confusion and hurt in her eyes. Those beautiful eyes that had been sanity to him in the chaos of politics. He jerked off his hat. Wanted to apologize but somehow knew it wouldn't come out right.

Head still not clear from what he'd let overtake them, Stone shifted away. "This can't ... I can't ..." He mumbled some excuse and shoved toward the doors. Moved fast, too afraid he'd throw himself back at her. The demons of his past were fierce and ravenous tonight. So was his passion. He plowed into the chilly night, the door thwacking and flinging back at him. "Augh!" He drove his heel into it.

Crack! The hinge popped free. Hung lopsided, slowly dipping forward until the final hinge surrendered. Wood thudded against the hardpacked ground.

He eyed the doors, stricken. Haunted by the look in her eyes, the hurt, betrayal ... he realized Brighton was just like that door. Hanging on by a thread, and now his irresponsible actions may have severed the only thread that kept her together.

CHAPTER
FOURTEEN

"*A gentleman should be ashamed when his deeds do not match his words.*"

While Mama wasn't known for profound sayings, she had loved that quote, especially throwing it at Dad when he did something wrong.

Brighton sat curled on the hotel bed, staring at the walls for the third day since Stone reminded her what it was like to be the center of his attention, to be in his arms, experiencing his passion. More than that—to have his strength encasing her—and she wasn't just thinking about those powerful arms and broad chest.

Though, yeah, *wow …*

It'd been the strength of his character that startled her when they'd first met and rang true and powerful even today. Granted, there was the tiny fact he'd been in bed with her back in Maryland, ready to complete what had been heating up between them for months. But he got that call and left with muttered apologies to answer it.

Hurt, dejected, she'd stared at the door for a good half hour, disbelieving she'd just been ditched. At first she thought it was because he'd figured out what Ladomer planned, but then came his two a.m. call, telling her he wanted to do things right. He wanted to honor her. It'd sounded a lot like commitment talk. She marveled that someone had really seen her, Brighton. Not a client with Lizzy. Or fans with a supermodel. He'd seen brash, broken Brighton.

Eight hours later, Ladomer destroyed everything.

No, you did that.

Stone hated her and that made sense, because so did she. What she had with Stone had been so very different from her clients. Every other intimate experience. He was better, kinder, funnier. And she was too weak to stand up to Ladomer.

That's why Stone could kiss her like a fool then walk away. Maybe he wanted to punish her the way he'd been punished. She'd deserve that and a heckuva lot more.

But ... that kiss the other night ... He wouldn't have kissed her like that if he hated her. Right? That kiss did not match the anger-filled words that said Stone Metcalfe was *stone cold* toward her. There'd been so much passion as he crushed her to himself. So much urgency wrapped in the hot little moment.

Then he'd ripped the door off the hinges trying to get away from her.

Just as Ladomer had ripped the door off their tête-à-tête and exposed Stone. Brought him down. Shamed him. Disgraced him.

He hadn't deserved it. Of all the men to get destroyed ...

God ... Please ... help me make this right.

A knock startled her. She swung her legs over, wiping away the tears and rushing to the mirror to make sure she looked fine. As her gaze connected with her reflection, she realized old habits died hard. Ladomer and Finch had always ripped her a new one if she wasn't in pristine shape when they arrived. She wasn't allowed to look tired or disheveled. Crying was worse.

Ladomer wasn't here. But he sure was in her head still.

Another rap yanked her toward the door. She drew in a

breath, glanced through the security hole. The guy at the front desk. The one who didn't like her.

Great.

Plastering on a smile, she opened the door.

"Sorry," he said gruffly. "I'm Oscar, from the front desk. I—" His mouth snapped shut, dark brown eyes swiftly taking her pulse. "You okay?"

"Absolutely. Sure. What can I do for you?" *A little too buttery, Brigh.*

He hesitated and checked the front desk, frowning.

What was going on? She looked there, too, but didn't see anything unusual. "Something wrong?"

He shook his head. "No, I—yes. Actually. We have a problem." He nodded into the room. "Look, I just ... I have a favor to ask."

"From me?" she balked.

"Yes, and I think it's the least you can do for him."

"Excuse me?"

"Look—the last time she was here, you were working the coffee bar and he nearly lost the café permit. Now she's back and if you don't help, we're all pretty much screwed."

Brighton blinked. Laughed. "I'm sorry. What're you talking about?"

He groaned. "I ... Okay, listen." He huffed. "You know how to work the espresso machine, right?"

She blinked again. "Yeah—I was a barista before ..." No need to go into all the gory details.

"Good. Yes. So, can you please come up and work the coffee bar?"

"You're kidding me."

"Look, there's this woman. She saw you there working it the last time she was here."

Awash in guilt, Brighton recalled Stone raging about the inspector who'd threatened to cancel a permit.

"She's back. And she's staying for a day or two—the boss doesn't know yet. He's in town this morning. And she wants a drink. Asked for you."

"But I don't work there. I'm supposed—"

"Right, but you can fake it, yes?" He fisted his hands eagerly. "For the boss. A favor. Since he's doing you a solid paying for your room. Right?"

"My room—"

"Really don't have time for this. Can you do it or not? He's in a bind and needs to smooth things over with her, so I thought if you could make her a drink, it'd help the boss and the lodge. And he really needs a break."

"The boss ..."

He nodded eagerly. "I think you know his real name, but we call him Mr. Mulroney."

Who would come unglued if he saw her out again. "And he's in town ...?"

"For supplies and—ya know what? Never mind." He slapped his thighs nervously. "Forget I asked. This is a bad idea. It's clearly too—"

"Espresso has been known to change people's lives," Brighton said with a small smile.

His faltered. "Yes. It has—can."

"I'll be there in five minutes. Need to change."

"Yes! Okay." He nodded and opened the door, then paused. "Thanks."

Brighton changed into a black top and jeans, then limped to the café, praying she got this over before Stone showed up. She had no idea where she stood with him at the moment.

The woman sat at the bar tapping dipped fingernails on a smartphone. She looked up. "Ah. You are here."

Brighton noted the machines were at least turned on—that'd save time. "What can I get for you?"

"I'm going to assume there's no cold brew," she said more as an accusation than a question. "So, how about a macchiato. Can you do that?"

"Sure, traditional or like you get from the siren?"

"Siren."

"Caramel?"

"Of course."

"Name for the order?"

The woman laughed. "It's not like you have a line."

"Yet," Brighton added ruefully.

After a long look, the woman smiled. "Chandra."

"One macchiato with caramel for Chandra coming right up." Brighton slid easily into the routine of preparing the macchiato—pulling the shots, steaming the milk, preparing the cup with caramel drizzle—and found that she missed this life. Missed who she was back then—fun-loving, carefree, full of dreams. Before she could deliver Chandra her macchiato, two more people were in line.

Brighton couldn't help arching her eyebrows toward them as she asked the woman, "You were saying?"

"Touché." Chandra lifted her cup in a toast but stayed at the counter.

After serving the next two, Brighton tidied up with the intent to return to her room before Stone saw her.

"How do you like working with ... *Mr. Mulroney?*"

"I don't." Wait. Oops. Working with Mr. Mulroney—Stone. Heat spiraled through Brighton, realizing her mistake. "I rarely see him," she amended. "That's why I'm here—he can't pull shots to save his life." Was that laugh too hollow?

"How on earth did he ever find such a beauty and convince you to come to our sleepy neck of the mountain?" Insinuation rich as the drink she consumed, Chandra took another sip. "This is delicious."

"Glad you approve." Brighton diverted the conversation. "The key is not leaving the shot too long before adding it to the drink or you kill it." When she turned, she was pleased to find Stone's mother in line. "Mrs. Clara, good to see you. Would you like something?"

"Tea, dear. Whatever kind you have."

"Hot or cold?"

"Hot."

"Sweet or unsweetened?"

"A little honey."

"Coming right up." After eying the supplies, she started a green tea. "How's Brooke?"

"Oh." She waved a hand. "Left days ago—got some urgent call and zipped out. Almost didn't even say good-bye. She's pretty important up in that New York City law firm where she's a partner at." She scanned the hotel lobby and lounge. "Have you seen my son?"

Brighton avoided looking at Chandra but felt the woman's interest pique. "I believe he's in town at the moment." She used a bear-shaped container to sweeten the hot tea.

"You're St—the owner's mother?" Chandra was a wolf stalking prey. But had she almost said Stone?

Mrs. Clara glanced over her shoulder at the taller woman and somehow seemed to assess things in that split-second examination. "I am."

"I … Can I ask, what do you think of his … conduct?"

Freezing, Brighton drew in a sharp breath, wondering if she'd been outed. Afraid his mom would mention her or maybe Mrs. Pellet already knew. Is that why she'd been hanging around the café?

Mrs. Clara didn't react as she faced the woman. In fact, it seemed she grew taller. "I've never been so proud of him."

Chandra gaped. "Proud? How can you say that? He—"

"He owned his mistakes and took responsibility. Can you say the same?"

"Me?" Chandra balked. "I didn't—"

"And you're sure *he* did?"

Nosy, mean-spirited woman faltered. "I ... It was all over the news."

"And that's so reliable, isn't it?" With a radiant smile, Mrs. Clara took the tea from Brighton. "Thank you, dear." She walked away, head high, back straight. Not too different from how Brighton had been taught to hold herself for modeling.

Can I be her when I grow up?

Biting back a smile, Brighton busied herself with the next customer, glad the aroma of espresso drew them from their suites and activities. A dozen more drinks served up before Stone stalked into the lodge. His gaze slid to the cluster of people, and he nearly tripped when he saw her working the coffee bar. That storm moved into his blues again as he angled in her direction. "What're you—"

"Boss!" Oscar called, diverting Stone and his attention.

Stone hesitated, glanced again at Brighton, then helped his employee.

"Is he always like that?" Chandra asked as Brighton poured hot tea for an elderly woman.

"Brusque?" Brighton supplied. "Yes, but it's just his business sense kicking in."

"What do you think of him—as a person?"

"He's the best man I've ever met." *Yeah, probably shouldn't have said it so fast.* But it wasn't a lie.

The woman's eyebrow arched. "But you're just a barista. How can you know that?"

"It doesn't take a genius to know a good man when you meet one, especially when you've known terrible ones." Wiping down the counter, Brighton heard laughter and glanced at the front desk. Saw a woman checking in, who held Stone's arm. Her fake, tittering laugh sang like metal on metal as she hung on to him. Leaned into him. Flirted.

Hussy.

Why hadn't he shoved her away as he'd done to Brighton?

She busied herself with tidying the bar, annoyed he'd let that woman hang all over him, but had shoved her away.

Because she *didn't destroy him.*

"Excuse me."

Brighton twitched, then realizing the flirty woman now stood at the counter. Swallowing her disgust, she managed a smile. At least, she hoped she had. "What would you like?"

The woman angled back toward the check-in counter, where Stone had planted his hands, his gaze sliding into Brighton's. "A scoop of tall, dark, and handsome," she giggled, "but I suppose he's not on the menu."

Irritation, hot and rank, flushed Brighton's good humor. "Afraid not."

The woman laughed again. "Sorry. I can't resist a man with a beard. And *oof*—those blue eyes." She sighed dramatically and scrunched her nose. "He's so suave, you know? Dreamy like that actor, George Cannon—or whatever his name is."

Brighton gave her a blank expression. Tried not to roll her eyes.

"Skinny vanilla latte, please—biggest you have."

She nearly snorted—sugar free and nonfat milk, yet she wanted the biggest. Hypocrite. Brighton scanned the syrup bottles to verify they even had a sugar-free bottle. Was there a poison bottle she could mix up? "Your name?"

"Rumor."

She blinked at the woman. "Seriously?"

That tittering laugh again. "Isn't it terrible? But it works perfectly for my career." But then she sobered. Stood.

Who cared what her career was? If this was the type of woman Stone wanted then Brighton really didn't know him. She stole another glance at the front desk and found his gaze flinging away from them again. Seriously? He liked this plastic-enhanced, platinum-dyed—

"How's the ankle?"

At the rich voice that feathered along her left ear, Brighton flinched toward Superman Jr, who'd helped wrap her ankle the other night. The night Stone had kissed her. What was his name again? Ross? Ray?

"Oh. Hi. It's good—fine." Though now that he reminded her about the injury, she realized it was starting to throb. Or maybe that was her anger. "Where'd you come from?"

"Stables." He whiffed his underarms. "Thought y'all could smell me coming."

She wrinkled her nose. "So that's what that was."

He laughed. "Harsh. But I can clean up nicely given the chance."

So not happening. Too young, too pretty. Too much like Leon Mueller. "Did you want a drink?"

"Uh, y'all serve coffee? You know, the real stuff. Not mouthfuls of sugar."

"Of course. How do you take it?"

"Sweet and blond," he said, more than a little suggestive. "Hey. You're—"

"Rowe." Stone's deep baritone thudded into her.

Brighton turned as he came up behind the property manager, and she busied herself preparing the drinks, all too aware of his larger-than-life presence. Remembering the way he'd crushed her to himself …

He just couldn't like the plastic bombshell.

Stone homed in on his employee. "Oscar said the first group is ready for the trail ride."

"Your coffee, Rowe." Brighton handed him a lidded cup with a bold black coffee.

"Yep, got my brew"—he hefted the cup to Stone—"and heading out now."

Stone ran a hand over his beard. "Find me when you get back. I'd like to know how it goes."

Soft. His beard had been softer than she'd expected, tickling her mouth and neck as he …

Steamy coffee, not steamy kisses, Brigh.

"Sure thing." Rowe tipped his ballcap at her. "Ma'am."

Brighton breathed a laugh, feeling too young for that moniker yet knowing he meant it respectfully. When he left, she looked at Stone, surprised to find him eyeing her. Her stomach squeezed, wishing things could be normal between them. But then … what was normal? It'd been romantic evenings binge-watching TV shows, kissing—

"You okay here?"

She jerked her gaze to the machine, as much to hide the heat in her face as to pay attention. "I am. Just pulling customers and helping shots." Wait. "Reverse that."

He almost grinned. "Let Oscar know if you need anything." His tone was surprisingly civil and hung in a long pause. "Appreciate what you're doing here."

Locked in his ice-blue gaze, she dug out a smile. It must've been hard for him to say that. To acknowledge that she helped him. "It's the least I can do." Aware that Chandra was still sitting nearby, listening, monitoring, she added, "Sir."

Disaster stalked him. This couldn't end well. It just couldn't. And sweet mercies, he'd hated hearing her call him "sir." Reminded him of their large age gap. Might as well be enough to be her dad. "I don't like this."

Oscar paused in reviewing reservations but didn't look up. "The inspector—"

"I meant Brighton," Stone bit out. "Working the bar. Her ankle is injured. She should be resting."

"She promised she would be okay."

"Maybe for a *while*, but she's been there hours." Should he intervene? Even as he thought to close the coffee bar early, more customers wandered toward it. Teeth grinding, Stone remained at the front desk to monitor what was happening in the coffee bar.

Inspector Pellet seemed to have grown roots around that chair where she sat chatting up Brighton well into the afternoon. Her ankle had to be aching by now. "I should close it." He had to admit, Brighton was a natural with customers, talking with ease and familiarity.

Rowe had grinned at her like a lost puppy.

Didn't like the way the guy had been looking at her, like he'd seen his first 1964½ Mustang. Too much interest. Too cozy. *Entirely* too cozy.

But she didn't seem to mind. She'd laughed with him, all ease and casualness. Was that the type of guy she was into? That was, when she wasn't being paid to ruin them.

"Definitely should close it soon."

Oscar opened his mouth, then suddenly closed it.

"You disagree."

"We have some great reviews about the café already, even though it's new."

"Reviews."

"Ratings—you know, on Google." He gave a shaky smile. "It'll bring in more business."

A two-edged sword now. Financially, he needed the business. But the more people visiting, the more risk he'd be exposed. Would the Mulroney surname keep him hidden well enough?

And Brighton ... he hadn't exactly treated her nicely since her arrival. Would that be his undoing? Would she spill her guts to this inspector and ruin yet another of his careers? She hadn't seemed the vindictive type, but with Pellet looking to expose the debauchery she believed him guilty of ...

He couldn't watch anymore. "I'm going to my office. Shut down the café at four."

Oscar nodded, but his eyes were large.

"The reviews can wait. At least until she's gone."

"Pellet or Brighton?"

"Both," he grunted.

"But … the inspector said she was looking forward a latte each morning."

He wanted to curse. Running a hand over his beard, he swore he was going to kill Cord for this. "Send Brighton to me when she's done."

"Will do."

"Wait." Stone didn't trust himself alone with her. "On second thought, just ask her if she can work tomorrow. I'll pay her. Time and a half."

"For that, *I'll* work the bar."

"If I thought you could do that without burning down the place, I'd let you."

Laughing, Oscar nodded. "Fair."

Stone started to leave, then hesitated. "By the way, next time you decide to help me out—ask first."

"Understood. I just wanted to look out for you—and in doing so, my job."

Stone smirked. "I hear you." Heading to his office, he eyed the café, the inspector, and the woman moving around that espresso bar as if she owned it, belonged there—like she did in his thoughts.

"Mr. Metcalfe."

Just shy of his door, he pivoted back, surprised to see the inspector stalking toward him. "Mrs. Pellet. Hope you like your room—it's the closest to the front lobby." It was his not-so-subtle jab that he knew why she was staying as a guest.

"It'll do, though I hope the pool closes promptly at ten p.m. as the rules state."

"Promptly." He held her gaze, waiting for the next challenge. Or for her to leave. The latter would be preferable.

"What of the waivers for those on the trail ride?"

"Waivers."

She gaped. "Surely you aren't letting people go out into the mountain on wild beasts without protecting yourself against lawsuits."

Wild beasts? "The horses are domesticated and trained not only for rides but to RTB."

Her gray eyes seemed to glaze over, but she drew up straight. "You didn't answer about the waiver."

"Inspector, what I do for insurance and safety is handled with the city licensing board. Your job—"

"Don't you dare tell me what my job is!" She seemed to struggle for breath.

"I wouldn't dream of it. If I can finish my statement?" He waited for her agreement.

Those dull irises dared him to prove her wrong.

"*Your job* is important, and I'm grateful for the direct attention you've given the Bexar-Wolfe Lodge." Too much? Maybe he *was* layering it on as thick as maple syrup. "I wouldn't waste your time or mine. In the many capacities in which you serve the community, you're responsible for overseeing the affairs of the county, including fiscal responsibilities, so I know you understand how precious each moment and dollar are." He gave a crisp nod. "So unless you have anything else, I have work to get done."

Not waiting for her to argue, he twisted the knob and let himself inside. Grief manifested out of nowhere and darted in as well. He closed the door and pushed himself across the room to his desk. Dropped onto the chair and buried himself in lodge invoices and statements, ignoring the plaguing question of how much penance he'd have to pay for his indiscretion with Brighton before his bill was paid in full.

Redirecting his thoughts, he trolled the websites of other family-centered lodges to see what they were doing, what worked, what didn't. Found one in southern Virginia that had the results he wanted, the focus he desired for the Bexar.

"We've got a problem."

At the sudden intrusion, Stone watched Oscar slide into the office and close the door. When had he even opened it? "Someday, you're going to walk in here and say you're so bored you quit."

Oscar frowned. "That is not this day."

"What's going on?"

"Inspector Pellet asked to extend her visit."

Pinching the bridge of his nose, he eased back in his chair. Not the best news, but not the worst either. So, what—

"The cybersecurity retreat."

Stone groaned. Leaned forward and cradled his head in his hands. They'd booked the whole lodge for that convention. The business of a respected corporation like that was crucial—not only would it elevate the Bexar-Wolfe on event-planners' radars, but it'd pay the bills through the next six months.

"Without your *guest*," Oscar went on, "the inspector wouldn't have been a problem—"

"But now we're overbooked."

Oscar nodded and lifted his hands. "No room at the inn."

"And we can't very well tell the inspector to take a flying leap."

"As much as I'd love to ..."

Stone pulled up the bookings schedule and stared at it. If Mom hadn't come, he could've given Brighton run of the one-bedroom condo. There was a couch, but he couldn't in good conscience ask her to camp out on a couch in his mom's new home. Could they get the inspector to leave? Probably not without ticking her off more.

He felt his employee waiting, watching. "I'll work on it."

With another nod, Oscar started for the door, but then

hesitated. Glanced at Stone, seemed to rethink and grabbed the knob.

"What?"

"I know where there's an extra room."

Hope surged. "Where?"

Oscar shifted, suddenly reticent.

Which connected the dots in Stone's brain. "No."

"Boss, I … I don't know what bad blood there is with you and Brighton, but that extra room in your cabin—"

"I said no!"

CHAPTER
FIFTEEN

BEXAR-WOLFE LODGE, *Northern Virginia*

Sleep had always been her enemy. Six years trapped in a life she didn't want, doing things she never dreamed of doing, made it hard to find the quiet places that let good, normal people sleep and dream. Fanciful dreams—the kind that made no sense but all the same brought laughter in the morning. Or stress-induced ones that had the dreamer walking the halls of their high school naked. But for her, she didn't let herself dream. Couldn't afford it. Dreaming meant being in the deepest sleep. Meant being vulnerable. Meant being … violated.

Brighton turned onto her side, peering out the curtain slit through which moonlight had snuck into her room. High and full, the moon hung so bright.

Just like the night I met him.

She got up and moved across the room, the carpet beneath her bare feet holding the chill of the mountain air. Her ankle ached as she stepped onto the balcony. Stared up at the night sky aglow and glittering with stars.

"Not the only one feeling smothered in there, I see."

On the terrace of the host mansion, she turned to him and smiled, tried to hide the jitters that erupted from being so close to the one man she'd watched all night. Dark blond hair, blue eyes, debonair with a side of rugged. It seemed contradictory yet so ... Stone Metcalfe. "Sad thing to feel smothered when it's your party."

"It's a means to an end and helps people." He shrugged. "So, I endure... this."

Later, she'd learned he hated those events. Hated being in the spotlight. Loved that he could do something about policy that hurt rather than helped constituents. He'd gone into politics to make a difference.

And he had. A massive one—in her life. Changed it. Changed her.

His gruff voice spiraled from the left. Far enough away that she wasn't worried about being discovered but she did not want to draw any more of his ire. She pulled into the shadows of her balcony and watched from a safe distance.

Leaning against the door jamb, he stared up at the stars as his dog circled the grounds, sniffing, relieving himself, darting after something in the copse of trees. "Grief! Come!" His dog bounded back and the two retreated inside. He shut the door ... and her out.

Like he had almost a year ago.

She crawled back into bed with *her* grief, which wasn't so cute and cuddly. It was painful and cruel, reminding her she didn't deserve a man like him. Never had. And she'd never have his attention again.

But wouldn't she? That kiss ... A mistake. One he'd run from so hard he'd broken the door. How could someone like him—someone with honor, integrity, a good family—want someone like her?

That was the rub, wasn't it? He didn't. Didn't want her.

Who would? She was dirty. Used up. No man wanted to marry a woman who'd been with so many men. It hadn't been willing—not really. But she'd long ago accepted that she'd be alone. For the rest of her life.

Tears blurred past and present, plunging her into nightmares, reliving the violence that had been hers. The beatings by Finch. The condemnation of Ladomer. The haunting terrors of her escort life chased her into the tormenting arms of sleep.

Bang! Bang! Bang!

Brighton shot up in the bed, her head weighing a thousand pounds. Dreams clinging like deadweight.

"Let me in!"

Ladomer. He found me. Her first instinct—submit—was quickly drowned out by the tastes of freedom and hope being here with Stone had injected into her aching heart.

She wasn't going to be used anymore. Amid the banging and shouts, she scrambled off the bed. Grabbed her packed bag and darted to the bathroom, locked the door. Heart racing, she shoved her legs into the pants. Stumbled. Threw open the patio door, half expecting Finch or Drex to be there but the room was empty. One more glance across it to the door, light stabbing through and broken only by shadowed feet firmed her resolve.

No. No more.

Brighton cleared the hip-high rail and sailed onto the path. Her ankle pinched, reminding her of the injury that had healed some. She shifted to avoid the pain, but lost her balance when her backpack caught on something. Spinning around with a yelp, she crashed forward—right into a solid mass. Felt like Finch.

"Let me go!"

Hands grabbed her shoulders.

She screamed. "Get off! I won't go back!" Brighton thrust the heel of her hand against the solid chest.

Oof!

The hands held tight. "Easy—"

"Stop!" She wriggled. "Let me go!"

"Brighton!"

Through the panic-driven chaos, she saw the face. Registered it. "Ray."

"Got the first letter," he said with a nervous chuckle. "Rowe."

"Right." She heaved breaths, still frantic. Glancing at the door. Shifting away, she did her best to control the panic but knew her time was short. "I … I have to go."

"Go where? You okay?"

The banging erupted again with more shouts from inside.

Brighton jerked and cried out. Her legs clipped on something and slipped. Rowe pulled her forward into his arms, saving her from a brutal fall.

She caught his biceps, gaze glued on the room. "They're here. I can't go back." She tried to tug free. To run. She wasn't doing that life again. Wasn't submitting to Ladomer. This time he'd brutalize her. Again. "No. I can't."

"Whoa, hang on th—"

"Let go! *Stop!*"

"Release her!" Stone's voice punched through the chaos, slamming into them like a brick wall.

Brighton spun toward him.

He was a storm. Fury and ferocity. Strength and violence. Gorgeous and terrifying. He barreled toward them, his rage focused on Rowe.

She threw herself at him, slammed into his chest, buried her face. "They're here. Help. Please. Don't let him take me. I don't want to go back. I want to stay with you. Please."

"Easy, Brighton. Easy." Large hands cradled her, held her fast in the storm thrashing her mind and thoughts. "What—"

Bang! Bang!

Stone pivoted from the room, protecting her as he looked in that direction. "What is—"

"It's him. Ladomer. He's here," she choked out.

A refuge formed as he pulled her close again. Scowled at

Rowe. "Go check it out. *Don't* mention her." He turned her toward the path. "C'mon." With an arm around her, he herded her up the path toward his cabin. Inside, he guided her to a chair and started to turn away.

"No!" Panic stabbed her common sense as she dug her nails into his biceps. "No. Pleasedon'tleaveme."

"Brighton." Calm reason filled his clear blue eyes as he spoke in a soothing voice. Warm hands cupped her face. "Hear me— you're safe. I'm not going to let anything happen to you."

She gulped the protection he offered, shocked. "Really?"

"On my word," he said, thumbing away a rogue tear. "And Grief is here. If I can't stop trouble, he will." He waited for that meaning to register, for her to nod. Her grip to ease. "I'm going to close the curtains."

"Oh. S–sorry."

"Don't be." There was a tenderness in his voice she hadn't heard in a very long time. And it broke her. Sobs vaulted out as if a dam had broken, unleashing tidal floods of grief and emotion she'd long ago buried combined with the adrenaline dump. She shoved back her hair and tried to get herself together. But the more she did, the more her control slipped.

He was there again, easing onto the couch next her, gathering her into his arms. Holding her. His deep rumbling voice offering a promise she'd never thought to hear from anyone, let alone him. "I won't let anyone hurt you again."

She believed he meant it. Believed he'd try. But ... she'd learned Ladomer's reach was iron and unstoppable. Freedom wasn't an illusion—it was a delusion. "He'll find me. Always does." Cheek against his chest, she heard the drumming of his heart. "I never should've come. What if he hurts someone in the lodge—or your mom! Or you! He won't stop looking for me. Ladomer never gives up what's his."

Stone's strength pulsed around her. His arm ensconced her as his hand caressed her head. "Neither do I."

Brighton stilled. *You misheard him.* He wouldn't have said that, not about her. She looked up at him, searching for the meaning behind his words. For him to confirm that wasn't what he meant. That it wasn't what she thought. His gaze was as steady as the rising sun, scattering darkness. When his expression remained the same, hope dared shoot between the cracks in the cement vault in which her heart hid.

Was it possible? Did he … did he think of her as *his?*

He'd said the words. And cursed himself, but refused to recant them. Because they were true. Sure, she was beautiful on the outside with her auburn hair and brown eyes, but her strength had always drawn him. Something twisted inside him at the vulnerability clouding her features. The watery eyes swimming in hope and desperation, half expecting him to take back the words. Stone cupped her face. "I won't let anyone take you back to that life if you don't want to go."

She jerked, a scowl scraping at her vulnerability. "Of course I don't. How could you—"

"Wait." *You're a piece of work.* "I worded that wrong."

But he had to admit … there was still a big chunk of anger blocking his path to freely taking her back. She'd been with other men—a lot of them. She'd known what her captor was going to do to him, and she didn't stop it. She'd chosen her brother over Stone. There was more to it, yeah, but … it knocked his feet out from under him in more ways than one.

Yet, seeing her terrified, watching that wild, fight-or-flight panic intrude on the strong, vibrant woman he'd fallen for …

And that's just it. He *had* fallen for her. When she was beautiful, intelligent, unassuming. Seeing that destroyed and her vulnerability explode had undone the knots he'd used to hold all that anger in.

And ultimately, he hated that his words just now hurt her. They'd both been through more than enough.

Several raps at the door had her leaping to her feet and whirling in that direction, her face white as flour.

"It's probably Rowe." Stone stood and moved between her and the front entry.

Unconvinced, she stared at the door, her eyes wide, her complexion blanched. She looked ready to run.

He couldn't stand it. Framed her face and brought those rich eyes to his. "I promise. Nobody's going to hurt you again or force you to do something you don't want to do."

Her bright eyes searched his, flushed with hope. He could see the struggle to believe what he said—in fact, he questioned himself about it. But ... he wouldn't go back on his word. With a smirk, he added, "Besides, I doubt someone coming after you is going to knock." When a smile wavered on those lips rosied from her crying, he resisted the urge to hug her. "Wait in the guest room. I'll see who it is."

Relief rippled through her, that tangle between her eyes loosened, and somehow it loosened something in him, too. With a quick nod, Brighton disappeared into the bedroom.

As the sound of her locking herself in reached him, Stone opened the front door.

Rowe stood there, annoyed, irritated.

"What'd you find out?"

"All that racket?" Rowe stepped back as Stone joined him on the front porch. "It was Mr. Blanton from one-two-seven. Apparently, he has flashbacks and thought he was in 'Nam or something searching for his buddies."

War took no prisoners, did it? Everyone came back affected, altered. His brothers, his father ... *Me.*

Rowe's gaze travelled the cabin, likely looking for Brighton. "Mrs. Blanton apologized profusely. Said he hasn't had one that bad in ages and had no idea what brought it on. Poor woman was beside herself. Offered to pay for psychological damages or something."

"No." The idea repulsed. He drew in a long breath and let it out, allowing himself to come down from high alert for the first time since Brighton's screams had yanked him from his project board.

"How's she doing?"

Stone considered his property manager. Rowe was closer to Brighton's age. Good looks. He'd seen her hug him, seen the way Rowe had taken a little too long wrapping her ankle. Immediately got the wrong impression as he sprinted down to the lodge and found the guy restraining a shrieking Brighton. "Shook up."

Silence stretched between them, questions not asked. Answers unnecessary.

Rowe eyeballed him. "Are we expecting trouble?"

Stone didn't want to compromise the trust Cord had placed in him, but if trouble was coming, then this was the man he'd face it with. Better to be prepared. "Yeah, probably." They were going to have a very long talk when he got back.

"I like her."

"I know. You had your hands all over her."

Rowe sniggered. "If you weren't so hung up on her—"

"Excuse me?"

"I wasn't touching her, not like that." With a huff, he shook his head. "She literally leapt into my arms—straight over the balcony from her room. She was terrified, injured—"

"Injured?"

"Her ankle. From when she tried to run. The first time."

Stone grunted.

"I tried to get her to slow down, tell me what was going on, but trying to calm and help her was like trying to hold a slippery, thrashing bass."

"She's been through a lot."

"Not exactly a secret." Rowe studied him from behind squinted eyes. "What's going on? What're we up against?"

Although he and Rowe had been through a combat tour together, Stone hesitated, not ready to lay that wound bare—even with his buddy.

"Not willing to connect some dots for me?"

"Need to know." This incident with Blanton was a good wake-up call. He'd gotten lazy, complacent. They needed to be prepared before they got caught with their pants down.

"Let's put it this way: the head of this beast is so far up the butts of so many VIPs that nobody has seen his face. They put me out of the game without batting an eye. If they come, it'll be a war zone."

The warning didn't faze Rowe. In fact, he seemed to have been waiting for it. "I'll set up more perimeter sensors and cameras. Have a couple of other tricks up my sleeve. And I know good operators I could recruit to—"

"No." When his buddy snapped his gaze to him, Stone tried to explain. "We keep it quiet. But the more people heading up here, the faster we draw attention. If we need help, I know who to call." They had to be smart because if—no, *when*—Ladomer Horvath came for her, he'd bring everything to bear, wouldn't he? "Do the sensors and cameras. Start there."

"On it." Rowe headed out.

Stone ran a hand over his beard and locked the doors.

"If you weren't so hung up on her ..."

Yeah, but he had a feeling that was only going to get worse, especially having her here on the property. Back inside, he spotted Grief popping up from a resting position. His black head swiveled toward Stone from his spot on the threshold. The guest room door sat ajar just enough for his Malinois to provide protection detail. Beyond his dog, on the bed and buried beneath a throw blanket, Brighton was asleep. Her position suggested she'd been watching the front door and sleep, greedy adversary that it was, seized hold. All the better—she needed the rest.

"Good boy." Stone rubbed Grief's velvety ears as he stood just outside the room, watching the woman who had once again upended his world. Forearm on the jamb, he recalled the terror in her expression, the trembling ... the way she'd thrown herself at him—and not romantically. Desperately. Terrified. Trusting him to protect her.

Her desperation, however, mirrored his need to make sure she was safe. His willingness to do violence on her behalf.

The thought startled him. Pushed him from the room. In the kitchen, he poured a drink then slumped onto the sofa. Alone with his thoughts, he went over the night's events. Tonight had been about a veteran wrestling his demons. What happened when the devil himself came looking for her? Danger inherently came with her.

Stone shifted on the sofa, his anger bubbling beneath the deceptive quiet of the night. It was too risky having her here. If the inspector saw what happened tonight ... Would she put the pieces together?

Yeah, that'd go over great. He'd be shut down faster than he could blink.

He resented thinking about that when Brighton's very life could be hanging in the balance. What was he supposed to do? Sacrifice his career this time? She'd taken it the last time—or rather, her captors had.

Stone set aside the drink and pinched the bridge of his nose, thinking. *Need to get her out of here. Uncomplicate things.*

He pulled out his phone and hit Cord's number. Pressed the phone to his ear as he kneaded the tension knot between his eyes. The call went to voicemail. "Hey. It's me. We need to talk. This isn't working. You need to retrieve the package."

He ended the call and leaned back against the sofa. Crossed his arms.

Moving her was risky. Increased the chances she'd be caught again.

Not my problem. Because keeping her here was riskier. He could lose the lodge if Pellet realized who Brighton was and what she was to him.

That was the question, wasn't it? The one that tormented him.

No ... the question didn't torment him.

It was the answer.

Stone shoved up, wiping away the haranguing guilt, and made his way to his bedroom. He considered calling in Grief but decided his dog's protection skills were better used guarding Brighton. He closed his door, pulled off his shirt, and noticed the laundry stacked on his bed. Mom must've done his laundry. That's when he saw the sweatshirt on top. The one Brighton borrowed a few nights ago. He lifted it from the stack and dropped onto the bed. Recalled how twisted up he felt inside seeing her wear it. All his idiocy and sentimentality in a size L shirt that swallowed her petite frame. Though it'd been laundered, he held it to his nose. Drifted back to the date ...

. . . . .

Baltimore, Maryland

She handed the small gift bag across the table to him.

He set down his fork and sat back. "What's this?"

"A memento," she said, grinning, the chiffon ruffle around her blouse making her seem an angel. "Just wanted to make sure you don't forget ..."

He reached in and found a sweatshirt. Pulled it out. Saw the lobster logo and laughed. "You seriously bought me a hoodie from this restaurant?"

"*Our* restaurant," she corrected, sipping her wine as he set the gift on the floor and went back to his meal. "You don't like it?"

"It's nice. Thank you."

"But you don't like it." She set down her glass. "But you love this place."

Stone swiped his tongue along his teeth and leaned on the table, bringing his face closer to hers. "I love being here. With you."

Though she grinned, it fell away suddenly. "Wait." Nudging aside her plate, she leaned forward too—but with a frown. "You don't like this place? But you love seafood."

He snickered. "Actually, I don't."

"But you set up our meets here."

Stone smirked. "Because *you* love seafood."

She drew back, lips parting as she stared at him. "I ..." Her shoulders drooped. "So you hate this place."

Now he laughed. "No. I love this place—and now the shirt. Because of you."

"Why would you repeatedly go to a restaurant you don't like and eat food you don't like?"

"I never said I didn't like it or the food," Stone countered.

Brighton huffed. "This is why you're having trouble with your cabinet."

Taken aback, Stone hesitated. He'd learned to listen, hear her out, since she so rarely offered thoughts about his position or career. "How's that?"

"Sorry," she said. "I know I'm not there, so I can't—"

"I want to hear what you're thinking."

"Okay. Well ... because you know what you mean when you say something, you assume they do, too. Or you assume the best of people, so you expect them to do the right thing."

"Expecting them to do the wrong thing is a jaded way of living."

"True, but ... sometimes ..." She twisted her diamond earring. "Sometimes, things aren't as simple as we'd prefer."

"True, but we always have a choice."

"That's oversimplified because ... people sometimes have to make choices that ... well, there's no good outcome no matter what they do."

"But they still have the choice."

BEXAR-WOLFE LODGE, NORTHERN VIRGINIA

Crap. She'd been trying to tell him even then. He dropped back against the bed and stared at the ceiling, hoodie still in hand. And just as she'd said, he'd assumed. Not technically a bad thing, but sometimes, he assumed and persisted with his plan not realizing what it might cost others.

God ...

What was there to pray? He had powerful feelings for Brighton. Didn't know which way was up. But she'd put a crater in his confidence, amplified the leftover resentment he felt toward his ex-wife and father. Everyone he loved betrayed him somehow. How was he supposed to expect it to be different this time? Why hand her his heart when she'd already bludgeoned it once?

But he couldn't freakin' stop thinking about her. Those kisses, her curled against his side, sharing good meals and conversation. Lazy evenings with the woman who made him happy. Thoughts of her teasing laughter and kisses luring him from consciousness.

Sunlight stabbed his corneas. He squinted, confused, and grunted. What was that? He lifted his head and felt something weighting his arm. "Grief, off," he muttered, his head feeling waterlogged. He shifted and felt the soft fur against his bicep. "Grief. Off."

An excited whine.

From his left. Not his right where he'd felt the soft tickle.

What ...? Stone propped up on his elbows. Squinted again, this time forcing himself to wake up. *Must've fallen asleep.* He looked to his right—and shot from the bed. Cursed, scrambling to cover himself.

"Stone." Brighton flushed.

"What the—"

"Wait, pl—"

"What's going on?" he growled, his head feeling like a thousand pounds.

Banging erupted from the front door. Was that what had awakened him—someone knocking?

He couldn't even look at the door. Couldn't tear his eyes from the sight before him. Acutely aware of his state of undress. Racked his brain to figure out what happened. How he'd ended up in bed with Brighton.

CHAPTER
SIXTEEN

Sleeping with Stone was not what she'd intended when she crawled into bed beside him. Well, not sleeping-sleeping. But *falling* asleep. "Nothing happened." Brighton held up her hands, trying to reassure him. "I promise." Man, she hated that crazed look on his face.

His bare chest rose and fell unevenly. "Then what are you doing"—he flicked a hand at the bed—"there? *How* …?"

Chagrined, she scooted off the mattress. "I startled awake, saw it was dark, realized you'd never returned like you promised." Her eyes were wide and vulnerable. "Then … I noticed Grief—and he's always with you. It didn't make sense. Scared me."

"Scared you, so the first thought was—*climb in bed with Stone?*" he balked, incredulous, as he slammed his arms into his shirt. "While I'm asleep! Is that how—"

"No!" Knowing how those razor-sharp accusations would shred her, she tried to slow her racing heart. "Nothing. Happened." Heat scratched into her cheeks. "Look."

Calm down. He doesn't know …

"Ladomer is swift with his vengeance. It wouldn't be the first time he cut the throat of someone who got in the way." Could he read between the lines? She didn't really want to tell him about Dan. But when he didn't respond, she knew she had no choice. "The man …" She could still see his blood everywhere…

"The bartender at the hotel where we met had … training. Knew the signs for persons being trafficked. I think he's the one who helped Cord find me. His name was Dan Duvall. We called him Double D." She wrung her hands, her heart feeling just as twisted. "Double D always liked me—he was older, a friend. Not an interested party. Always said I deserved better. Anyway, one night after meeting a client, he tried to get me to leave with him. Escape."

She touched her forehead, remembering the metallic smell of his blood all over the alley. "It was bad timing. Ladomer just happened to show up. They took us into the back alley … Double D … Ladomer killed him. For trying to help me." She tried to shove her meaning into her eyes. "So, when Grief was with *me*"—she put a hand on her heart—"I swear I could smell blood. Came running in here. It didn't look like you were breathing …"

Swallowing, she lowered her head. "When I realized you were, I couldn't leave, afraid they'd kill you. I know you're bigger and stronger, but somehow … somehow it felt like I was protecting you, too, by staying." She swallowed. "You said you'd never let anyone hurt me again, that Grief would also protect me … and you were both in here, so it just felt safer in here."

"This isn't cool." His gaze bounced to the bed and he blinked several times, angry.

No, not angry. "You're scared."

His gaze hit hers then ricocheted away. "God rescued me from compromising us once before. I'm doing the best I can to honor Him for that help."

"So, being with me … God stopped you?" Her throat felt raw. Anger sprouted barbed tendrils that coiled around her heart. "Which would make sense since, to you, to Him, I'm just basically a prostitute."

"*No*," he said, his words raw and vehement. "Stop right there."

"This"—he stabbed a finger at the bed—"is sacred."

"It's sex."

"It's our souls," he said, turning to her, "entwining. It's far more than just sex. It's the most intimate, beautiful thing I can give you or vice versa."

Bang-bang-bang.

The visitor at the front door was getting irritated.

But so was she. Fed up. "I … know you can't get over my past, what I did, was forced to do, but contrary to what you think, I am *not* wanton or a slut—"

"Tizzy, stop. Please."

"—but I didn't come in here to seduce you."

"I never thought that. I just—"

More knocks.

Growling Stone flashed a palm at her. "Please, hold … that thought." He looked down, seemed to take stock of himself and then ran a hand through his disheveled hair as he started for the door.

Realizing he intended to answer the door, Brighton hurried into the front bedroom. From the sliver of space between the jamb and the door, she watched Stone.

He drew up. "Oscar. What's wrong?"

"Nothing, Boss." The front desk manager suddenly stilled, his gaze on something. His eyebrows winged up. "Ah. Well. Very good. Question answered. I'll get back to work."

"What question?"

What had he seen? Brighton strained to peek into the living room and spotted Grief chewing on her bright pink hair scrunchie. Oh no.

Oscar faltered. "The, uh, inspector was still checked in …"

Quietly, she slipped into the guest bathroom but didn't turn on the light, afraid it'd be noticed, too. She met her reflection in the mirror. "You fool," she hissed. Things seemed to be changing between her and Stone, for the good. She'd dared to hope that maybe … But … "You ruined it. Like everything else."

Yet the confusion in the dead of night had given way to more of the same panic that sent her flying into Stone's arms … She'd just wanted him to hold her again. Somehow, *there*, with his arms around her, threats fell away. The world seemed like it wasn't out to destroy her—or at least, that it couldn't get to her. Because of him. It was stupid—she'd told herself that even as she sat on the edge of the mattress as he slept.

She *was* wanton, wasn't she? Was there no hope for her? To be happy? To be … normal.

What does that even look like?

"Brighton."

Startled, she glanced in the mirror to the door behind her where his voice had come from.

"Let's talk."

He's going to make you leave. Never wanted you here anyway. Climbing into bed with him … it was the last straw. He was done with her. Angry.

"I'm … not mad."

Frozen that he'd so thoroughly known her thoughts—as he had so often during their time in Baltimore, she blinked. Why wasn't he mad?

"I'll be in the kitchen when you're ready."

It's a trap. It's always *a trap*. Men were nice only to manipulate her into what they wanted.

Somehow, she found herself standing outside the guest room, watching him stir something in a pan on the cooktop. Just like old times.

He looked up and something twisted through his expression.

"Eggs? Bacon?" His tone gave no hint at what he wanted to talk about.

What is happening here? Why's he being so ... nice?

"I know you prefer breakfast sausage, but I'm fresh out." He wiped his hands on a towel and switched to another pan. "I'll pick some up later this morning."

"I'm sorry, what?" What changed him so drastically?

"Long story. I'll explain over breakfast."

Over breakfast. They'd met for breakfast many times when they were seeing each other. And here he was, cooking and acting like things were ... normal. Gingerly, she slipped onto a stool at his large kitchen island, afraid if she moved too fast or said the wrong thing, this bubble would burst.

"Ground rules." Stone popped bread into a toaster. "You sleep in the guest room, and I stay in mine. Doors closed. No deviation. Understood?"

"Sleep here?" What was he talking about? "What about my room at the lodge?"

"Change of plans." He still hadn't looked her in the eye since she sat down. "Big conference hit today, and all the rooms are occupied. Then, by mistake, Oscar rented your room last night."

"How does that happen?"

"Another long story not worth going into."

She glanced to the door, as if she could find answers there. Instead, she spotted her backpack slumped against the wall. "Guess that explains my things at the door."

"Doubt he didn't realize it was all you owned. Thought it got left behind on accident and brought it up here to see if I could get them to you." Stone sipped a mug of coffee, but still hadn't met her gaze.

He doesn't want me here. "I'll ... leave. Figure something out. Get a room in town—"

"Can't risk you being seen." He was all business, then grunted. "Look, we're adults. We can handle this. Also, you said you didn't want to be locked up, so … what do you say to continuing to tend the café?"

She raised her eyebrows, stunned.

"You'll be paid, of course." He divided the food onto two plates.

"I … Yeah. Sure."

"Okay, so that creates some logistical issues. Don't want people thinking we're living together or seeing you coming/going and connect some dots, so I suggest using the kitchen backdoor to get to the café. Try to avoid Inspector Pellet, who's staying to spy on me."

First. Her brain was still catching up to the little fact she was supposed to stay with him in his home. Second. He was okay with it.

Well, not *okay-okay*, but … okay. But why wasn't he throwing her out on her rump?

She should feel bad, yet she couldn't help but hope this could give her a chance to prove to him that she was no longer Lizzy, the girl owned by Ladomer, the escort who serviced clients.

The thought made her skin crawl. Only ten days and she couldn't stand the thought of being trapped in that again. *Please, God …*

"We clear?" He set a plate in front of her with eggs, bacon, and a slice of toast—no butter but slathered with jam.

Just the way I like it.

He'd remembered. The thought drew out a tremulous smile.

"That a yes?"

She started. "Yes."

He hesitated, taking her in. "You look like you're about to cry."

"I …" What could she say? How was she to explain what she was feeling—that she'd never expected to have this again, that she was awestruck being here in his home, him talking to her in a manner reminiscent of their past. Did he have any idea what that smirk and blue eyes did to this girl? But it couldn't be that he was forgiving her. That … it'd never happen. "Why are you being nice to me?"

Stone tensed, his lips tight amid that thick, trimmed beard. "Because," he said with a huff and planted his hands on the island. "I can either fight this or I can roll with the punches and get on with it."

Fight this. Punches. Exactly what was he fighting? "Get on with what?"

"This. You here. In my life." He shrugged, grabbing his own plate and fork. Keeping the island between them, he started eating. "Besides, Cord's coming back in two days. We just have to survive till then."

Survive. So. He *did* want her out of here. She felt foolish now for seeking comfort from him. Should've known better. He was out of her league. Always had been.

But that kiss … his promises to protect her … Did all that expire at "midnight"—with Cord showing up—like Cinderella's carriage and coachmen? Why had she gotten her hopes up?

But that kiss she thought for the millionth time. The way he'd held her last night. Maybe to him she was just a bad habit. An addiction. She'd serviced men like that. But she hadn't thought Stone would be one of them. Hope died among the pile of eggs and bacon.

He'd said something wrong at breakfast. Had no idea what, but the change in her was like night and day. Maybe it was his mention of Cord's return. Had to admit, that thought had even rankled him. Just as she was starting to wonder how to make peace with what happened, how to let her back in … He'd messed it up. And dang, if he didn't want that door of conversation between them opened again.

After a shower, he found her sitting at the island, using his laptop. "Have you ever thought of opening a water park?"

Stone faltered. "Here?"

"Yeah," she said, nodding over her shoulder. "You could do it on the north side of the pool. Enclose it. Keep the water shallow and you eliminate risks." She spun it toward him. "There's a lodge a few hours south that does something similar."

Taken aback at the suggestion, that she was even thinking about the Bexar-Wolfe, he palmed the granite and the back of her chair as he bent toward the laptop. "I'd looked at that facility for ideas, but never considered a water park."

"It'd draw families—and parents that can leave their kids to a program while they ski are more likely to come. There are also families that will want to come together, so maybe have an adult slide or two as well."

"It'd be big, gaudy."

"Possibly," she said with a shrug. "If you find a good architect, it could blend in."

Stone studied the pictures, clicked through and noted not only the equipment but the people. "Crowded."

"And crowded means more money to do something else, like maybe start a program for veterans."

Stone marveled at her. "I think it's my turn to ask why you're being so nice to me."

She grinned. "Turnabout's fair play."

"I don't quite think that's what the phrase meant."

She shrugged with that quirky smile he loved.

The instinct to kiss her was crazy powerful. "I'm running into town for some things."

"Oh." Her smile faded and she turned back to the laptop.

"Why don't you come with me?" *Stupid idea, Metcalfe.* She could be seen, exposed.

Maybe, but it was a small town. He knew the people and they knew him—as Jackson Mulroney, granted. But he should be able to suss out if there was trouble.

She was on her feet, her excitement all too apparent. "Ready." Clearly she wasn't going to give him a chance to change his mind.

"Grab a hat," he instructed, pointing to the closet. "Something to shield your eyes."

Complying, she dug out a Coast Guard ballcap and threaded her ponytail through the back hole.

Man, she looked good in that. He grunted.

"What? I think they're underrated."

"Don't let Canyon hear you say that." He motioned her toward the door. "C'mon."

They headed into town with Grief, who trotted along with them—the benefits of small-town favor. Everyone knew the beast and loved him.

"First stop—the bakery."

Brighton followed him into the shop, but Grief waited outside, knowing he'd get a dog cookie. "Thought you didn't eat sweets."

"I don't," he said, stepping up to the counter. "A dozen assorted donuts and a half dozen jam tarts."

"And a cookie for Grief?"

"Of course."

Brighton wrinkled her brow at him.

"Did you want something?"

"No," but then she hesitated. "Actually—"

"Boston crème," they said together.

Stone grinned, but realized he probably shouldn't.

The worker added one to the box and checked them out. As they left, he handed her the Boston crème, tossed Grief his cookie, then snagged a chocolate glazed for himself. He tucked the box with the rest in the truck and started down the sidewalk.

Pulling the donut apart, the gooey middle stretching between her fingers, she eyed the truck. "Who are all those for?"

"Donuts for the staff, tarts for my mom. The move to the lodge has been tough on her, so I wanted to do something nice to cheer her up."

Brighton smiled, and it twisted up his insides in a different way. "Was it recent, her move?" She plucked a piece of pastry and ate it.

"Same day you showed up."

"Wow. That was a *really* bad day for you." When she tore another chunk, she swiped it into some of the crème before sliding it in her mouth.

"A game changer."

From the top, she peeled more donut. Angling her head so she didn't drip the filling, she ate another piece. "Hey. How's your son?"

He hadn't expected Jack to get brought up. "Good." He stopped in front of the hardware store and watched her.

Licking her fingers, she balanced what was left of the shredded pastry. Creamy goop landed on her thumb and she licked it off with a giggle.

He shook his head. "Plan to finish that sometime today?"

"Eventually," she said with a little of that playful streak that had lured him when they first met. "Why?"

He pointed to the sign on the window: No food or drink.

"Whoops." She stuffed the last bit in her mouth, but looked at her palms.

He sighed. "Towels and sanitizer inside."

She bunched her shoulders sheepishly and availed herself of the supplies, while he grabbed a new bolt lock and went to the cashier.

"How's it going with the lodge?" Darrell, the manager, rang up his purchase.

"Good. You?"

"Better since that ray of sunshine came into the store." Darrell grinned, bobbing his head toward the front.

Stone looked in that direction and found Brighton thumbing through a brochure. He scowled at Darrell. "How much?" His growl had the intended effect, snapping the clerk's eyes back to the register.

"Twenty-two-fifteen." He shifted as Stone dropped the money on the counter. "So … she with you?"

"Yes."

"Ah."

"Thanks." He snatched up the brown paper bag with the bolt and stalked toward Brighton. "Let's go."

She hurried behind him, oblivious to the attention or his irritation. "Did you see this?"

"No."

"It's that indoor aquatic center I'd told you about."

"Can't afford it right now."

She paused in the middle of the sidewalk.

"Keep moving," Stone muttered.

Confused at his tone, she hustled to catch up. "What's wrong?"

"Nothing." He crossed the street to the grocery store and tugged out his list.

"I feel like I missed something back there." Brighton peered through the window. "Like something happen?"

Darn fool of a clerk now stood in front of his store, staring back in their direction.

"*Did* something happen?"

"Why?"

"Because you're prowling up and down these aisles like a panther guarding its territory."

"I'm not." He grabbed another item, crossed it off, and started for the next item.

Skipping a step to stay with him, she gave a laugh. "My calves are *literally* aching from trying to keep up." She sounded out of breath.

"I always shop this way."

"Like it's the Indianapolis 500?"

"In and out," he said, stabbing a knifehand motion toward the registers at the front. "No need to waste time."

"What if you forgot something? Taking your time will help you remember."

"I have a list."

She laughed. "I know. You *always* have a list. And a plan."

"Now you sound like my mother."

"Does that mean I get jam tarts, too?" Now she was taunting him.

"I told you, sweets will rot your teeth."

"And I told you," she said, leaning in and catching his arm, poking a finger at his bicep, "sweets will do much to soften *your* rough edge."

He grinned like a fool at the way she laughed as they approached the check-out stands. She slipped closer, and his arm—with a mind of its own—coiled around her waist.

Casually, she tiptoed up and kissed him. Her lips were soft and teasing. Achingly familiar. Sweet. It surprised both of them, but neither pulled away.

"Welcome to Groce's Grocer! Do you have a super saver card?" The all-too-cheery voice of the cashier crashed between them. "Oh. Hi, Mr. Mulroney."

Face bright with embarrassment, Brighton eased out of his hold with a shy-but-guilty look that also said she hadn't minded.

And really, neither had he. Because his brain wasn't working. Kissing her, being with her, was as natural as grocery shopping.

He also hoped Darrell had seen that kiss. After paying for the groceries, he started for the door, her hand slipping stealthily into his. He glanced at her, once again realizing how much he'd missed this. Missed her. Them.

The staccato barks of Grief jerked Stone to a stop. He glanced across the street, saw his Malinois tearing up the road toward the truck. A shadow spirited away from the vehicle, heading down an alley.

Stone nudged Brighton back into the store and passed her the bags. "Wait here. I—"

"No!" She grabbed his arm. "No way. This is what they do— distract and snatch."

Stone realized she was right. Nodded. "Okay, c'mon." He took her hand and led her across the street, stowed the groceries inside the truck box in the bed, and reached for his weapon. "I—"

Grief rounded the corner, trotting lazily as if he'd been out for a stroll.

Stone scanned the alley, the sidewalks, for sign of someone he didn't recognize. For trouble, his internal alarms still ringing.

"The pastries are gone," Brighton said. "Did you lock the truck after you put them inside?"

"Of course." Startled by the pronouncement, he checked the cab of the truck. Sure enough, the box of pastries and tarts were gone. Had he locked it?

"The Knave of Hearts has struck this sleepy little town," Brighton said, her voice tinged with nerves though she sought to make light of it.

Stone wasn't convinced that this was just about someone stealing donuts. That tingling on the back of his neck told him there was trouble. He just didn't know who or where it was. "Why don't you get more donuts and tarts," he said absently, going for his wallet.

"Why? So you can hunt down the thief?" She shook her head. "I told you—I'm not leaving your side."

So, she wasn't convinced either. "We'll both go." They restocked the pastries and then headed back to the lodge in silence. Well, save Grief's panting and whining as he nudged the box of donuts.

CHAPTER
SEVENTEEN

Surreal. Crazy. Wonderful. That's what that kiss was. In Maryland, that's how every minute with Stone had been. No wonder she'd fallen in love with him, hard and fast. No wonder she looked forward to every moment they were together.

Even when the specter of death came to call.

Is that what'd happened in town? She didn't want to believe, but then … how could she not? She knew Ladomer would not give up. She'd serviced too many VIPs, knew too many names and places and deals.

"You okay?" he asked as they hit the main route between town and the lodge.

"Yeah." Mostly.

"Look, neither of us believes it was about pastries."

She swallowed.

"So, we stay alert. Eyes out."

She nodded. This—the business, the down-to-action—was what he preferred. Romance, soft moments were wonderful, but he never lingered there long. It didn't surprise her that he didn't mention her accidental kiss in the store. She hadn't meant to do it. Things had just been so comfortable and natural between them, so like before, that her lips were on his before she realized it. And remembered they weren't at that stage in this refreshed relationship yet.

Since being thrown back into his life, she hadn't seen the side of him that had been like stepping into a natural hot spring—the warmth eased aches and the silkiness of the water calmed her. That. That was Stone Metcalfe.

Even with the beard.

Which was a nice one, granted. Nothing could make him look bad, but … "Why'd you grow a beard?"

Right arm hooked over the steering wheel as they headed back to the lodge, he glanced at her. Ran a hand over the face fur. "What's wrong with it?"

"Nothing," she said, lifting her shoulder. "It just …"

"What?" His eyes were a darker blue beneath the rim of that black cowboy hat. He shot her a glance, the winding curves back to the lodge forcing him to keep his eyes on the road.

Another nonchalant shoulder lift. "You're handsome either way, but it's … scruffier, gruffer than the man I knew. Seems like you're hiding something behind it."

His expression shifted. Though that fuzz shielded the planes of his face, it couldn't hide the change in demeanor. "I was." He motioned around them. "Coming up here …" His gaze stayed on the road for several long seconds.

And she understood. Chastised herself for bringing it up.

"Had to change a few things to eke out my living up here and to not be the man everyone knew as Governor Metcalfe."

"Including your name." The weight of what she'd cost him once again seared the air between them. "I really am sorry"—she forced herself to meet his eyes—"for everything. For not figuring out some way to stop Ladomer. I should've stood up to him."

The truck bounced and rocked as they hit the country road outside the city limits. "You got away," she said around a raw throat, "rebuilt your life … and then I crash into it again. I …" She shook her head and swallowed. "I hate that he used me to ruin you."

"I'm not ruined."

"But your career—"

"Needed to end."

Surprised, she gaped. "You were *governor*."

"I was full of myself. You remember how I was when we first met," he said. "God toppled the tower I built."

"But you were *good* at what you did. You cared about the people."

"I agree." He nodded, his black hat dipping and hiding his eyes. "But I lost my way."

She wanted to rip off that hat. "I … I don't understand. How can you be so calm about what we did to you?"

"Calm?" He snorted. "If you'll recall the night you showed up with Cord, I doubt you could call that calm."

"I'll never forget it or the way you shouted at me to get out."

Stone winced. "Not my greatest moment." He eased up to the security gate, rolled down the window, and entered a code, letting them back onto the property. They ambled the back road to the workshop and his cabin. "I'd built a new life and it was on the verge of being toppled again. I felt I had everything to lose." He aimed the truck into his private driveway. "I'm a firm believer in God directing our paths."

"So, God wanted Ladomer to ruin you?"

"No," Stone sniffed. "I'm saying God knew I needed a reset. He let my choices and mistakes run their natural course."

"But *I* was that mistake. So … what, God used me to destroy you?" She heard the panic in her own words, the fear as he parked by the workshop and let the truck idle. If God had allowed the mistakes of a man of character to follow their natural course, which effectively destroyed him, what would the last six years cost *her*?

My life.

It only made sense. The natural end result was Ladomer finding her. She'd pay for what happened. What she'd done. Oh man. Why had she ever started this conversation? She tucked her chin.

The truck shifted as Stone angled toward her, tipping up the brim to see her clearly. Set his large hand on his chest. "*I* did this. *I* caused my downfall. It was *my* choice to stay with you, to see you, to … be with you that night. To compromise my core values. Hard as my fall was, as ticked off as I was, the only person I can blame is myself."

"But you *did* blame me."

His beard twitched, evidence of his jaw muscle working.

"I think you still do, though you have the diplomatic words to cover the pain."

His gaze snapped to hers, then bounced away, out the windshield. He killed the engine and grabbed the keys before climbing out of the truck.

Way to kill the mood. She hopped out and hurried around the truck as he grabbed the groceries from the back of the truck.

"Stone, wait." She caught his arm, but he resisted, reaching for the box of pastries, but she wasn't giving up. Not this time. Not with him. "Please."

"What do you want from me, Tizzy? I'm trying to figure this out. Trying to demonstrate some character. I'm doing the best I can."

He'd called her Tizzy again, a nickname that sparked hope— but she knew better than to go that route. Yet every time she tried to squash that rebellious thread of hope, he went and did something that shoved her square into its grasp. "You've always shown your character—good character. Always. And I see it now, that you even give me the time of day is more than I deserve. I just … I miss *us*," she whispered.

Lips taut, he stared at the pastry boxes sitting on the seat of the king cab.

"How we were in town, it was like … before. And I really liked that, *us*."

His gaze skidded into hers like a slow-moving storm cloud. "Me, too."

That treacherous hope leapt onto a trampoline and flipped high into the sky. Her heart was doing the mamba as they stood, afraid to move, afraid to do the wrong thing. But his face was closer—he was closer and she felt herself easing into him. "Forgive me?"

"Already have." His warm words dusted her cheek, and her heart jostled as his gaze drifted to her lips.

"Maybe shave the beard?"

He smirked. "That's going a bit far."

"Then—though I prefer your smooth skin—I yield, Sir Metcalfe, and will take you as I find you." She angled in closer, wanting the kiss that dangled between them.

"Need help?" A cheery voice punctured the moment.

Stone straightened and looked back over his shoulder.

On the grass with his burly dog stood a tall, beautiful woman Brighton recognized as her aftercare specialist and felt a shot of adrenaline. What was *she* doing here? Was there danger? Or worse—had Cord made good on his promise to find Brighton a more permanent placement? Was Willow here to take her away

Castration might be a bit extreme, but Willow would take whatever measures necessary to get the point across to Stone that Brighton needed time to heal after six years of trafficking and, therefore, was *hands-off*.

"Willow." His greeting was gruff and tight. Pretty normal for her eldest sibling, but that shadow hanging over the strong ridge of his Metcalfe brow told her he knew a lecture was coming. And deserved one.

Holstering her anger, she hugged him, getting buried in the muscled mass that was his oversized self. "I'm going to kill you."

"Later."

"Count on it." She broke away and met Brighton's worried expression. "Hi, sweetie. How are you?"

"Good." Brighton nodded as she hefted up a box. "Donuts solve everything." The way she held the confections between them like a barrier said she felt guilty.

Willow smiled. "It's the Metcalfe way." She took a bag, threaded her arm through Brighton's as they followed her brother back to the cabin. "Mom wants us to eat together tonight."

Stone didn't hesitate, but irritation scratched his eyes. "I'll cook."

"I thought you'd never offer." Willow stepped inside. Immediately, two things hit her—the bags sitting inside the guestroom and the way Brighton suddenly stiffened, knowing her things had been discovered there.

Did she need to beat her brother into next week?

Setting the grocery bag on the island, Willow turned her glower on Stone. "Oh. Saw Oscar at the front desk. He was looking for you." It was true. Mostly. "Said he needed something."

Stone swiped a hand over his beard. Classic move that said he wanted to say something but wouldn't. His focus flicked to Brighton, then back. "Y'all good here?"

"Why wouldn't we be?"

He eyed the grocery bags. Stalling.

"I can put them away," she stated. "Shouldn't keep your desk manager waiting. Bad for morale, I hear."

He held her gaze—hard. Clearly didn't like this, but he'd yield. "Understood." Another swipe of his beard. "Grief, stay."

When he headed toward the door, Willow rolled her eyes at Brighton, who seemed amused with the exchange. She started putting away the food, noting the strawberries. Sausage. "Thought he liked bacon."

Brighton awkwardly helped. "Uh, that's … for me."

Willow closed the refrigerator, folded her arms, and met the brown eyes that had bewitched her brother. "How're you doing?"

Shoulders bunched, Brighton pursed her lips. "Good."

"And the ogre? He's not making life awful, is he?" Not if that near-kiss was any indication.

"No," Brighton said, tucking her hands in her back pockets. "I mean, it was rough at first. He couldn't stop barking and telling me I shouldn't be here."

"Sounds like Stone. With that deep voice, he's got a lotta bark." Willow stole an orange and started peeling it. "And back there?"

The girl's cheeks pinked. "What?"

Rind tossed, Willow slipped around the corner of the island. "You don't owe him anything. You know that, right?"

"Owe?" Brighton frowned. "What—" Her eyebrows winged up. "Oh. No. That's not …" She flushed. "He's not like that." She touched her throat. "Neither am I." She flinched.

"Hey, whoa there. I never meant to imply anyone was that way. I simply meant that there are times when we feel we've wronged someone and want to make it up to them. We'll do anything to make the situation better or help their anger go away." Willow held her gaze. "I do know Stone enough to know he wouldn't want you to feel like you needed to do that. Sometimes, in the heat of a moment, things can get out of hand…"

Brighton swallowed, not meeting her gaze.

Her brother had gotten himself tangled in a very complicated situation with a very beautiful woman who was enmeshed in a nightmare. What had transpired between the two since Brighton arrived here that they had gone from him yelling at her to them being out on a grocery run that ended in a near-kiss?

"Can we sit and talk?" She led the sweet girl over to the sofa and sat down. "Really. How are you?"

"You asked that already, and my answer hasn't changed." She seemed defensive. "I'm fine. Good." She frowned. "Is that why you came here? You didn't have to—because I'm okay. Honest. Things have been fine here, too."

"I heard a very different story," Willow said softly. "You didn't exactly have a welcome party when you arrived."

Brighton shrugged, drawing her hands into her sleeves. "It wasn't fair to Stone—Cord ambushed him, and in a way, me." She wrinkled her nose. "I was the last person on earth Stone wanted to see."

"He yelled at you, and that's not okay."

Another shrug. "Yeah, maybe. But I understood."

"You were traumatized and sobbing afterward."

"It's ... You don't understand." Pools of brown looked up at him. "I ... really hurt him, ruined his life." She lifted her chin. "I never thought I'd see him again, and to be honest, I deserved everything he yelled and much more."

Willow reached across the sofa and touched her knee. "*Nobody* deserves that. I know Stone and I've never seen his anger like that, but regardless, he shouldn't have treated you like that."

Brighton sniffled and nodded. "That's what he said."

Startled, Willow stilled. "My brother said that?"

"Never thought he'd talk to me again. But after I ran away, he brought me back and we ... talked." With another nod, Brighton sat cross-legged on the couch and propped her elbows on her knees.

She's comfortable here. But Willow's thoughts snagged on two words. "Ran away? What happened?"

Brighton gave her a shrug. "I couldn't take it anymore. Just wanted to get out of here."

"Couldn't take what?"

She chewed the inside of her lip. "It's been over a year, and I was okay until I came here and had to see him every day. Then he was so mad ... yelling and angry ... It just all—I couldn't take it."

And here the girl had just been defending Stone. "I tried to tell Cord this was too much."

"No." Brighton raised a hand. "I mean—yeah, it was rough at first. But it needed to be worked out, and we've done that. Mostly."

"Want to elaborate?"

She tugged on her sleeve. "Not really." She looked sheepish. "Is that okay?"

"Of course." What on earth was going on between them? Mom said Stone had a lot of anger, which was unlike him. And anger was a masking emotion, so what was it masking? Did he really care about her? "I want you to know I'm here to talk. You should feel safe where you live, and I'm not sure this place—"

"I do feel safe." Her answer was quick and assured. "He's always made me feel that way."

Willow nodded, watching, wondering. Ultimately and ideally, she should get to a place where safety was not defined by a man or any other person. But that was a long journey of healing. And what on earth was she doing living in Stone's cabin? Granted, her clothes were in the guest room, but still ... it was too few steps to his bedroom.

Clearly, she needed to punch some sense into him. Warn him of impeding the healing process. Guilt had been scrawled all over his face and his rigidity when he turned away from nearly kissing

Brighton and found Willow there. Honestly, it was priceless. Something she could lord over her big brother for a very long time. Siblings. What was life without a little sibling mercilessness?

"I'm glad you feel safe. Cord is still working on your placement."

Brighton sat up, her expression open. "So, you're not here to take me away?"

Take me away. Those words were replete with a mentality of bondage and no sense of control. "When a place has been found, moving will be up to you. Nobody is—nor should be—forcing you to do anything you do not want to do."

A flicker of a smile washed through her face. "Right. Okay. He said that, too."

Shook. That Stone could be volatilely angry then speak such healing words to Brighton ... was he just saying them?

No, that wasn't like Stone.

From her backpack, Willow retrieved a packet and slid it over to her. "In there, you'll find a notebook, pen, and a devotional. All are optional." She laughed. "However, I'd really encourage you to start dream-building. Think about your future, your career, school, whatever. Where you'd like to live, what you'd like to do, own, be. This is your time to dream and plan. When we talk next time, we'll do what we can do to start the process of helping you realize them."

Brighton looked at the packet. "I ... I just thought with them still out there and me ... hiding ..." She squinted at her. "Isn't this a bit premature?"

Willow's heart broke for her, giving the enemy, her captor, the power over her future. And for once in this whole crazy mess, she was glad Brighton was here with Stone. "First, I know my brother is not going to let anything happen to you. But more importantly, we need to put the power over your future back in your hands."

With a slow nod, Brighton pressed the packet to her chest. "When will you be back?"

"Once Cord sends me your placement."

Deflating, she seemed to clutch that packet tighter. "*Tomorrow*? I thought—"

"Ah." Willow cringed. "No, sorry. I know that was the plan, but Cord is tied up on the other side of the world." Thinking through how much longer this would take, Willow couldn't help but wonder if it was a mistake to leave Brighton here. The girl was fragile, though she didn't want anyone thinking that, and Stone was ... Stone. "You'll probably be here another week or two."

Brighton's lips parted, her gaze wandering to the windows. "He's going to be mad."

Definitely need to kill my brother.

Tomorrow. He's coming for her tomorrow.

Something twisted in Stone's gut.

No. It was better this way. Especially since his nerves hadn't stopped buzzing since the incident in town. And he didn't mean the kiss in Groce's. Or the near-kiss at the truck—witnessed by Willow.

Two in one day. He was getting too comfortable around Brighton. Too familiar.

God, get her out of here before I do something stupid ... again.

More often than not, God didn't outright remove temptation or a problem. Instead, He provided opportunities for escape. So, where was his exit? Dad said it was always there, if we were willing to look for it.

Willing? I'm desperate!

He needed an exfil strategy. Now. This—him and her—couldn't happen.

Why not? He wasn't a governor anymore and she wasn't an escort anymore.

But she *had* been one, being paid for sexual favors. The thought infuriated and disgusted him. He hated himself for wondering how many she had been with.

What about you?

He hadn't been with anyone!

Yet ... something reverberated against his conscience. His gaze fell on his desk.

No, not his desk. His planner.

All his plans. Lists.

He hadn't been with anyone except Marie, but he'd made his planner his lover. Iron-grip control on what happened in his life to the point nothing was as important. By planning, keeping people and love at bay ... he made sure he wasn't betrayed. And yet ... he had been. Dad. Marie. Brighton.

But doing this ... keeping the plans, the lists was smart. Right? He who fails to plan—

"The heart of man plans his way, but the Lord establishes his steps."

The chastisement rippled through him. He hadn't planned for Brighton to be here. Hated that she was.

No, he didn't hate it. He'd been so adamant about avoiding her, cutting her out of his life—the scandal necessitated that— but hearing her laugh ... seeing how she fit into his life and arms like his Glock in its holster ... So perfect. So molded to his life and heart.

Could it work?

Yes—fiercely. You saw the fruits of it.

He had to be an idiot to consider this, open his heart and life back up to her.

But he *was* considering it, wasn't he?

I'm too old for her anyway.

Not really. There *was* an age gap, yet ... it somehow worked for them. His conversations with her had always been good, filled with theological, eschatological, psychological explorations and so on. She'd offered so much, filled a companionship hole he hadn't even known existed. He'd learned and appreciated that Brighton wasn't the average twenty-something woman. She had a lifetime of experience and pain that knocked her solidly into a mid-thirties mindset and personality. Now that she was back, she was showing him that betrayal had many forms and histories.

Mature—that was the word for her. How could she not be after all that had been done to her? All she'd been forced to do? She had betrayed him that one time, but hadn't she been betrayed time and again by men who should've been protecting her?

He tucked his chin. Stroked his beard, recalling his vow after Marie's infidelity to never again be protector to anyone. Never fall in love or marry. But then, Brighton plowed into his life. Her abuse she'd suffered made him want to hurt someone. Bad. And protect her, make sure nobody ever hurt her again. Here at the lodge, he could keep her safe. They could …

Man, could they make it work?

So, guess this makes me an idiot.

The phone rang violently, jerking Stone from the conviction dogging his thoughts. "Hello."

"How's it going?" Cord sounded way too casual.

"Nobody's dead, if that's what you're asking." Man, this was it—wasn't it? He was calling to say Brighton would be leaving. Stone wanted to say good riddance … His fingers curled into a fist.

"Good," Cord laughed. "Wasn't sure after that introduction."

"You mean ambush."

More laughter, but it was … off. "Fair enough."

Watching the clock, Stone felt every tick of the hands like hammers chipping away what little time remained. They'd had ten days, and he'd wasted most of it being angry. Yelling. And now, with Cord calling, she'd be gone in less than twenty-four hours.

He shifted his gaze back to the planner and the call. "Did you manage to save the world in time?" Where Stone expected even more laughter, there was instead an ominous pause. Suddenly his plans seemed like ravenous wolves. "Things good? You okay?"

"Yeah, yeah. Sure. But uh …"

Familiar with that hesitation, Stone stilled. Knew what was coming. Conflicted, he held his breath. Half of him needed Brighton out of here. Half hoped—

"Look," Cord said, "I know we said a week or two."

"You swore." There was no conviction in Stone's words.

"Things here are taking longer than expected. There are complications."

Tell me about it. At some point, he'd stood, unsure whether he was angry or relieved. "How long?" That's what Cord was saying, right? That he couldn't come for Brighton yet.

"Two more weeks."

Stone closed his eyes, not sure how to feel. Nah, not true. He was *relieved*. Which made no sense. Absently, he traced the planner entry for tomorrow. He'd have time to fix things with her. Figure out how to wade through his grief, see past all his well-laid plans to … her. He stroked his beard, a move that this time teased her words about liking him better without it through his chest. "Two."

"Maybe three."

"Cord—"

"I hear you. I do. But you know me, man. I wouldn't do this unless absolutely necessary. And, you have to admit, moving her, drawing attention to yourself or that location would put both of you at risk. They're looking for her—and I think that's why we're having issues here."

Not liking the sound of that, Stone frowned. "How so?"

"We've got some heat on us right now, tails and such. Gotta play it smart, and going anywhere near her ..."

"This call—"

"Secure."

Stone nodded to himself. It was secure on Cord's end, but what about here?

Willow had come ... Did that mean she'd endangered Brighton? He suddenly felt paranoid, protective. Especially with Willow added to the mix. "My sister is here." That shouldn't tip off anyone listening, yet Cord would know who and what he meant.

"That's secure, too." Cord cleared his throat. "So. We good with the extended-stay?"

With a sigh, Stone again looked down at his planner. His lists. This was royally messing with his plans ...

Are they more important than a broken soul?

Ouch.

"You there?"

"No—yeah." He straightened, nodded, and pinched the bridge of his nose. Scratched his beard. "Fine. Three weeks."

"That ... was too easy."

"Don't have to like it to know it's smart, keeps her—everyone—safe."

Cord grunted. "Always said you had a good, if not big, head on your shoulders."

"Just be ready to pay up." Stone ended the call and bent forward, fingertips bracing him as he stared at the litter of plans and lists.

What're You doing, God?

A text chimed on his phone—Willow, reminding him they were hungry and he'd said he'd make dinner. Smoothing a hand over his beard, he scanned his short- and long-term goals written in the planner. All now compromised because he had to watch the traffic coming into the lodge. Protect an asset. It was entirely possible that Brighton might mess up his newest career, too. Not intentionally, of course. He was big enough to admit that.

He tapped the planner and shifted his gaze beyond the windows to where night had fallen. A light flickered and bobbed in the trees up the hill from the workshop. What on earth ...? Nobody should be up that way.

Stone grabbed his hat, locked the door leading into the lodge, then headed out the back, almost calling for Grief before realizing he'd left his partner with the ladies. He scanned the wooded area for the light but didn't see anything.

A shadow shifted between the trees.

Stone stopped. Wished he'd gotten back in the habit of carrying a weapon after his days of politicking. He angled his head as he eased forward, head ringing with Cord's words about being watched, about Horvath looking for Brighton. As he moved up the hill, he snagged a broom propped against the side of the workshop to use as a weapon. He stopped, heart whooshing as he listened to the noises around him. Settled into his skin, processing the native chatter of wildlife.

A soft pop spun him around.

Shadowed and fast-moving, a shape came at him.

He swung the broom handle.

"Whoa!" Rowe ducked and narrowly missed getting whacked across the head. "Holy *what?*"

Stone nearly cursed himself. "What're you doing here?"

"Working," Rowe balked.

"Not at nearly nine p.m."

Rowe's brow dug into his dark eyes, made darker by the late hour. "A racoon was down by the hot tub, so I relocated it away from the guests. Guess I'll leave him next time if it's after nine." He shifted around Stone. "Or maybe hang a 'No Vacancy' sign so he knows it's after hours."

Stone sniffed. "Sorry." He hefted the broom and returned it to the wall. "Just ... keep your eyes open."

Rowe paused. "Everything okay?"

"Not in a long time," Stone said, slapping the back of the guy's shoulder as he started around him toward the cabin.

"This about that chick you're all scary-protector over?"

"Just do your job."

"Understood." Rowe grinned. "She's worth it."

Stone hesitated, glanced to the side. Then to Rowe. "Worth what?"

"Anything—everything. This side of you," Rowe said quietly, "I haven't seen it in a long time." He nodded. "It's good to see."

No idea how to respond, Stone let himself into the cabin. Grief greeted him with an excited whine as a peal of laughter yanked his attention from locking the door.

Hair like a waterfall, Brighton bent over, cradling Grief's thick skull.

He shook his head—unbelievable. "First time I tried to get near his face, he nearly took mine off."

Brighton smiled at him as she crouched next to his Belgian Malinois, giving his ears a massage. "Dogs know good people."

"I'm not sure if you just called me a bad person or not."

"It's our secret, huh, Grief?"

"Wow, with my own dog even ..." He scanned the cabin. "Where is everyone?"

"Ah." Brighton washed her hands at the kitchen sink. "Willow had to take a call, and your mom needed an oven"—she indicated to where cookies were baking—"so they said they'd be back."

Stone rolled up his sleeves and washed his hands. "Cord called."

Leaning back against the island, Brighton seemed to be bolstering herself. "Willow said there'd been a delay ..."

He grabbed the towel and dried his hands. "He can't make it back for a few of weeks."

"You angry?"

Palming the edge of the island, Stone stared into the sink. He should be. Would've been a few days ago. But ... "No. Not really."

"Seriously?" Her voice was small as she pressed in closer.

"I've spent a lot of time angry since ... since our photos were leaked. Since my shame was spilled across the headlines."

She touched his shoulder.

"And I think maybe"—he peered down into those brown eyes he loved so much—"I need to do some rolling."

A smile teased her lips. "'When you're pinned against a wall, you can fight it or roll with it.'"

"Guess I said it a few times around you, too. Time to live up to it. Learn from it."

Her face was in line with his, softened by the lights over the island. "What have you learned from it?"

Stone brushed her hair aside and traced her cheek. "I think I've been fighting the wrong fight." His hand slipped to her nape. "Instead of fighting what I feel for you, I need to fight *for* you."

Her lips parted with a stunned intake.

"You got me majorly mixed up, Tizzy."

She smiled. "I love when you call me that."

Stone set a light but firm kiss on her lips, hovering there. Wanting more. Remembering more—what they'd had together, the fun, the laughter, the ... yeah, even the love. "I'm sorry, Brighton. Sorry for my part in what happened to you."

Her eyes widened. "*You're* sorry? I—"

He pressed a finger to her lips. "The danger you've lived with, the cruelty, the perversion—you didn't deserve that. Nobody does."

"But I—"

"You. Didn't. Deserve. It." He almost smiled. "You *do* deserve so much more. A good life. A man who will honor and respect you. And if I could gut some men to erase that pain, I would."

She wrapped her arms around his neck and hugged tight, faced buried in his shoulder. He felt her slight frame trembling as she cried.

His phone buzzed. As he reached for it, she eased aside—but not completely out of his arms. Man, she twisted his mind up good. He dropped another kiss on her lips. She gave him that sultry smile that turned his brain to goo.

"Hello?"

Stone twitched. Angled his head aside and paid attention to the call. "Yeah?"

"Heeeey, Rocky."

Stone started, that voice and nickname so jarringly familiar. "*Boone?*"

A deep, resonant laugh carried through the line. "Been a while, eh?"

"*Long* time." What on earth was Boone Ramage doing calling him? "What's going on, brother?"

"Well," Boone said with his Northern Virginia country twang, "Sure do hate to be the bearer of bad news, but I think ya might have some trouble coming your way."

Stone straightened, moving around Brighton and making his way to the windows. He'd known this was coming. Why hadn't he listened to his instinct? "What do you know?"

"Not sure ya heard, but I moved back to NoVA and have been working contract with a team. All female. They're—epic, I'm telling ya. Anyway, I was out getting gas when I bumped into a surly fella who had his manners backwards and his pants inside out, if you know what I'm saying."

Stone rarely did.

"But ya know how rich folk are, and he was chatting loud on

his phone cuz the signal was bad—ain't that hilarious? People think talking louder improves a bad signal." He snorted. "Anywho, ya know I'm not really one to get up in someone's business until they make it mine, but this fella left no doubt of his intentions and making it my business when he dropped your name."

"My name." A guy at a gas station in Northern Virginia just happened to say his name? In front of Boone? What were the chances?

"Yep, and that's why I'm calling because I know there ain't many Stone Metcalfes out in the world. Least not up this way."

Ice dumped down Stone's spine. "Where'd this happen again?" Northern Virginia. But where?

"Little nothin' of a town called Lucketts. One light. Blink and you'll miss it. But I didn't miss his phone when I somehow lost control of my coffee and spilled it all over that fella's device. Hoo-ee. He was pretty ticked. Doubt he'll be able to report back in like he promised—least not for a while. Then, wouldn't ya know? I *dropped* my durn knife. Straight into his tire." He clicked his tongue. "Dang if those hilts aren't slick. Thing just flicked right outta my hand. Never seen nothin' like it, if ya know what I'm saying."

Boone had bought him time. "I owe you."

"That ya do, brother."

Stone strode into his bedroom and unlocked his gun safe. "I've got to run."

"That ya do, too. But listen here. If you're planning on getting noisy up that way, I know a brother or two nearby who'd be glad to come party."

"Thanks, Boone. Might need that help. I'll keep you posted."

"Anytime, brother."

Brighton was at his side—she hadn't touched him, but he felt her presence.

He dragged a hand over his beard, thinking. Planning.

"What's wrong?" she asked quietly.

Stone lifted his phone. Hit a programmed number. Reached for Brighton and drew her to himself. No way he was going to let anything happen to her.

"Yo, big bro!"

"Hey." Stone peered into Brighton's worried eyes and said words he never thought he'd voice. "I think I'm going to need your help, Canyon."

CHAPTER
EIGHTEEN

"So, he's coming." Her heart thrashed and Brighton moved away from Stone.

He eased onto a barstool and held out a hand.

Right now, she didn't want romance. She didn't want his charm. Because she'd never forgive herself if Ladomer got to Stone. Because it wouldn't just be his career slaughtered this time. Ladomer would make sure Stone's body was unrecognizable—if it was ever found.

"C'mere."

Reluctantly, she moved toward him.

He laced their fingers and drew her closer, peering up at her.

Brighton ran her fingers over his beard. It was soft, but also scritchy. Realizing what they were facing, what was coming, she let herself kiss him again. Breathed her relief that at least she had known this one more time.

He tilted his head and frowned at her. "That was a kiss of death."

She startled that he understood what she was thinking.

"Had no passion. That was a kiss of saying good-bye."

She smoothed his beard and traced his cheek, feeling raw

over the noose around their necks. "He never loses, Stone. And if he's coming—"

"I take exception to that. He lost you the night we met."

What …?

"Because while he got in the way, separated us once, I'm not letting it happen again."

"I don't deserve you."

"Can you promise to remember that the next time we fight?" She frowned.

"Because I don't know what it's going to look like, Tizzy, us working through this. You have a lot of healing to do. I do, too. It's going to be messy."

She nodded. Smiled. "My agent always said messy is good. Messy hair, messy clothes—too much perfection draws the attention away."

"Well, we don't have to worry about perfection with me in the mix."

"I don't know," she said. "You are pretty perfect. Even with the beard."

He groaned. "Leave a guy some dignity, will you?"

Overwhelmed at what they were facing, what was coming, she threw her arms around his neck and locked them tight. "I'm scared."

His embrace tightened. "I know. It's going to be okay. I promise."

"You *can't* promise that," she breathed against his neck. "You haven't faced off with him. He's powerful. He gets his way."

"Not this time." He urged her back and touched her cheek. "He's not getting you back. If I have to die to make sure—"

"No!" Brighton choked a sob. "Don't say that. Please. I'm not worth it."

He grunted and frowned. "Tizzy, you're worth way more." He wanted to seal that with a kiss but—

She leaned in and kissed him. Faltered, but then caught his mouth again.

Man, she undid his willpower.

"Woo-hoo! What's is this? My big bro hot and heavy with a pretty?"

Stone groaned again. "Canyon."

Face hot, Brighton winced away as Stone straightened to his six-two height and hugged the man who strode into the cabin as if he owned it.

Brothers.

After backs were slapped, they parted and that's when Brighton saw a black man standing at the door. As big as the door. Hands clasped in front of him. Who ...? Feeling outnumbered and uncertain, she started for the guest room that was hers. But Stone caught her hand and drew her to his side. "Brighton, this is my brother Canyon." Then he indicated to the larger man. "And that's longtime family friend, Griffin Riddell."

Canyon smirked—*good grief, do all the Metcalfes do that?*—and extended his hand. "Ma'am."

She accepted it and nodded. "I've heard a lot about you." She then shook Griffin's hand. "Hi."

"Well, I learned a long time ago not to trust anything my brother says when there's a football game on or a beautiful woman in the room."

Brighton eyed Stone. "Were there a lot of beautiful women?"

Canyon laughed. "We're Metcalfes. Of course there were."

"Easy," Stone said gruffly. "Don't scare her off." His hand slid around her waist in a surprising show of both affection and ownership. Which didn't upset her somehow. "Canyon's good with smooth talk."

"And blood and guts," Griffin added.

"Canyon's a combat medic," Stone said around a laugh.

"But baby girl," Griffin continued, "don't let either of these two sweet talk you. Make them earn their keep. Just smile and bat those eyes and you'll have them begging. Trust me, they're Metcalfes."

"Hey, I'm a happily married man now," Canyon said. He pointed to his buddy. "Make sure you tell Roark that when you tell her about this, because we all know you'll rat me out."

"Just keeping you in line, Midas."

Brighton had no idea what to say. She felt outnumbered— and yet, she'd never felt safer because these three men felt like six.

"Mercy!" the jovial voice of Mrs. Clara pushed into the room. "What is this? A Nightshade reunion? I feel the need to pull out my barbecue skills before the rest of the team gets here."

Nightshade?

Stone hovered close and nodded to the others. "Canyon and Griffin were—"

"*Are*," Canyon interjected.

"—part of a paramilitary team called Nightshade."

Paramilitary. She eyed the two men. "Are ... are the ... others coming?"

"On call." Canyon gave a nod that was so reminiscent of Stone. He cocked his head toward his friend. "Legend and I were at a briefing about an hour away, so we headed over."

The Metcalfe genes were strong. And gorgeous. It wasn't just that they were blond and blue-eyed, but the thick air of masculinity and owning a scene they entered ... Wow.

"I think," Mrs. Clara said with a laugh, "this means you've only lacked meeting two of my children now. Right?"

Brighton shrugged. "I ..." She'd met Brooke. Willow. Now Canyon. "I suppose so."

"With Range there's no loss there," Canyon snarked.

"Canyon!" Mrs. Clara gave his arm a swat. "Range has really come into his own—"

"If you say so."

"I do." She shook her head in mock annoyance. "And Leif has…well, he's doing really well now that he's met Iskra."

"Marrying a woman with a kid grows a guy up real fast." Canyon smirked and eyed her. Then Stone. Back to her. "You got any?"

"Kids?" Brighton balked. "No."

"Stand down, Midas," Stone growled, his hand on her shoulder firming.

Canyon chuckled and swiped a hand over his face as he looked at his brother who was a couple of inches taller. "So … how about you get us up to speed over some of those waffles you're known for?"

"I'm not known for waffles, punk."

"Yeah, well, keep perfecting those skills—like tonight—and you will be."

Stone rolled his eyes. Motioned to the kitchen. "C'mon. Let's get this going."

The next morning after a shower, Stone considered himself in the fogged mirror. Had the same debate he'd always had about the fur lining his jaw. Three weeks ago when Mom showed up, he hadn't been willing to shave.

"You never look bad, but I miss your soft skin."

Scissors in hand, he began the process of clearing away the scruff. Had nothing to do with a pair of brown eyes and the way they looked at him. The lips that screwed up his thinking.

Last night, he'd gotten Griffin and Canyon updated. The ladies had gone to bed, and while Stone knew the security measures had been upgraded—both by Rowe's efforts and with the addition of Griffin and Canyon—he hadn't been able to sleep. Danger was breathing down their necks. The same people who shoved him out of office were coming for the woman he loved.

He paused, safety razor in hand. Water running. He did love her. And he'd be hanged if he let anyone touch her again. The price this time might be his life. Not just his career. Somehow, he didn't care. As long as she was safe.

Maybe he should make some arrangements in case he was mortally wounded. He wanted her protected, taken care of.

He cleaned up, threaded on a shirt and jeans, then headed back into the living room. After pouring a cup of coffee, he saw Canyon and Griffin standing on the front porch. So, they hadn't slept either. He joined them, steam spiraling off his mug.

"Going to walk the property," Griffin said as he left the porch.

That felt like a planned exfil, but Stone sipped his brew without comment.

Hands in his pockets, Canyon stared out at the predawn morning, the mountain covered in dew. "Give it to me."

Stone glanced at him. "What?"

"You swore you'd never marry again."

"Who said anything about marriage?"

"The way you couldn't keep your eyes or hands off her last night said everything. The way you kept her close." He side-eyed him. "The way you shaved."

"Beard itched."

"Mm-hm." His brother folded his arms. "Seems I got a powerful lecture from you when Dani and I told the family she was pregnant. I'll never forget that look on your face. How I'd let you down."

Stone stared into the black coffee, recalling the stinging rebuke he'd delivered. "You let yourself down."

"No, that's not what you said. You said I'd let *you* down. Turned out just like Dad."

Stone winced.

"What did that mean?"

"It didn't mean anything. I was just mad you betrayed Range."

"Hold up. I didn't betray anyone—I let Dani choose. Isn't that what you're letting Brighton do?"

Stone tensed.

"See, I think these are connected—what's happening with you and this girl, and Dad. So read me in."

"Leave it alone."

"Yeah, thought so. But"—his brother pursed his lips—"no."

He glared at him.

"You're about to engage in a life-and-death battle for this woman, so I think you need to clean out the trunks weighing you down."

Stone sighed. "It's best left in the past."

"You and I both know the past won't stay there. Hurl it out, dude. Never seen you this crazy about someone that you'd go to war. Heck, you *left* war for politics." Canyon snorted and shook his head. "Explain that to me—no. Never mind. I don't want to know."

"She was an escort."

"Nope."

He squinted at his brother.

"You're past that."

"How—"

"You were eating her face when I walked in last night. There was no propriety in your positions, so no—you're not hung up on how many men she's been with."

Leave it to his brother to be blunt. "Dad ..." He dropped into a wooden rocking chair, rocked a few times, then shoved to his feet. "Dad. Marie. Brighton. They all betrayed me. I loved them. And they betrayed me."

Canyon's arrogance slipped, his brow knotting. "How did Dad betray you?"

Eying his brother, Stone wondered if he should let someone else share that burden. "Doesn't matter—"

"Hold up. Yeah, it does. You just accused our father of betrayal. He was hero, earned the Bronze Star and Purple Heart—"

"He had an affair."

Stricken, Canyon gaped. "No. No way."

"Happened first time he was deployed."

"Then how on earth do you know?"

"Somehow, some of his Army mail got misdirected to me while I was in Balad. I didn't really pay attention—thought it was from Marie. Opened it. Read it. I confronted him." He'd never forget that night. The rage in his father's face that slowly drained out. "He was so livid, but he finally confessed. Said it was over. A lapse in judgment."

Canyon looked like he was going to be sick.

"Mom was here, holding down the fort with six kids, and he's out there sowing wild oats."

"Why didn't you tell me?"

"He said it was over, in the past. I didn't see the point."

"He was our father!"

"And he's dead now. It'd change nothing—except maybe do to you what it did to me and irrevocably alter what 'hero' and 'love' looks like." He ran a hand over his head. "Dad was a hero, but he was also unfaithful. Both sides. No reason to destroy anyone else's view of him."

Canyon stared at him. "That's why you didn't re-up."

"Wasn't sure why I was in anymore. Joined to follow in his footsteps ..."

"And that wasn't a path you wanted to follow."

"But ... I did." Stone squinted into the darkness. Was something moving in the trees? Maybe Rowe or Griffin. "Dad's priority was his career. Separated him from Mom long enough that he forgot what it was like to be in her arms, and he ended up with another woman. So, I got out, buried myself in law enforcement ...” He sneered. “Drove Marie into the arms of another. I did the marriage and military thing all to continue the Metcalfe legacy. Only ...”

“That legacy wasn’t what you thought it was.”

With a slow nod, Stone glanced down.

“That’s why you didn’t even blink when Marie cheated on you and left.”

Stone snorted. “Figured it was my Metcalfe inheritance. Then I dared get involved with Brighton while in office. My arrogance—another thing we Metcalfes are good at—convinced me it’d be different this time.”

“Well.” Canyon wheeled around and leaned against the rail. “You were right. *Hello*—an escort and sex scandal.” He cocked his head and gave a one-shoulder shrug. “Can’t get more different than that.”

Stone socked his brother.

Canyon grunted a laugh, then sobered. “You really like her. I mean—heck. Of course you do. You called *me* in and you never want my help.”

“More of that prideful arrogance, I guess.”

The door creaked open and Stone glanced over his shoulder. Saw Brighton, her hair messily mounded atop her head. “Hey.” He instinctively reached for her and liked the way she stepped closer. “What’re you—”

“Your mom—” She drew in a sharp breath, then her smile brightened the morning. “You shaved.”

Heat chugged through his face, all too aware of his little brother listening and watching. “Got on my nerves.”

She trailed those delicate fingers along his freshly shaven jaw, her expression entirely too inviting. “Better.”

Dang if he wasn’t homing in on another kiss when Canyon cleared his throat.

He glowered at his little brother, resenting the intrusion and the snigger that came after it.

Brighton blushed and tucked her chin. "Sorry. Your mom … she needs buttermilk from the condo, so I volunteered to run and get it."

It was strange, her being here, part of his life, interacting with Mom. "I'll go with you."

"No," she said softly, glancing at Canyon with a shy smile. "You two keep chatting. It won't take a minute." She was hustling off the steps by the time he found his brain again.

"Be right back," he muttered to his brother, then strode after her, ignoring Canyon's snicker.

He was almost to where the path banked when he heard voices. Lengthening his stride, he rounded the corner. Saw the forms ahead in the glare of the condo porch light.

Crap. Pellet and that woman who was none too shy about flirting. What were they saying to her? He didn't like the way Brighton's eyes glinted with anger, the way her lips thinned.

"Excuse me!" He quickened his step. "This is private property. You're not allowed back here."

"Private property? This is a lodge," Inspector Pellet said.

"And if you check the paperwork, you'll see this condo and back patio defined as private property, exclusive from the lodge." He flared his nostrils, moving to Brighton's side but glowering at the other woman. "Ma'am. Anything you need—"

"Is this her?"

No. No way he'd tell this woman a—

"She's a reporter." Brighton's words were leaden with implication, her hand bunching the shirt at the small of his back. "Rumor works for the Times Tribune."

Son of a—

"I'm right, aren't I?" Rumor said breathlessly, nodding. "That's her—the prostitute you were with."

God forgive him, he'd never punched a woman, but he really wanted to right now.

"The one you left office for? I mean, that wasn't the story that ran, but it will now."

"No," he barked, shouldering into her. He'd dealt with journos like her too often in Baltimore. "There is no story here, and if you print anything about me or that scandal, I will make sure you can't get a job anywhere again."

"It's too late."

Stone faltered. "What—"

"My story about you and this lodge will go to print—"

Stone surged forward but was stopped by a powerful right arm. He glowered, ready to throw a punch when he saw Griffin.

"Ma'am." The big guy powered up all six-four of himself and stepped between them. Kept moving in, forcing the journalist back. "I'd like to have a talk with you."

"You can't threaten me!"

"Hey." Canyon was there. "C'mon. Let's go." He guided them away as Griffin made the woman head back toward the front of the lodge.

"Crap," Stone hissed. "She went to press about the lodge." He ran a hand through his hair and noticed his brother putting his phone to his ear.

"This is Midas," Canyon said. "General, we need to swing some of your Potomac Two-Step savviness." He nodded to Stone, letting him know this was taken care of.

Anger churning, Stone turned.

Looking defeated, Brighton had tears slipping down her cheeks. "I'm sorry. I didn't … I'm sorry. I'm ruining your life all over again."

"You're not that powerful, Tizzy." He pulled her into his arms and held her as they trudged back to the cabin. "Besides, Canyon might be my *little* brother, but he has big connections. Don't worry. They'll get it silenced."

"We're never going to get away from this, what I did. It's always going to hang over our heads."

By the time they reached the cabin, Willow was out front. Stone nodded to her, urging her to take Brighton inside. But first, he whispered against her ear, "It's going to be okay. I swear."

She went with his sister reluctantly.

On the porch, he sagged against the rail. Roughed a hand over his face. She was right—it just seemed relentless, the trouble from that scandal. Just wouldn't go away.

"You *really* like her." Canyon jutted his jaw. "Followed you and saw you about to come go to blows—with a woman! My big brother, the unflappable, even-keeled Metcalfe."

"Not since Baltimore." He scratched his jaw and heaved a sigh. "What can I say? She's important to me. I think I love her."

"Little slow on the uptake there, dude. I could've told you that yesterday."

Stone smirked, but then saw a shifting in that patch of shadows again. He went for the weapon at the small of his back. "Someone's out there."

Glock cradled in both hands, finger along the trigger guide, Canyon stalked forward, keying a mic Stone hadn't noticed. "Legend, what's your twenty?"

Despite his three-year stint in the Army and his short law enforcement career, Stone was not as skilled as his Green Beret brother. Pulse jacked, he moved in sync with him, letting Canyon lead. Praying to God they could handle whatever this night was about to throw at them.

"There." Canyon hustled forward with the honed experience of the special operator that he was. With two fingers, he signaled Stone to the side. Indicated he should come up and around.

Heart thundering, he moved quickly. Thought of Brighton

back in the lodge. Prayed he could make it back to her. Stop whoever was coming for her.

Branches rustled. He jerked to the right—limbs thwapped his face. Stung his cheek. He grunted as a blur collided with him. Knocked him to the ground with a thud that rattle his teeth. Sent the weapon tumbling. A weight dropped on him. He grunted and threw a punch, connecting solidly with a gut. Heard the oof of wind knocked out from his assailant.

Shots cracked the night.

"He's going to take you apart, limb by limb," the man hissed. "She belongs to him."

Rage coursed through Stone. He drove an uppercut into the man's jaw. Connected solidly with him.

"Stand down! Stand down or I'll shoot!" Canyon's voice echoed in the small valley of the mountain. "Down! Down!"

The man reared and aimed a weapon at Stone.

Ice poured through his veins. Froze him.

Crack!

Warmth splatted his face. The man grunted and struggled to get free … then crumpled.

"If this casserole is going to be ready and still warm by the time the biscuits are done, I should probably take it to the condo and cook it there."

Willow nodded. "True. I can't leave the bacon, and the eggs will need to be started before you get back."

"Then I had better be on my way." Mrs. Clara gathered up the casserole dish, which seemed a bit heavy.

"I can help," Brighton said, hoping to see where Stone and his brother went. She took the dish from his mother and followed her out the door, scanning the hillside awash in predawn light. She didn't even spot Grief.

"I'm sure they're alright, dear." Mrs. Clara let them into the back door of her condo. "Now," she said, hurrying to the oven, "let's get this warmed up. Maybe I can make some French toast. The boys sure loved that growing up. Now, Willow—she wanted Belgian waffles. Every Saturday."

Brighton set the dish on the island. "Stone likes French toast?"

"With powdered sugar."

"Of course."

"And snickerdoodles. That boy could eat me out of house and home—well, they all could, really. Even Range." She smiled at Brighton. "What about you? What's your favorite cookie?"

"Guess it's not really a cookie, but a bar—Rocky Road. My brother, Aston, loves chocolate chunk. The bigger the better." Aww, that tweaked her heart. She hadn't seen him in ages. Missed him.

"Why does that make you sad?"

"The memory doesn't," Brighton clarified. "But I haven't seen him in almost a year. We used to be close."

"Oh sweetheart. I hope you see him soon. Nothing hurts more than bitterness in a family. Rots the soul and fabric of the family." She shook her finger. "Trust me. I saw it with my boys. Range and Canyon especially."

Mrs. Clara was moving around the kitchen, pulling out pans, cracking eggs in a bowl. She invited Brighton to help and the two of them made quick work of an entire loaf of French toast by the time the casserole was done.

After gathering the cooked food, Mrs. Clara suddenly stopped. "Oh no."

"What?"

"I don't have powdered sugar. Stone won't touch them without it."

"I ..." How could she help? "I could ask Alvaro for some from the kitchen. I'm sure he'd have it."

"Okay, then meet us up at the cabin?"

"Sure." Brighton made her way down the private hall, then rounded the corner and headed toward the front.

"Miss Brighton?" the girl at the front desk called. "Mr. Mulroney said you should stay inside."

She smiled. "Just going to the kitchen for some powdered sugar." But even as the words left her mouth, Brighton stopped cold at the familiar face outside the vestibule. Beyond the revolving doors.

Oh no.

Air trapped in her lungs, she couldn't move. Stomach roiling, ears ringing, she saw Death had come for her.

Saw Finch with a gun to Mari's head. He motioned Brighton outside. Somehow, he stood at an angle that hid him from the front desk.

Run. Just run.

Finch must've read her thoughts because he hauled Mari up tighter. Though the distance was too far to hear Mari's cries, they made it to Brighton's soul. Stone ... she did not want to leave him. If she went out that door, she'd never see him again. Either because Ladomer would make sure. Or because she'd be dead.

But Stone wouldn't be.

"You okay, ma'am?" Olivia called from the front desk.

"I ..."

CHAPTER
NINETEEN

What Willow wouldn't do for a wide-open plain. To take a long walk in tall grass. Have a moment alone to connect with nature and find some peace. A thousand pieces of information were stinging her attention, making it impossible to figure out the source. Since it was late and wilderness—along with its inherent wildlife—surrounded the lodge, she instead opted to bake. A poor substitute, especially considering her poor baking skills. But a girl did what she could with what she had.

"Where's Brighton?"

Licking cookie batter from her thumb, she pivoted to her brother. "Barking a question like that in a terse tone doesn't exactly entice people into answering." That's when she noticed the cut across his cheek. The bruise swelling his eye. "What happened?"

"*Where* is she?" he growled.

Swallowing more than a little nerves, Willow scowled. "She went to help Mom in the condo. What's going on?"

"We had an intruder." Stone stalked to the door with Grief aimed in that direction, too. "Tried to kill me. Said they were taking her back. Canyon and Griffin are scouting the property for more trouble."

"No," she said slowly, evenly. Trying to breathe ... and failing.

"Lock the doors after me. Let nobody in unless they're family. Clear?"

The door swung open, and Stone pivoted toward the door with his weapon trained on it.

Mom stepped in, humming and carrying a casserole dish. She bent to greet Grief. She started when she finally noticed Stone and the gun he lowered. "What's wrong?"

"Where's Brighton?"

Faltering halfway to the island, Mom glanced between them. "She was cooking with me, then went to get powdered sugar from your chef. She'll be right up."

Stone bolted out the door and down the hill to the lodge. Not seeing her in the foyer, he grew frantic. Checked the condo, darting from one room to the next. "She's not here." He barreled past his sister and pulled out his phone as he stormed to the front desk. "Olivia."

The woman's head yanked from her work, startled at his tone. "Sir?"

"You seen Brighton?"

"Yes, sir." Olivia pointed toward the front. "She went out to get a better signal and saw her friend out there."

"What friend?" Willow balked.

"The one outside."

"She doesn't have a phone!" Stone sprinted for the vestibule door. "Did she come back in?"

"I ... I don't know." Olivia looked ready to cry.

Willow's heart thundered. Who had Brighton left with? She pitched herself at the counter. "The girl you saw outside— what'd she look like?"

"Fourteen, fifteen. Blunt cut. She was shorter than Brighton."

"Oh no." Willow darted to the front where Stone met her with a tight expression. His eyes were shadowed, warning of his anger. "She's with Mari. And that means one thing."

"Horvath." Stone ran toward the back, up past the cabin.

"Horvath doesn't get his hands dirty. Has to be one of his goons," his sister's shout chased him to the truck.

He yanked open the door. "Either way, they're as good as dead."

"Stone!" Willow slipped on the gravel drive as she tried to catch up with him. "Stone, please—be careful. They play for keeps. They will not hesitate to do whatever it takes to stop you, including killing. These men don't mess around."

"Neither do I."

Not when it came to Brighton.

As he tore down the gravel road, probing ahead for taillights, he couldn't help but wonder—had she really just walked out of the lodge? Walked away from him?

It didn't make sense.

Didn't have to. Haunted by the hollow screams when she'd thought her captor had found her again, Stone refused to let that life reclaim her. Wasn't going to allow men to treat her like a slab of meat. Ever. Again. He punched the gas pedal. Rocks and dirt sprayed, peppering the truck as he spun toward the main gate.

Phone in the dash holder, he had to shout over the din of engine and road noise. "Call Cord."

Beep beep beep.

He glanced at the screen as he nailed a sharp curve, nearly

ate a ditch and had to correct his trajectory. Back on the road, he eyed the screen. Signal Lost.

Stone bit back a curse and again gunned it.

God, please …

Ahead, red blips winked in the darkness. His pulse ratcheted. He shoved his foot against the pedal, but he had already maxed out the acceleration. Hands curled tight around the steering wheel, he knew there was a series of switchbacks coming up, along with offshoot roads that would lead in different directions. He'd lose them if he couldn't erase this distance. But even as he realized that, the taillights winked out of sight.

"No!" He banged the steering wheel.

"If that's your lover," Finch snipped, "you'd better hope he doesn't catch up."

Lover? Brighton glanced out the back window. High beams of a big vehicle stabbed into the inky darkness. It was barreling toward them.

He had come. He'd come after her. Relief seared across her betrayal. She'd left the lodge with Mari, gotten into the back seat of the car, all knowing if she didn't, they'd kill Stone, Willow, and Mari. "He's not afraid of you."

"I'm so sorry," Mari whimpered. "They made me."

Gripping the teen's hands tightly, Brighton glanced out the rear window to the headlamps glowing in the distance. Her beacon of hope. And yet, if Stone got too close … She'd seen Finch's handiwork before in protecting Ladomer's interests and did not want Stone to end up in a morgue because of her.

What surprised her is that Finch didn't have his partner with him. He rarely operated without Drex. "Why're you alone?"

Finch's beady eyes found her in the rear-view mirror, but

then shifted to the truck closing in on them. "I swear I'll make hamburger of him."

"I'm so sorry," Mari cried again, burying her face in Brighton's shoulder. "I didn't have a choice. They took me … I don't want to die."

Brighton cradled the girl close. "Shh. It's okay." She knew it wasn't her fault. In fact, if it was anyone's fault, it was Brighton's because Ladomer wanted her, and the only way they could find Brighton was through Mari. "He'll save us." Eying the truck behind them, she didn't know how to hope or pray. For Mari's sake, she prayed Stone could intervene. But for Stone's sake, she prayed he didn't catch up.

Maybe … maybe *she* should die. It'd solve everything, wouldn't it? They'd leave Stone and Mari alone.

First, she'd need to make sure Mari got away.

Her heart thudded as a plan formed in her mind. If she could just … She eyed the narrow country road stretching before them. The SUV's lights streaked ahead. Ditches lined both sides. But they were thick with weeds and grass, not concrete. Better chance of—

"Don't even think about it," sneered Finch. "There's nowhere to go, and if you even try, you kill her." His gaze hit Mari, but the road demanded his attention.

When the car slowed for a sharp turn, Brighton slid her hand to the seatbelt release.

"Ha!" Finch shouted. "See? You're not worth it! Too much work. He knows when he's been outdone."

Brighton snapped her gaze back, heart plummeting at the dark road bathed in the ominous glow of their taillights. But no headlamps. No truck. No Stone. "No," she whispered, twisting around to search the road. The ditches. The fields.

How …? Why had he left?

Well. Okay then. All the more important she do this. She

reached across and grabbed the door handle and met the girl's shocked expression. "I'm sorry."

"What do you know?" Cord demanded.

"Not much," Willow shouted as she raced her little Prius down the bumpy road. "But I'm pretty sure Horvath's thugs have both girls again."

"Son of a—"

"Stone has gone after them. I'm trying to catch up, but I'm pretty far behind. And not even sure which direction I should be driving at this point."

"Toward the nearest airport."

"It's pitch black out here, and I've only been to the lodge a few times." She eyed her in-car navigation. "I'll use Siri to find the nearest airport once I can get a Wi-Fi signal again."

Cord muttered something she couldn't hear. "I'll call you back. I need to notify the authorities."

The call ended and Willow took a corner. "Siri, find—"

A shape appeared in the road.

With a scream, Willow yanked the steering wheel to the right and nailed the brakes. The car dipped down and slid to a stop with a thump. Nerves tangled, she took several long breaths, shoved the car into park, and glanced back to the road.

A woman stumbled toward the car.

Willow unfolded herself and felt some relief, until she saw the girl was beat up. "Mari?" She sprinted to her. "What happened? Are you okay?"

"She pushed me out." Wailing, Mari fell into Willow's arms. "He's going to kill her!"

"That was very stupid."

Heart crashing as she pulled the door closed, Brighton tightened her own belt. Straightened and felt a tinge of both terror and relief as the car sped back up after Finch's initial slamming of the brakes. "You wanted me. You have me."

He sneered. "You cost him too much. I don't know why he doesn't let me end you."

"Because he knows what I can bring in." She hated the truth of that, and that even though he made a killing off her Lizzy persona, he would punish her for escaping. For helping Mari.

"You bring trouble. A lot of it!"

"Not anymore." She swallowed again, tasting the bile at returning to this life. To …

No, push it away. Think about Stone. About the lodge. About the laughter. The good times. Reality would find her soon enough. Right now, she wanted to immerse herself in the last few weeks. Memorize them. Every detail. Every word—even the bad ones from Stone because those … those were his heart speaking. His broken heart. The heart she'd broken. Because he cared about her. She cared about him. They might've had a chance …

But not anymore.

He'd never understand this.

Maybe … maybe Mari would tell him she hadn't had a choice. That they'd forced her back.

You always have a choice. How many times had he said that?

No, no, no. Remember the positives. More of those. The kisses. The way he'd responded in the workshop, sliding her against his chest. The way he'd chosen to endure her presence because he'd said it was safer for her. That he had started after her, even if he'd turned back. Probably knew she was a lost cause.

Oh, Stone. I love you. Always have. Clearly, I didn't deserve you.

Was that why she kept getting ripped away from him? Was even God protecting him from her?

Yeah. Had to be.

Though tears stung, she silenced them. No more. She'd made her choices. Had her answer about the possibility of "them." She accepted the futility of ever hoping to be with him again. It was over.

Light exploded from the left, where Mari had been sitting. Brighton cringed and jerked away from the blinding light. A violent impact catapulted the car into a frenzy of noise and weightless. Spinning. Her head whacked hard against something. Darkness.

CHAPTER
TWENTY

BEXAR-WOLFE LODGE, *Northern Virginia*

"God in heaven, protect her!" Shock rocketed through Stone as he realized what he'd done. Adrenaline spiraled as the SUV with her in it went airborne. Cartwheeling off the road and across the field.

What have I done?

When too much distance had grown between his truck and the SUV, he'd known he had to take another route. He yanked his truck off the road and shot across a horse farm. The truck bounded up over the final rise just in time to see them coming around the bend. He gunned it, the jouncing turning his dinner to liquid as he barreled down the slope, narrowly avoiding the horses, and shot through a fence. Broadsided the SUV. Sent it into a ditch. Over an embankment. Flipping into the field across the street.

It was risky. Dangerous. But he knew if they got away, Brighton would likely never again be recovered. In law enforcement, he'd done women's advocacy meetings where he warned them to do whatever was in their power to avoid being put in a vehicle by a kidnapper. Chances were slim once they were in a car that they'd be recovered.

And he wasn't good with those odds when it came to Brighton. He'd rather her be injured than dead. Considering the SUV was a late-model, he guessed it had side-impact airbags.

Ears and head ringing from the impact, he slammed the gear into park and vaulted out of the truck. Sprinted over the uneven field toward the SUV that'd landed upside down. No smell of fuel. No fires. Just smoke, broken glass, and spinning tires.

On the road behind him, he heard tires crunching. Sirens wailed in the distance because he'd called 9-1-1. One way or another, he knew someone would need an ambulance.

Approaching the SUV, he drew out his weapon. Felt warmth sliding down his temple. "Brighton!" Crouching, he used the Glock to trace the driver's side. Squinted inside but couldn't see anyone in the front. He squat-moved toward the rear. "Brighton, you okay?"

A shadowy form in the haze shifted. An arm raised.

His breath jacked into his throat as he tried to make out the shape.

"Here," came a weak reply followed by a cough.

He angled close, his adrenaline dumping as he strained to see around the air pillows that had rapid-inflated/deflated upon impact. Part of the haze in the air was from the chemical that had saved her life.

In the darkened interior, her hazy form moved. Still strapped in. Upside down. Brighton whimpered. "I ... I can't move."

"Hang on." Stone shone a flashlight into the front. Empty. Where was the driver?

"Stone!"

Weapon snapped up, he wheeled around, losing his balance and falling against the upended vehicle as the dark mass rushed him. Canyon. Thank God!

His agile brother negotiated the scene and reached his side. "Just like you, throwing a party and not inviting the relatives. Sorry I'm late."

"No. Just in time." Relief whooshed through him, his brain arguing over his brother being here and yet glad he was. "Driver's MIA." Even as his brother communicated that information to someone else, Stone dropped to his knees, then all fours next to the SUV. "She's trapped." He angled inside and inched over to her. "Are you hurt?"

Blood trickled down her temple. "I … I don't know."

Stone gently probed her neck and shoulders. "Paramedics are on their way. It's tricky to move you."

"No," she whimpered, catching his hand. "Don't leave me. Please."

Her words had a way of squeezing his heart tight. "I'm not going anywhere, Tizzy."

"Finch—where is he? Oh, God. Get me out. He swore to kill me."

"Stone, think we got a problem here."

Crack. Pop!

A whoosh of another kind erupted, sending smoke and the fetor of fuel into the SUV.

Crap!

"Taking fire!" Canyon hunkered against the incoming barrage.

"Get me out. Get me out!"

Stone jerked to Brighton. "Can you release the seat belt?"

She whimpered, blood on her face and side. "No. It won't—" She cried out in pain.

"Okay, easy. Easy." He levered himself into the back and retrieved his pocketknife. Sliding beneath her, their faces nearly touching, he reached the belt. "Lean on me and hold still."

Her hands found his shoulders and she grunted softly as he started sawing through the strap. A few more slices and she dropped a few inches, but was yanked tight. She yelped.

"Sorry. Sorry." Stone shifted to support her weight more with his shoulder. "I've got you." Working around her, he felt the time slipping away before this thing blew or a bullet found its way into one or both of them.

"You came," she whispered. "You hit the Tahoe."

"Told you." He sawed the strap a few more times. "You got me all jangled. Not thinking straight."

Whoosh! A strange whistle rent the air in the same moment Brighton dropped into him. Crashed hard against his shoulder. She screamed through the pain, but her arms were a vise around his shoulders, her breaths jagged rasps against his neck.

Hooking an arm around her waist, he scrambled backward. Glass dug into his palms. He didn't care. Only sought escape. As he hiked his tail over the lip of the upside-down roof, he felt assistance dragging them backward. Thank God.

Free of the fire, he shifted to the right—straight into the barrel of an M4.

"That doesn't belong to you. She's Horvath's property," the man leered as his bloody finger grabbed the trigger.

The report of the gun rattled the night.

Stone jerked. Braced for the pain. But it didn't come. He mentally patted himself down, then saw Canyon closing in, his weapon cradled confidently in both hands as he sent several rounds into the goon.

Shielding Brighton, Stone guided them to the side where paramedics met them. They drew her away.

"No! Please—Stone!"

"Easy," He knelt at her side. "Let them do their job—saving you. I'd like that." He brushed the bloodied strands from her face as she lay back on the backboard. "Don't worry. I won't let you get away that easily."

EPILOGUE

A dozen stitches and a painkiller prescription later, Brighton was back at the cabin, resting on his sofa. She was numb, but it wasn't the painkillers. It was shock over Stone coming for her. Saving her. Violently.

"Still can't believe you came for me."

He perched on the coffee table in front of her, his hands threaded. "I was afraid if I didn't, I'd never see you again."

"Would that have been so bad?" she asked, sad. Thinking of Mari, who had—once again—been returned to her parents. Since Mari's kidnappers crossed state lines with her, the FBI had been called, and they'd put the family in a safehouse with the intention to set them up with new names and a new life to protect the teen. "I've only brought you trouble."

"Not true." He slipped from the table onto the floor, on his knees. "You brought love back into my life. Granted, at my age, I—"

"Please." Her heart thudded. "Please stop referencing our ages. Okay? I mean, we're both adults. Considering what we've been through, age matters little."

"Yes," he said with a firm nod. "With all *you* have been

through, all the times you've been forced into … things. How can …" He swiped a hand over his face. "How can you do this? Even want to be with me, let alone anyone."

"With *anyone*?" She shook her head. "Unlikely. With *you*?" She drew in a deep, soul-entrenched breath, then let it out slowly. "I think because *of* you, I am able to consider love and a relationship, something I never thought I'd ever do again. But Stone, you've always respected me, protected—and yes, even loved me. I saw—*felt* it. It's night and day compared to that life I was trapped in. You cared about *me*, not my body or buying time with me."

He cringed.

"I know it's crude, but that's what most men wanted from me. I know it's not the same with you. In fact, it's very different. Everything is different."

Even with his large hands, his touch was gentle as he brushed her hair from her face. "In all seriousness, thank you. Thank you for saying that." He traced her jawline with a finger. "What we have is different for me, too. I don't want you out of my life again. Ever."

Unshed tears burned her eyes. "You can't mean that."

"Never meant anything more in my life."

"You might want to listen to the oaf," came a resonant voice. "He's not big on grand gestures, so if he's offering, I'd accept before he realizes what he's doing."

"Canyon, be nice," Willow chided. "I mean, after all, maybe it's that knot on his head. Paramedics said the concussion could make him act strange."

"*Act* strange? He *is* strange. He's a Metcalfe!"

Stone smirked. "On second thought, maybe you should escape while you can. I'm not sure this is a family you want to join."

Brighton startled, searching his eyes. *Join? Join the family?* Was he saying what she thought he was saying?

"Dude! Did my big brother just break his vow of singlehood?" Canyon taunted. "Stone, maybe you *should* have that knot checked out. I'm a combat medic. I can take a look. Better yet—give you a bigger one for taking so long to see what was right in front of you."

Stone hung his head, pinching the bridge of his nose. "You're going to scare her off."

"Not possible," Brighton said, the words tremoring past hope that dared shove itself into her life. "I'm pretty sure I have to stay here. Indefinitely. To make sure my stitches heal properly."

Canyon sniggered. "The lady has a point. Although, if you try to get her in bed again without a ring and marriage certificate, we all might give you a knot on the other side of your head."

"And your backside, young man, " Mom promised.

"Man," Stone muttered as he buried his face in the crook of her shoulder. "Maybe we should all go into witness protection—from my family!" He stood. "But first ... I thought a little surprise might help."

Brighton's brow rippled in confusion. "What surprise?

He nodded to the opening door. In walked Griffin and—

"Aston!" With a shriek, she launched at her brother. Hugged him. Bawled. Then turned to Stone, who stood back, hands clasped respectfully. "Thank you. Thank you so much."

"Seemed the perfect ending to the past, the start of a new beginning."

"I honestly didn't think you'd agree to dinner."

Brooke Holloway slid into the seat across from Cord in all her dark-hair-and-icy-eyes glory. There was, of course, just as much ice in her heart, but he was determined to help that thaw. "Since, unlike Stone, I don't cook, I had to eat somewhere."

He grinned, impressed with himself for several reasons: one, he'd gotten her to come; two, she'd legit showed up; and three, he'd remembered to change out of his tac gear into jeans and a blazer. He was looking mighty fine, if he said so himself. And he did.

She casually laid the black linen napkin across her lap. "You are, however, underdressed for Giuseppe's." With an air of indifference, she motioned to the waiter.

"You kidding me?" Cord laughed. "This is my best t-shirt, and I brought my best girl."

Lasers had nothing on that glare, and he was glad the waiter showed up to distract her. "Whatever sweet red you have tonight," she ordered. "And rye bread to start."

"Right away, Ms. Holloway."

Cord faltered. The guy knew her name? "So, you come here a lot."

Finally—a smile but it was dripping with condescension. "One of our partners is Giuseppe's brother-in-law."

Huh.

"Look, let's just set the record straight." She was poised and in control. "I'm not here to be romanced or wined and dined. This is where I eat with regularity, and coming is something I felt was owed to you after what you did for Brighton—who is apparently about to become my sister-in-law. This is merely a gesture of appreciation."

"Right."

"I ... agreed to meet you because—" She fell silent when the waiter delivered the wine and bread to the table, then started talking with him about the evening's specials.

What would it take to impress her? How could he win her over? Because he would. Somehow. Some way.

He'd worked with two of her brothers and her sister was an

integral part of Mission: Liberate Everyone—MiLE. They were good people, hard-hitters. Heroes. But Brooke ... Brooke was very different. And she had completely ensnared him. Trying to win her, though, was probably a lot like trying to catch an electric eel with bare hands during a lightning storm. No way to avoid getting that bolt through the heart.

Why her, God? Why make her the one I can't walk away from? And he should. She was cold, abrasive, rude, blunt ... passionate, beautiful.

As the waiter left, she sipped wine and met his gaze over the rim. Vulnerability flickered through her expression as she set down the glass.

Couldn't fool him—she wouldn't have agreed if she didn't have a reason. This wasn't just a *we're both humans who need to consume carbs* thing. This was ... What was this, really?

"How'd you get into this?"

"Into the restaurant? You mean looking like this?"

She sniffed. "Trafficking."

"Ah." He took a chug of water. "That's a long story."

"Give me the brief on it." She wasn't going to take no for an answer, was she?

"Okay," he yielded. "I'd been in the Navy and saw a lot of bad things in combat—friends blown up, missing limbs, loyalties betrayed." He jutted his jaw. "But it paled to what I encountered when I got out and did border patrol for a few years. I know there are some powerful feelings about the wall, but—"

"Oh, come on. Don't tell me you support it. America was built on immigrants."

He wasn't going to be baited. "Politics aside," he said evenly, "the wall would go a long way in making the sex-trade business more difficult for those who profit off it." He pointed out the window. "There are thousands of girls in this city right now who are being abused thirty, sixty times *per day*. And they were brought across the southern border. A wall forces traffickers to enter through ports, walk through security where the agents are trained to spot victims."

She eyed him warily. Took a long sip of wine. Held the glass close, as if she needed it for reinforcement. "Is that true …?" Her eyes met his. "They're abused that … much?"

Reading body language had been one of his specialties. And hers was screaming. "It is. And those are only the times we know about it. Some are a hundred times a day. Can you imagine? A five-year-old girl being raped by grown men—"

"Please—don't." She took another mouthful of wine and nodded to the waiter to refill the glass. "Sorry. I just …"

"No, I get it. It's hard to hear. Hard to believe. But we need to fight for them. Be their voices." He folded his arms on the table. "That's why I'm doing this—for them. To be the tangibility of God to a hurting world. It's why I can't—*won't* give up."

"How … how do you find them?"

"Them?"

"The girls—victims. Trafficked."

"Training. There are signs. Things I recognize from my years working to tear this infrastructure apart. Dismantle it." He nodded. "There's a site online—Exoduscry.com. Check them out. They have a sort of Cliff's Notes on trafficking information and how to recognize it. Read up. It's worth it, but I warn you: it'll change how you see the world around you."

"But …" She straightened the fork and knife at the table, the bread and butter untouched. "How do you find them? The victims, I mean." More wine. "Like Brighton—how did you find her?"

"First—Brighton isn't a victim now. She's a survivor. But the operation involving her was pretty straightforward. I traced a leak and followed it back to the source. Led me to Horvath's organization."

"So, Horvath's thug was the one who tried to kill my brother and Brighton. What do you do when they aren't … killed?"

Her questions were specific and direct. Like they had a point. She was an attorney—was she looking to get involved? "Some organizations use back doors, do things under the radar. But MiLE uses the front door via legal, legitimate channels. Through cooperation and respect, we work with the local government and authorities. MiLE goes the extra mile. We have operators who can carry out the rescue, but even if our guys are hands-on, we never overstep local authority.

"We've worked too hard to gain trust in countries that have been, prior to MiLE, closed to cooperation. Here in the States, we prosecute to the fullest extent possible when arrests are made, and we work with the survivors to help them get their lives back on track."

She nodded. Tracing the rim of her glass.

"Are you thinking about donating some legal hours to help?"

Her eyes widened in surprise. "Oh. Yeah …" She eased back as their meals were delivered, body language telling him she had not asked with the intent to volunteer. "Martinek, Deluca, and Santiago does a lot of pro bono work here. I might be able to recommend we donate hours to MiLE."

"That'd be great." But he could tell she had asked for another reason. One Cord was pretty sure had a very personal component.

Cutting her salad, she didn't meet his gaze. "So, how many MiLE countries do you work with?"

"At this time, close to thirty." He carved into his steak.

Her eyebrows winged up. "That's a lot. Is that list available online?"

Cord slowed. "Not sure. I don't handle our website." He set down his knife. "If you want to ask me, Brooke, shoot."

She gave him a stern look. "I was curious since this struck so close to our family—w-with Stone and his now-fiancée. And of course, since Willow works for you, too."

"Of course."

"I talked to her last night."

He peered up through his eyebrows, unsettled, worried about what she was hiding. "Yeah?"

"She said she's heading out of the country soon. Is that related to MiLE?"

Now it was his turn to be evasive. "Do you think I'd be sitting here eating a steak with the most beautiful woman in New York if it were?"

The look she gave him said she'd read his mail. She wasn't fooled. Which was fine. But he'd have to talk to Willow about divulging mission-sensitive information. For now, he'd play along. Finish the steak. Then catch up with Willow on that midnight flight to Nigeria.

After he dented the steel vault around her sister's heart.

O.U.R. PROMISE

To the children
who we pray for daily, we say:
Your long night is coming to an end.

Hold on. We are on our way.

And to those **captors and perpetrators,**
even you monsters who dare offend God's
precious children, we declare to you:
Be afraid. We are coming for you

To Those Who Have Read This Far
we plead with you: Donate to our cause

Donate. We can't do this without you.

OPERATION UNDERGROUND RAILROAD

MORE INFORMATION ON
OPERATION UNDERGROUND RAILROAD

Within the Metcalfes Series, you will meet Cord Taggart and his organization, Mission: Liberate Everyone (MiLE), an organization I've loosely modeled after Tim Ballard's Operation Underground Railroad. A couple of years ago, I stumbled upon a video about a young boy name Gardy (check out Gardy's story here https://ourrescue.org/blog/search?search=gardy), stolen from his church in Haiti's Port-au-Prince and from his father, who has never given up the fight to find his son. The heart-wrenching story gripped me and wouldn't let me go. I watched hours of videos, which invariably led to Tim Ballard and his backstory, and his organization, Operation Underground Railroad. This fight against trafficking wouldn't leave me alone. So, I reached out to O.U.R. and asked if someone would talk to me, so I could be sure to write with accuracy and authenticity. I was in awe of how responsive they were, how willing they were to share their organization and their hearts. Not to brag on themselves. But rather to add to the voices screaming out against trafficking. O.U.R. has my heart. I can't venture around the globe, but I can write. And that is my contribution to O.U.R.'s endeavor and the fight against monsters selling people for sex. PLEASE. DONATE.

From the O.U.R website (www.ourrescue.org):

WE WORK WITH LAW ENFORCEMENT TO FREE SURVIVORS OF HUMAN TRAFFICKING AND EXPLOITATION. THEN WE WORK TO BREAK THE CYCLE.

Operation Underground Railroad currently supports operation and aftercare efforts in 22 countries and 34 U.S. States. Since our group is privately run, we are able to quickly respond to foreign government requests and institute investigative measures, develop intelligence and assist in enforcement operations and rescue efforts.

The O.U.R. Ops Team primarily consists of highly experienced and extensively trained current and former law enforcement personnel. Other members have a background in either the military or in intelligence work. Our goal is to develop long-term relationships with foreign governments and their law enforcement agencies responsible for combatting human trafficking and child sexual exploitation; working closely with O.U.R. Aftercare in anticipation of their rescue.

O.U.R. does not conduct or participate in investigations, operations or enforcement action in the United States. This important work is conducted by the brave men and women in law enforcement.

Domestically, O.U.R. develops relationships with law enforcement agencies and offers resources to assist them in their local efforts against human trafficking and sexual exploitation.

THE PROCESS

1. Assess the feasibility of rescue. This must take into account the willingness of local authorities to work with us since we not only want to save the children but arrest the perpetrators as well. We also want everything to be done legally and above board.

2. Research the location, the children and the background of those who are running the sex ring. We also search for vetted care facilities that will take the children once they are rescued and not only give them food and shelter but rehabilitate them as well. In some instances the children are able to return to their families.

3. Design a strategy for rescuing the children. This is the logistical part of the process. As former CIA, Navy Seals, Special Agents, etc., we have a very unique skill set to make this happen safely, efficiently and legally. We provide local law enforcement training to support and sustain anti-trafficking operations.

4. Take action. Obviously this is the most dangerous part of the operation but one well worth taking. In some instances we go undercover and arrange to "buy" a child as if we were a customer. After the purchase, we move in with the police, arrest those responsible and rescue the children. In other cases, we may act as a "client" looking for favors, etc. Again, we work with local authorities to make sure everything is done to protect the children and that the perpetrators are arrested.

5. Recover the children. These children's lives will never be the same. Their innocence has been stolen and they need help to readjust to a better world. Therapy can be provided as well as food and shelter at a pre-screened facility.

6. Arrest, try, and convict the perpetrators. We follow this process every step of the way to make sure they don't traffic children again. In many cases the perpetrators were sex slaves and victims of trafficking themselves and know no better way to survive. We hope to break this cycle.

She's been around the world, seen it all, and has come to easily recognize heroes—her four brothers, after all, are some of the world's finest. For that reason, she's confounded by one of the Nigerian mafia holding her, her team, and two dozen other hostage. The man seems ... familiar.

Join Willow Metcalfe as she and her friends fight for
freedom in Spring 2022.

ACKNOWLEDGMENTS

Many thanks to dear friends who helped bring this book to fruition: Rel Mollet, Kim Gradeless, Mikal Dawn, and Katie Donovan. Thank you, Bethany Kaczmarek, for proofing this story and your amusing comments that kept me from tears (mostly). I am very grateful to Susan May Warren for helping me strengthen this story when I grew blind to the forest for the trees.

Thank you to Jenny from Seedlings Studio for designing such perfect covers for The Metcalfes.

Again, a million thanks to Jessica Mass and Tyler Schwab of Operation Underground Railroad for taking the time to talk to me and share from your hearts. You are warriors!

ABOUT THE AUTHOR

Ronie Kendig is an bestselling, award-winning author of over thirty books. She grew up an Army brat, and now she and her Army-veteran husband have returned to their beloved Texas after a nearly ten-year stint in the Northeast. They survive on Sonic runs, barbecue, and peach cobbler that they share—sometimes—with Benning the Stealth Golden. Ronie's degree in psychology has helped her pen novels of intense, raw characters.

Website: www.roniekendig.com
Instagram: (www.instagram.com/kendigronie)
Facebook (www.facebook.com/rapidfirefiction)
Twitter (www.twitter.com/roniekendig)
Goodreads (www.goodreads.com/RonieK)
BookBub (bookbub.com/authors/ronie-kendig)
Amazon (www.amazon.com/Ronie-Kendig/e/B002SFLGQ2)

ALSO BY RONIE KENDIG

The Metcalfes

Stone

Willow

Range

Brook

The Discarded Heroes

Nightshade

Digitalis

Wolfsbane

Firethorn

Lygos: A Novella

The Book of the Wars

Storm Rising

Kings Falling

Soul Raging

The Tox Files

The Warrior's Seal

Conspiracy of Silence

Crown of Souls

Thirst of Steel

The Quiet Professionals

Raptor 6

Hawk

Falcon

Titanis: A Novella

A Breed Apart

Trinity

Talon

Beowulf

The Droseran Saga

Brand of Light

Dawn of Vengeance

Shadow of Honor

Abiassa's Fire Fantasy Series

Embers

Accelerant

Fierian

Standalone Titles

Operation Zulu: Redemption

Dead Reckoning